CW00642859

The Bright
Fabric
of
Life

Mhairi Collie

MACLEAN DUBOIS

First published in hardback in Great Britain
in 2024 by Maclean Dubois
14/2 Gloucester Place
Edinburgh, EH3 6EF

9 8 7 6 5 4 3 2 1

Copyright © Mhairi Collie, 2024

The right of Mhairi Collie to be identified as
the author of this work has been asserted in
accordance with the Copyright, Designs
and Patents Act 1988.

All rights reserved. No part of this publication may be
reproduced, stored, or transmitted in any form, or by
any means electronic, mechanical or photocopying,
recording or otherwise, without the express written
permission of the publisher.

ISBN 978 0 95652 783 7
eBook ISBN 978 1 78885 727 7

British Library Cataloguing-in-Publication Data
A catalogue record for this book is available on
request from the British Library.

Typeset in Bembo Book MT Pro by The Foundry, Edinburgh
Printed and bound in Great Britain by Clays Ltd, Elcograf S.p.A.

THE BRIGHT FABRIC OF LIFE

All the people and places in this book are entirely fictional;
most of the events happened and continue to happen.

Proceeds from this book will go towards treating fistula –
so thank you for helping!

'Whoever and wherever you are, you stand at the end of a long line of women, each born of the one before – with love, with pain, sometimes with loss. Lines which stretch back and back, beyond the reach of imagination, weaving the bright fabric of our human race.'

MC

Chapter 1

Juliet

From London to Ethiopia

JULIET LOOKED OUT OF the kitchen window into the hot tumult of Addis Ababa. Cold, rainy London was a million miles away; this was a different world of colour, heat and mayhem. A boy in the street caught her eye – skinny and purposeful. She watched as he carefully unpacked his wooden box, removing various bottles, a filthy cloth, a less filthy cloth and a worn brush. He turned the box upside down, putting it in front of a foldup deckchair, which he positioned precisely in the centre of the walkway. He then lined the bottles and brush neatly in front of the box and tucked the cloths into the back pocket of his jeans, hauling them back up over his scrawny hips as he did so.

Once satisfied with that, he started calling out to passers-by: 'Sir! Madam! Shoe shine! Please sit!' and to Juliet's surprise, breaking into song – a hymn, she thought, in between shouts. Intermittently he rearranged the bottles and brush, as if the order of them was the sticking point preventing Madam or Sir from sitting.

Quite quickly he had custom; he flourished his cloth to welcome the lady and ushered her flamboyantly into his chair, while he attended to her muddy shoes. Red high heels, noted Juliet, very glam, but maybe not ideal for the dusty clay track at the side of the main thoroughfare into the capital. The pedestrian walkway was shared with wildly overladen bicycles, cows on long tethers and goats on shorter ones; they were hoovering up whatever they could; there were motorcyclists trying to dodge the traffic, and sometimes indeed the traffic trying to dodge the traffic.

Job done; red shoes and the boy had a spirited haggle before she sashayed off. He almost immediately found client number two: a young man, nervous in an ill-fitting suit, wanting to make the best of his worn brown shoes. The boy switched in an instant from insistent barterer to welcoming helpmate for his new best friend. So much human theatre being played out right in the middle of the street in broad daylight.

It was all so different to London, thought Juliet, where people stayed buttoned up, keeping their stories tidily hidden away. There was plenty of drama at her work of course, behind the big doors of the hospital, down the interminable corridors. A bit too much drama sometimes . . . she pulled her mind back before it launched an exploration of recent events. No time for that – she had to enter the fray here. She had a new hospital to find today.

She turned away from the window and picked up her bag.

She had to commute across the centre of Addis from her lodging in the suburbs. There did not seem to be any type of map or A–Z of the sprawling mass of higgledy-piggledy clay lanes all clustered around the main thoroughfares, but she knew the huge Black Lion government hospital would be well known. Hopefully, all she had to do was shout Black Lion? at the Toyota taxi rank until one of them decided to take her.

She called 'Bye!' to the housekeeper and let herself out the side gate, blinking in the surprisingly strong sun, the heat already formidable at eight in the morning. The shoeshine singer brightened at the sight of her and enthusiastically waved her to his seat. She shook her head, pointing to her trainers, but this was no barrier to shoe improvement it seemed. She found a coin in her pocket for him and backed away smiling. Her shoes could probably do with a clean, but sitting while he knelt at her feet seemed impossibly awkward for her. Weird, she thought, considering the far more intimate things she did for people in the name of medicine.

At the roadside, four Toyota taxis were scooping up passengers, each with its own cockney-style wide boy conductor trying to ensure they got the custom.

'Hey, *mzungu*!' grinned one of the lads, revealing some major gaps in his teeth.

'Black Lion?' she called back.

He flapped his hands dismissively at the taxi in front and turned his attention back to a large woman trying to force her over-sized bag through the door. Yelling, the driver

3

jumped down and pulled it out; he then pulled out another passenger, and with much instruction from the large lady, the two of them managed to wedge the bag through the door and into the taxi. She followed suit, surprisingly nimble, and the displaced passenger was left to squeeze in beside them.

Juliet nipped past them to the next taxi, shouting, 'Black Lion?'

The conductor of this one looked to be about ten years old.

'Yes, yes, you come in, plenty of room, no problem!'

He gestured to the door. There seemed to be about fifty people already in there, plus many bags and a number of live chickens, but they gamely pushed closer together to leave a few inches of seat for Juliet.

'Oh! Aren't you full?' She hesitated.

'No madam, plenty of room, we're leaving now!'

The small conductor had a tiny moustache, she noted, which pleased him greatly – he smoothed it down with every sentence. Maybe slightly older than ten then, and certainly quite set in his view that there was enough room for her. He grabbed her wrist and hauled her aboard with more strength than she had expected. The door was somehow closed, and the Toyota lurched off to join the crazy cavalcade charging into the city. She wasn't able to say how many lanes were in the road – it seemed completely fluid, dependent on the daring of the drivers.

Being in the taxi alongside a significant number of squashed Addis inhabitants was quite an experience. As packed as the Tube at rush hour, but much noisier. She was perched on the end of a banquette designed for three people, and now with five sizeable bottoms squeezed onto it plus her at the end. There were no embarrassed silences – almost everyone was talking, dramatising, gesticulating. Everyone seemed completely alive and out there; engaging with everyone else, telling stories. Juliet drank it all in.

The conductor was crouched in the door space and would regularly jump up to holler out the door – for what she was unsure, as you couldn't have fitted even one more tiny baby chicken inside. Intermittently, when shutting the door again and yelling updates to the driver, he actually sat on her knee. The driver was supremely relaxed despite the utter chaos in the roads – it was like rally driving, only with five million other assorted vehicles. There seemed to be no rules, and certainly no traffic lights or signs. Every few seconds Juliet could not help but give an audible yelp, as they narrowly avoided certain death with a last-minute swerve.

Finally, she was spewed out of the taxi along with three of her neighbouring bottoms and two of the chickens. They were right in front of the Black Lion Hospital and the bottoms waddled off slightly anxiously towards the front gate. It looked as if the chickens were going in there, too. Juliet wondered why – if they were for visiting, for presents or for lunch. Perhaps best not to wonder too much.

She walked up to the railings to peer in. This was not her final destination in fact, but the nearest landmark. Even though it was in the middle of Africa, it still felt a bit like home. Probably because for the last eight years she had spent more hours inside hospitals than out of them, immersed in surgical training. She scanned the buildings, the connecting corridors, the complicated signs and busy doors. She could imagine herself tearing through that place, chasing emergencies as she did back home.

She leaned against the fence, and now her thoughts were off on an unstoppable rerun of her last week in London. The stabbing.

It was a wild ride through the emergency department that Friday night, culminating in a crazy operation at top speed to try to save the man. Blood everywhere: a large knife in the middle of the man's abdomen; a cacophony of beepings, ringings and alarms; some cardiac resuscitation in the middle of the operation; losing, winning, losing again. Andy, the balding anaesthetist, becoming pinker and sweatier by the minute, looking as though he himself might pop, and finally after a tough few hours: success.

The bleeding was stopped, the various bits and pieces of the guy repaired and returned to the inside, and everything sewn up. And he wasn't dead.

With a tremendous flurry of machines and people, he was trundled off to the intensive care unit. Juliet sat for a few minutes in the vacuum left behind, letting the shakes and the what-ifs pass through her. She could feel her heart still pumping hard, her eyes wide with acute, almost painful awareness of everything around her. She knew the adrenalin high would soon wear off, leaving her hollowed out somehow, a slow headache starting up, a little nausea lingering on.

She deliberately thought over what she had done, visualised all the nice snug stitches stopping the bleeding and mending all the injuries, the dry swabs at the end. The mental recap was okay. It was better than okay: tidy and dry, and, she repeated: he was not dead.

She let herself feel the relief, enjoying the delicious warm thrill of it coursing through her. Each tired muscle was tingling, as she sipped at the pure joy of having *Done the Thing* . . . She quickly stopped herself. It was best to never feel too pleased – that was just asking for trouble.

Because there was the other danger: of waking the malevolent vengeful beast slumbering inside her. That monster which sniffed out the triumphs and disasters, always ready to pounce. An ever-threatening Cerberus, trying to overpower her with memories. The ones that had got away: the man from two years ago; the lady from her first month. Smaller operations that had gone wrong, but also the memories of failures that could barely be borne, that had to be carried with the gaze averted. The baggage every doctor carried.

Firmly, she sealed the underworld barriers shut again, skirted past the beast and moved her mind onto the next item on her rather long to-do list, chanting her usual mantra: *Keep moving, keep working*.

The next day was a glorious sunny Saturday. Juliet was

running through Highbury fields on a wave of satisfaction. All around her unfolded a mini tableau of summer in the city. Lovers lounging over each other, their bodies learning how to fit together, managing the mismatches. Young mothers laughing on a blanket, intermittently reeling one of the small children, orbiting them into the middle for snacks, cuddles, band-aids. Older children doing handstands, playing tag, playing catch. A bunch of students half-heartedly throwing a frisbee. Readers here and there had gravitated to the dapply green light of the generous leafy trees. Everywhere wispy trails of contentment meandered lazily upwards to the July sun.

She wondered which group would be for her in future years? Would she be one of the lovers, or readers or even mothers? It was unimaginable. She didn't see how she would fit any of these lives. Perhaps she could wear one anyway, make do with some pinching here, some bagginess there.

No. She wouldn't. She had a good going addiction to surgery now – to the rushing around, the emergencies, the lurching fear that she would not be able to deal with whatever came crashing through the doors, and the intense satisfaction of finding a sturdy path through the morass. This was where she belonged.

But then the text arrived. It was from Zaid, her colleague on duty that day. She came to a stop, fumbling with her phone anxiously, her heart starting to beat fast as she read:

Sorry mate – your stabbed man's fine but your cancer from

Monday isn't – has a complication – infection in the abdomen.
We are about to start another case, then taking him back to
theatre. He's stable.

She took in a deep, long breath, feeling the nasty plunging
of her stomach as she assimilated the information. That
dreaded word: complication. Meaning something had gone
wrong – probably the intestine she had painstakingly sewn
together had fallen apart. Yet the patient looked perfectly
fine only yesterday morning . . . they all had! It had been a
very positive reassuring ward round. She had basked in the
warmth of everyone doing well.

And now she was back in the cold dark; the spectre of failure
spreading its shadow everywhere. This was the flipside of the
coin, the payment extracted for the satisfaction of yesterday:
hubris and Nemesis.

She shook her head to clear her thoughts. She had to focus.
They needed to get the poor man off the downhill track,
which meant going back to the operating theatre, opening
the wounds again, and cleaning out the mess within. Hoping
it would heal, hoping he would overcome it.

Oh, God, not good. And how ill was he? Zaid had said
stable. Stably bad or stably good?

Get a grip, Juliet, she admonished herself. Stable means
stable, can wait a bit. You can run home, shower, change and
be at the hospital in time to help.

Sensible words, but the double-headed monster of fear and
guilt was at her back. She had to get out of here. She started

to run again, trying to ignore the rampaging taunts in her head. Running normally smoothed out the creases in her mind, but now rhythmic chants were biting at her in time with her steps: 'So now it's out – you're no good; maybe you'll be sacked; they'll think you don't belong there, you're not good enough; soon they'll all see that . . . ' On and on.

She could bat away most of these trollish jibes, could answer that she was no different to anyone else – no worse; she knew her results were as good as theirs, maybe better. She worked harder than anyone, earned everything; was always there, doing the extra mile, putting in the effort: completely committed.

Rounds one and two went to Juliet. But when there was a third . . . that always felled her.

Round three was given over to that small insistent voice buried inside which could not be silenced by arguments. A voice which ran deep and true, cutting through the very core of her, stirring up a foul black spectre: 'You couldn't even save your own brother,' it said. 'Your own brother. Poor boy, poor Drewie.'

She stopped, held onto a flashing advertisement for McDonald's Happy Meals at the back of a bus stop and bent over, momentarily paralysed by the tide of grief crashing down, pulling her under. Sweat ran into her eyes. She wiped them shakily with her T-shirt, made herself breathe, waited for it to pass.

Keep running, insisted the survivor part of Juliet. Come on, move, keep moving, work your way away through it. Build a house of work to stand against it. Run, work, move. Run home, then go to the hospital, and fight to save your patient. Keep going. Run, move, work.

The following day, she was walking out of the hospital, when the portraits in the entrance hall caught her eye. She paused for a moment to survey the collection of overdressed old men, all staring blankly ahead, unexcited by London's mind-blowing skyscrapers and wailing traffic crowding around them. She couldn't imagine any of them living, breathing or working. In fact, she bristled a little in their presence, aware that they would have absolutely disapproved of her: a woman in the holy sanctum of surgery. Yet, they had all toiled along the path she was travelling; each making some sort of contribution to medicine; each probably treating some patients successfully and some not.

A lot not if they were surgeons in the dirty pre-Lister years, she thought. How did they bear it, so many dying – almost all? Of course, those guys had no understanding of why so many of their patients died – no inkling of what infection even *was*. No one understood until Dr Lister worked it out and explained it to the world. Why didn't they give up?

Lots of them probably did, but not the ones who made it to a portrait. Those must have felt the same ambition which burned in her, always hungry for more work, to do better operations. Fuelled, rather than satisfied, by every case. The undeniable compulsion of surgery.

She certainly felt that compulsion, although this week it was getting somewhat overwhelmed by self-doubt. It was quite the battle to save her cancer patient, who was now languishing rather than truly recovering in the intensive care unit. Her repair of his intestines had indeed fallen apart. He was frail, not a good healer, but she was the one who had performed the surgery. She felt the responsibility for the complication, she took the blame. A heavy weight on the bad side of the scale.

It was a struggle to tidy up the mess in her head this time, compounded by the unexpected escape of some of her Drewie trauma. It was all caught and packed away again now, though, compartments bulging somewhat, but shut.

And she knew, of course, that things did go wrong in surgery – you would have to be an idiot not to notice that. But it was natural to always hope it wouldn't be you, wouldn't be your patient. How to deal with it when it did happen, that was the question.

Her boss, the Professor, was trying to teach her, she thought. He found her in the unit late that night, staring at the depressing charts of her patient, willing the lines to start going up.

He produced a ripe apple from his pocket and gave it to her. 'It's a good one, from my garden, the perfect mix of sweet and tart. Always a tricky balance. I've been experimenting with different trees, you know.'

'Oh – thanks.' She pocketed the apple, ready to leave, but he wasn't quite done.

'Balance, yes. Important. Keep the humanity, be upset, but also be brave. Do it all again.'

She looked up to meet his grey eyes, brimming with intelligence. That was probably the longest psychological pep talk she'd ever heard from him. Possibly the only one, in fact.

'Yes. Thank you,' she managed, a little stunned.

'You know, if your lifetime complication rate is only half of mine, which would be ridiculously optimistic, that's a lot of heartache to shoulder.'

Juliet let his words sink in. He was right of course, which didn't mean she was about to forgive herself. She understood the importance of this conversation though. These were the true secret bonds of the surgical fraternity, and this was the unavoidable initiation rite: dealing with bad things which you have caused, albeit unintentionally.

So, she was in the club; that was something. But there were still many uncertainties in the road ahead, including the need to get a consultant job – the last hoop she had to jump through. Prof would be interviewing her for that next week, and had notably not discussed it with her. Unless you counted the 'Hmmm' sound he made when she told him she would apply. Not very encouraging.

The committee of grey-haired black-suited men on the interview panel turned out not to be very encouraging either. They smiled at her, but in a way that suggested mild pain rather than pleasure. She was not for them, for this post, in this place. And to be fair, she wasn't sure that they were for her. But what was, then? Surgery? Yes, but how and where and with whom? She had no answers, and felt she was chasing something without being quite able to see it.

Then a little miracle maybe – the offer of a post with Médecins Sans Frontières in the north of Ethiopia. It arrived with perfect timing, the day of the interview.

An escape? Yes. No. Maybe? A vision flashed in front of her eyes, a straight long road of bright red earth, a wide-open landscape, a vast sky.

It was that strange thing of having an almost-memory of a place without ever having been there. Yet it lived in her head, waiting for her to catch up. In the vision, warm air was blowing through her hair, breathing *Africa* to her, and she felt calm, good. Such an enticing whisper, such an inviting name. It invoked all that long, long time from way back in the beginning of everything to far into the future. A whole new story for her, a promise of infinite possibilities.

At the very least, it was a chance to pause and work out what sort of future she wanted.

Caitlin, her best friend from medical school, had understood – sort of. 'Médecins Sans Frontières?' she shrieked. 'Oh, my God, are you really going to do it? I mean, I know you've talked about it on and off since for ever, but now, really? Are you going to leave?'

'Not leave for ever . . . but maybe a gap year? MSF or "Doctors Without Borders", as the Yanks call it, might be a good gappy thing to do. I don't know. I'm thinking about it, that's all. I love surgery. I know that's going to be my life, but, how can I put it? I haven't found my place yet. Can't imagine where it is for some reason. Can't settle. I guess Prof knows that, too, which is why he didn't give me the job,' Juliet added ruefully, kicking off her heels and sticking her feet up on Caitlin's sofa, having retreated there after the interview for commiseration and vodka.

'Anyway, it won't be so different to here. It's still surgery; still people to treat.'

Still complications and worrying about everything all the time, she added in her head, avoiding voicing these truths.

'Just a bit hotter and sweatier and further from the number eight bus to your place.'

Caitlin eyed her for a moment, thinking that the issue was probably not really geography. Although she supposed that changing the external things could give new perspective to the internal things. She sat up, business-like.

'Well, if you're off for a year to somewhere out of range of cosmetic deliveries, I shall gift you a year's supply of mascara. Can't have you frightening the natives if you run out. They'll think you're a ghost.'

Juliet started laughing. 'You're so kind! To spare people you don't even know that sight. You know, I don't think I've been out of the house without mascara since I was ten. Up to that point, I'm pretty sure my own mother continually thought I was a very unhealthy child, awash with undiagnosed noxious diseases. It's amazing the anxiety blonde eyelashes can cause.'

'It's not generosity – it's basic humanity,' snorted Caitlin.

'God, I will never forget the first time I saw you coming out of the shower make-up free. You looked like a cross between a zombie and the white rabbit. Terrifying.'

Juliet grinned. 'Dr Fitzgerald, I think you might have nailed my problem, my inner conflict. I think I am actually a cross between a zombie and the white rabbit.'

'Chrrrrist!' mock frowned Caitlin, her own smile breaking through. 'I can't unpick that – way beyond my psychiatric paygrade. Repress away, darling, is what I suggest. You just repress it! And also, let's get some Abba on and get sloshed. Some traditions have to be upheld, even if you are off on some crazy jaunt, you desperate ship-jumping traitor.'

And now she had jumped. She was about to join the MSF team and head for the far north, for a refugee camp and hospital near the border with Eritrea, but first she had three weeks to spend here in Addis Ababa. Oddly enough, it was the Prof who recommended that she go to the Fistula Hospital in Addis – *a place like no other,* he had said, *don't miss the chance to go there*. They had moved on to something else, and she didn't ask him anymore about it.

Later, though, she thought, why not? And emailed the superintendent, receiving an agreement for a visit to observe. She had very little time to find out much more about it, what with all the preparations and courses for Médecins Sans Frontières. Anyway, she was used to dealing with bowel fistula in the UK – usually fairly innocuous little tunnels between anus and skin. But perhaps there was something more to explore – certainly medical history books were full of drawings of bygone barber-surgeons proclaiming how they treated fistula with unfeasibly long pointy sticks.

She decided to give Prof the benefit of the doubt – and also take a few weeks to acclimatise in the capital city before heading off to the turbulent borderlands in the north. There were landmines up there, she knew.

So here she was – all set to acclimatise, and to learn. She let the memory reel spin to a stop then turned her back on the sprawling Black Lion Hospital, and walked over to a little wooden shack, stuffed full of toys, juice bottles, snacks, toiletries and sundries. There was a small man in the shack, popping up and down behind the counter like Punch.

'Excuse me, do you know the way to the Fistula Hospital please?' she asked, addressing the shack as he dived under the counter again.

He popped up and stared wide-eyed at her. 'Yes of course, madam!' She gave a surprised reflex laugh at his beaming face.

He leaned out of the shack towards her, almost falling out of it in his eagerness to help. 'Take that road over there beside the white car. Go on up, not far, maybe few minutes only, to the black gates on the left. Very nice. Good day!' He waved his arms at her and popped back inside, up and down again in a trice.

'Thank you so much, you too.' She beamed back, thinking

how un-London everything was, and then how stupid she was to still be in London mode. This was the fresh start, remember? A lighter Juliet, some of the baggage jettisoned, at least. She gave herself a little shake, looked around her.

The street itself made for complete sensory overload. Apart from the ongoing morning jam carnival, a kaleidoscopic spectrum of humanity filled every corner. Straight-backed ladies walking majestically with a mountain of buckets perfectly balanced on their heads; mums with their super cute infants strapped to their backs; schoolchildren with uniforms all the colours of the rainbow; guys hawking drinks, oranges, newspapers; guys frying up pancakes, kebabs, chicken and corn on the roadside braziers while joking and shouting to their mates as they lounged on purring motorcycles; smells of fruit and diesel and goats and sweat and perfume – everything imaginable in a few cubic metres of sun-baked air.

Life overflowing everywhere, and it felt just great to be in it.

She let the usual Monday morning knot of anxiety melt away. No need to worry about what anyone was thinking here, or to strive to look like the serious professional surgeon she thought was expected. It was impossible to imagine how to fit into this wild maelstrom. She was free to be anything, even an adventurous highland girl, with a secret hankering for mischief. Is that who I want to be? She thought, making a mocking smile at such a cheesy dating profile summary. Go the whole hog and add fun-loving or GSOH, why don't you? She let a smile open up freely onto her face and pursued it to the precious little nub of happiness at the root. Yes, a joyful self was waiting here, in this new life. She could enjoy that self, maybe not erect so many barriers and façades in front of it.

Onwards.

Chapter 2

Juliet

The Fistula Hospital

JULIET FOLLOWED THE INSTRUCTIONS and arrived at the large black gates.

'Oh,' she thought, as the security guard swung open the gate. 'I've gone wrong somewhere.' She was looking at a beautiful wide, white single-storey house, surrounded by gardens in full bloom. There was a veranda all around the building, draped in a Carmen-worthy flounce of red and purple bougainvillaea. The house itself looked like some place out of *Gone with the Wind*. There were figures seated in the shade of each tree and even two relaxed looking golden Labradors lolling beside a flowering bush near the house.

She was about to ask the guard where she was, when a sweaty man pushing a wheelbarrow steered past her to the steps in front of the house. In the barrow lay a weak figure of a girl: large blank eyes, registering nothing at the sight of Juliet or the beautiful white house. The man lifted her out of the barrow and, supporting her, tried to walk her up the stairs. Her wasted legs had no strength in them, and he was struggling to keep her upright.

Juliet dropped her bag and ran over to help, catching the girl's other arm and giving her a small smile of encouragement. The man looked over, surprised, but nodded a thank you. The girl gave no sign of noticing anyone, staring at the ground, her ankles almost completely flaccid as Juliet and the man practically lifted her up the veranda steps. It was as though there was a barrier all around her. Juliet wrinkled her nose involuntarily at the strong smell of ammonia, a pungent waft of it blasting upwards when they managed to sit her down on a wobbly chair. Within a few seconds, a bustling lady in a white dress appeared: a nurse perhaps, if this truly was the fistula hospital, and started talking to them, presumably in Amharic. They all sat down at a table, and the nurse began filling out a long form. The girl did not speak. Her eyes were cast down; her head bent.

Juliet retreated to collect her bag, noticing on the way that there was a dark trail of liquid marking their walk, and a small puddle in the wheelbarrow, where the girl had been lying. She frowned – none of this made sense yet. She looked up and found herself being studied by some wide dark intelligent eyes in the face of a tall, elegant Ethiopian woman.

She smiled up at her: 'Hi! I'm Dr Macleod, visiting from the UK, not sure if you were expecting me?'

The Ethiopian woman nodded. 'Yes, you are welcome to our hospital,' she said softly, her voice rich and low. 'I am

Dr Valentine.' She followed Juliet's gaze which had been drawn back to the miserable girl at the table.

'Ah, a new fistula patient.' She inclined her head towards them. 'Depressed, thin, bad walking, wet and smelling of urine. Instant diagnosis, although we don't know yet how bad it is and what can be done.'

Juliet looked confused. 'I'm sorry, I don't think I quite understand – what has happened to her?'

'I'll tell you – you will never forget it. The same tragic story for nearly all of these girls. They've been left to try to give birth in the village with no help, no midwife. The baby gets stuck, then after maybe two whole days of fruitless pushing, if the mother survives, their baby dies—'

'Oh, no,' Juliet gasped.

Dr Valentine nodded and went on slowly, deliberately, 'Eventually its poor little skull bones collapse, and then it's not stuck anymore and can be delivered. But, there is a terrible but, by then there is a hole worn between the baby's head and the mother's pelvis – meaning there is now a connection between bladder and vagina or even bowel—'

'The fistula,' Juliet interposed.

'Yes. If the mother lives, she will be marked by having this never-ending leakage of urine or stool. Stigmatised. Bereaved. In pain, smelling bad, shunned by all—'

'That's just so awful, I had no idea.' Juliet gazed at the broken girl on the veranda. 'I've never seen such a thing – we don't see this at home. The fistulae I am used to are usually tiny wee things at the bottom, temporary, hardly bother anyone.'

She paused, acute sorrow for the girl making her eyes swell. 'I guess no one waits for days with a baby stuck, wearing away their flesh. The pain must be awful. Horrible.' She shuddered at the thought of it, unable to help herself.

Dr Valentine pursed her lips, 'Very horrible. And the horror goes on. These girls lose everything: baby, health, husband usually—'

'Husband? Why is that?' interrupted Juliet.

'They don't tend to stay around. They need a strong wife, to give them plenty of children, not an ill and barren one with bad smells and leaks.'

She saw the anger in Juliet's face and gracefully lifted a hand to gesture – wait, hear more, 'You know in Ethiopia, a farmer needs children to help him survive, and later to tend to him and his wife when they are old or sick. It's very hard for them all. But the girls lose everything: health, baby, their role and home too.'

Juliet was silent, rage still coursing through her at the thought of these girls discarded and abandoned.

Dr Val was watching the new girl, slumped on her chair. She turned back to Juliet. 'They still matter to us, you know.'

Juliet nodded her head slowly, feeling the flame die down a little, but sure she would always feel anger at the appalling story she was hearing. 'Does this happen a lot?' she asked, finally.

'I'm afraid so, yes, everywhere in Africa. So many new cases every year here in Ethiopia and they say over a million women worldwide living with a fistula. If you can call it living.'

'Oh, my God,' said Juliet, the enormity of it flooring her anew. 'How can I not have known? Have I been living on a different planet?'

Dr Valentine smiled at her slightly ruefully. 'All these different worlds under one sky. Although, this is about time and money, not race.'

Juliet's face betrayed her confusion.

Dr Valentine went on. 'Fistula following disastrous childbirth has been around forever – in your country, too. The first women's hospital in the US was built over a century ago mainly to treat fistula. The collective memory of rich countries has lost fistula though – it's now almost always in poor countries with poor women having their babies in a village hut, without help. And these women are outside of society, with no voice.'

They were joined by two giggling girls in matching long blue dresses. Holding hands, they gave a slight curtsey to Dr Valentine, and one held out a flower.

'Thank you, my dears – jasmine! My favourite – did you know?' They giggled even more before disappearing in a stream of laughter.

Juliet was still reeling from the new version of the world she had been shown, but the girls caught her attention, with their open happy faces, so different to the girl on the veranda.

'What about these two – are they fistula patients? They seem so happy!'

'Ah, yes, they are. They've had successful surgery and will go home soon. We do offer treatment and hope here. You see, we can mend many of them. Although, it can be a long slow process for them. It's a long slow process for us, too: a complicated surgical procedure to master. This is what you are here to see, yes?'

'Oh, yes!' Juliet made an instant decision. She might not have known about this five minutes ago (for which blindness she sent a mental apology to Womankind), but she wanted in. Wanted to be part of something fighting against this huge awful thing.

'I should love to help you if I can. And find out what I should do if I have these patients during my year near Adigrat.'

'Ah, yes, we will make a plan. You are working for MSF, yes? I know they want me to come to the north for a week or two next year, to do some cases. There is a great shortage of doctors and surgeons up there in these rural areas. No one who can repair fistula, which means many women unable to get any treatment are left with this.' Her face was stern as she spoke, but then she broke into a genuine smile, warming up.

'So. You'll be my assistant there, too. Now, let me show you around before we start the first case.'

Juliet followed her into the white building. They walked through a bright nightingale ward, about thirty patients in tidy white beds, the floor sparkling clean, sun coming gently through lightly curtained windows. There were girls scattered all around, mopping the pristine floor, murmuring with the patients in the beds, folding swabs and rolling bandages at the nurses' desk. There were four or five white-starched nurses moving amongst the patients, too – chatting to them, fiddling with tubes, straightening sheets. They all smiled widely at Dr Valentine as she walked through. There was a warm atmosphere of tenderness, as though the patients were enveloped in a special healing fug, this continually being woven by every little smile, word of reassurance, tuck in of a sheet, mop of a brow, check of a catheter. A real oasis of care in the midst of a hard country – a hard continent.

'Some of these girls helping on the ward and cleaning have had surgery and some are still waiting – getting stronger, having physio,' explained Dr Val. 'Everyone is involved in the whole process; everyone helps. It's a boost for the patients and assists the staff. In fact, many of the staff are ex-fistula patients. And here is theatre.'

Juliet breathed in and out slowly, recognising her milieu like an old friend, as she viewed the shiny theatre, the bustling In-Charge organising instruments in readiness. She could hardly wait to see how Dr Valentine fixed these girls. Would she be able to learn it? The desire to do so was already beginning to burn in her, already becoming intense.

Chapter 3

Juliet

Fistula Operation

DAYS FLEW BY, PACKED with learning about all the different cases, talking and tending to the patients, assisting Dr Val in theatre and generally immersing herself in all things Fistula.

Now, on this day, it was Juliet's first fistula operation, under the calm supervision of Dr Val.

Juliet picked up the knife, stilled her hand, breathed and focussed; imagining how the cut should be; how the flesh of the girl should give way to her. She took a minute to let her eyes and her mind align. Anatomy was usually such a beautiful, perfectly planned thing. However, this most assuredly was not. What was the old joke about a man likening childbirth to watching his favourite pub burning down? No joke to live with ruins like this, though. Fistula seemed far too clean a word for the mess this represented, the horrors which caused it, and the desperate misery of the reduced life it caused.

She could feel the convoluted histories which had

brought her and the girl to this point looming over her. The unchangeable past. And in front, the scarier unknown future, ready to be carved out, quite literally by this gleaming blade. Maybe another chance at life for the lovely girl.

She shook off these weighty thoughts of past and future – she needed to hone all her consciousness into this moment.

She let her intent flow into her steady fingers. She should concentrate on each physical step of it, make it good. She had to ignore the sweat running down in between her breasts, the ache already starting in her back from having to bend too much to see, the itchy lock of hair at her ear which she would not be able to scratch for the next few hours.

She peered up at the fistula, thinking furiously through the operation again. Dr Valentine came over to look, bringing along her force field of confidence.

'There is more scarring on the left. You'll need to do more work on that side to free it up,' she murmured.

Juliet nodded and adjusted her grip on the knife – time to start. Come on then, make the cut. Then stay in control of the operation; don't allow too much bleeding, keep the vision clear. Every movement counted: every stitch; every knot. It only took one bad thing, even one slightly suboptimal stitch or knot for the whole thing to be lost.

There was a little more tension than normal in the operating theatre. It was the usual thing when a new surgeon was in the hot seat, but Dr Valentine was cool and collected, and as the operation proceeded, the staff started to relax and chat a little. Juliet remained focussed and quiet until the end.

It took almost two hours, but she barely noticed the time, concentrating hard in her operative bubble. She cut the final stitch, put the dressing in and turned to look at Dr Val, checking her miss-nothing eyes for an assessment.

Dr Val nodded. 'It looks good. We'll leave the catheter for ten days while it heals.'

Juliet gave her a slightly crooked smile. 'And I will worry about her for the whole time.'

Dr Val smiled back. 'Yes, this is surgery, is it not? Always worrying about someone: no sooner are you freed from worrying about one than there are three more to take her place.' She peeled off her mask and rolled her shoulders to stretch them out.

Juliet gave a little nod of agreement. 'Yup. What a career choice. But thank you very much for helping me do it.'

'You're welcome. We are making you into a fistula surgeon! The world certainly needs more of these. I'll do the next one, then maybe we'll share the third case. Coffee first, though?'

'Yes please!'

Yes to the gorgeous Ethiopian coffee, and yes to becoming a fistula surgeon. The words sang out in her head. How fast life was changing – a couple of short weeks ago she had barely heard of this condition, and now it filled her mind. She sent a silent thank you to Prof. His seemingly casual off-the-cuff recommendation might actually lead her to her path forward. Typical of him, to spot this for her. Somehow, he had more vision than ordinary mortals; she might have to forgive him for not giving her a job in London after all.

Email to Caitlin:
This place is wild. Traffic is mad, hospital is flowery. Great coffee, dubious antenatal care. Recommend we shy away from any birth plan with the word natural in it. Anyway, I've got no time for that sort of stuff — am very busy finding my true calling in life. Will keep you updated!
Love from Ethiopia

Chapter 4

Juliet

Meeting Jan and Jeff

JULIET LEANED AGAINST A pillar on the veranda, enjoying the protection it gave from the late afternoon sun, and watched the activity around her. The pace was relaxed in the heat, but nonetheless there was much going on. A pretty girl in a long pink skirt was carefully mopping the veranda; two others were sitting on the steps, heads together, intermittently giggling, winding cotton. The gardener was tying up wayward strands of the fabulous red bougainvillaea, trying to prevent it from flinging exuberant limbs over the entrance gate. On the lawn in front of the hospital she could see one of the patients from the physio lab, sitting under the large shady acacia tree, stretching out her sticklike little legs and trying to get her ankles to bend.

She thought about the three weeks she had spent here. Only three weeks since she had arrived – and what an amazing, life-changing experience. She had gone from ignorance to obsession!

The most amazing thing, though, was the transformation of the patients from depressed, lost-in-lifeless-limbo shades of themselves, to being animated lovely girls again. It was as if they had woken up from a never-ending nightmare, and were now all full of character: some joking and teasing, some peaceful, all with a smile for her on her rounds, all radiating hope again.

Well, not quite all – those whose surgery had not worked were still shackled by their disability, unable yet to be free of it. They had a little hope, the flame small, but fierce. They waited to find out what could be done for them. There was no question of them leaving yet.

She had learned much about how to repair these injuries, the intricate movements required, the retraining of her eye to understand what the injury was exactly and what needed to be done to repair it. She had also learned so much about treating patients in general. To be in an environment where fully committed loving care was freely given by all the doctors and nurses, indeed by everyone involved, was truly eye-opening. It was incredible to gauge the benefits of that generous care to these love-starved girls, previously all out of chances.

At a table on the cool balcony, Agnes, the theatre nurse, was carefully cutting swabs from lengths of gauze from a long roll and folding them up.

'Can I help you?' asked Juliet, pulling a stool up to the table and holding out her hands.

Agnes gave a trill of laughter.

'You want to help, doctor? Yes, thank you! If you can hold the roll of gauze for me . . .'

She heaved the roll towards Juliet, who grasped it, held it up in front of her and with some difficulty allowed it to unravel slowly, depositing white clouds of gauze onto the table. Agnes deftly straightened, measured and cut it, her head bent in concentration.

Alix, one of the Ethiopian junior doctors, came out of the ward and paused at the table to watch. 'You are helping, doctor!' he pronounced.

'Only a little,' smiled Juliet, peeking out from behind the large roll.

'Agnes will be happy with a little,' he nodded placidly, slipping past them to greet some visitors.

'Alix, man. How are you?' There was the sound of hands being slapped together and laughter. Juliet kept her eyes on the gauze and on Agnes, but she registered an accented European voice.

'I'm glad to see you here – you can help me find our new surgeon. Dr Jools Macleod. He's probably one of those overconfident big London boys – you know the type – bit thrusty, bit too much testosterone, always wanting his case done before the poor gynaecologist's—'

'Excuse me,' Juliet said quietly to Agnes. Jools! she thought in exasperation. That was most likely courtesy of the plummy voiced chap who had interviewed her in London for the MSF job. No one ever called her Jools. She stood up and turned to see a smiling, tall and lean but strong-looking man, gripping

Alix's shoulder with one hand, while the other twirled his sunglasses. He had an unruly mop of dirty blond hair, twinkly eyes and an MSF T-shirt which had clearly seen better days.

'It'll be more tits than testosterone, but I'm sure I can fit your stereotype otherwise,' she drawled, eyebrows raised. Alix looked discomfited at this, but the tall messy-headed man next to him gave a resounding bark of laughter, slapped his leg and stuck his hand out to Juliet.

'But this is most excellent; a girl surgeon with a boy's name! You are most welcome to our top humanitarian team!'

His infectious grin seemed to encompass all of him: the mad hair, eyes the rich blue of the Mediterranean, prominent nose and high cheekbones above deep laughter lines. He continued to hold out his hand to her, while the other arm waved wildly in the air as if ready to embrace her, anyone else, everyone else. Juliet felt her frosty tight-lipped smile melt into a genuine one. She kept her lips together, but felt her own dimples deepening.

'Pleased to meet you, I'm sure,' she clipped in her best Royal Family accent, daintily taking the ends of his big fingers in her own as though they were a fragile china teacup.

He gave another ridiculously loud bark of laughter, inclined his head and curtseyed, holding her hand above his head and wobbling clownishly. Juliet started to chuckle.

Jan stood up, winking at Juliet, and pointedly relinquished her hand, after just a few seconds too many.

'Jeff! This is our new surgeon and he's a girl,' he announced theatrically.

A smaller tidier man with combed dark hair and a tanned face stepped up to them, giving a nice flash of his white American teeth.

'No shit, Sherlock! Those ten years you spent training in obstetrics and gynaecology are finally bearing fruit.'

He took off his mirrored sunglasses, screwed up his soft brown eyes in the sun and extended his hand to Juliet. She shook it, noticing his pressed, almost shiny MSF T-shirt.

'Juliet Macleod. Which is actually a girl's name, as is Jan.'

'Jan with a Y sound!' expostulated Jan. 'It's a very fine manly Viking name, given to me as I am a fine manly Viking man!'

'From Slovakia?' Jeff looked inquiringly.

'Yes, the ancestors . . . you know – Ich bin ein Viking and all that . . . Not that you Yanks understand.'

'We might need to have a little history chat one of these days. Anyway—'

Jeff turned his attention back to Juliet. 'You've met our Visiting Obstetrician and Gynaecologist, known as the VOG, Jan – pronounced manly Yan, and I'm Jeff the Log.'

'Right, lovely to meet you,' Juliet hesitated. 'Sorry, what do you mean "Log"? Is that a Viking thing too?'

Jeff puffed out his chest a little. 'No. No Viking nonsense – logistics! I am the strategy and operations manager, also in charge of safety, supplies, vital logistical challenges—'

Jan cut across him. 'He fills the cars with diesel and sources the beer. Very important actually.'

'. . . And I fill the cars with diesel and source the beer,' finished Jeff, giving a triumphant performer's flourish with his cap.

'Talking of cars, we're here to offer you a lift back to HQ if you like?' Jeff opened his palms towards Juliet as though giving an offering.

'What a flirt,' snorted Jan. 'Let me go and find Dr V to talk about the fistula camp, which is the real reason we came.'

'Yeah, yeah, whatever – two birds one stone,' replied Jeff, replacing his sunglasses with unruffled equanimity. 'You two trot along now and chat fisty-whatsits.'

'Fistulae,' said Juliet, carefully following this little comedy. 'It's a hole in the vagina leaking ur . . . '

'Aaargh nee naw, emergency button! No revolting anatomical chat to the Log please. That will be one beer from you, letting you off lightly as you're new.' Jeff pulled his sunglasses down his nose to look sternly at Juliet, hands on hips.

'Oh, yeah?' Juliet squared her shoulders, up for the challenge, and with a dark glint in her eyes. 'How much is it for crusted carbuncle oozing faeculent maggoty pus?'

Jan rubbed his hands gleefully and looked approvingly at Juliet. 'I'd say three beers, but maybe I can beat it with—'

'No!' shrieked Jeff. 'I'll get you each two beers not to have this contest. I'll tell Man-U to be ready to take us to a bar in fifteen.' He trotted off surprisingly sharply for one so previously laconic.

Amused, but still not a hundred per cent sure of what was going on, Juliet turned to Jan who was watching her, an interested and somewhat pleased expression on his open face.

'Man-U?' she asked.

'Emmanuel, driver. Known to all as Man-U. And fifteen minutes? Pah – African time, nothing's ever done in fifteen. Shall we go find Dr V? I'll follow you, Mrs Surgeon.' His eyes widened at her, innocently.

Juliet would normally have narrowed her own eyes suspiciously at this, but instead to her surprise she felt the irrepressible joy of the place surging up again as she looked into the ward. She wanted to share the specialness of it with someone else, someone able to understand how extraordinary it was.

'Okay, have you had the tour here before?'

He shook his head, smiling at the excitement he could hear in her voice.

'Well, this is the entrance of course . . . Here's Agnes, working hard.'

'Hi, Agnes, good to meet you.'

She stood up, smiling shyly. 'You are welcome, doctor.'

'But let's go round the outside way,' continued Juliet. She turned to him and beckoned, the sun catching her hair in bright gold streaks.

They walked along the veranda and around the corner to enter a green, gently sloping garden, bathed in sunlight and sprinkled with shady trees, blue-gowned patients and brightly flowering bushes. The Labradors lay stretched out under a bench in the shade. She was feasting her eyes on the

Cézanne-worthy scene; he was looking at her rather than the garden.

'This is what we need in our hospitals in the UK: gardens, flowers, dogs. It's got to be better for recovery than busy carparks and grumpy security guards. More sunshine would be good too, obviously.'

'Yes. It seems too nice to be a hospital.' He paused. 'Wish there were more like this.'

'Me too,' said Juliet. 'Anyway, come in and see the ward. Dr V will be in her office. I will leave you with her after our tour, then come back and meet you here.'

Half an hour later, Juliet came hurrying back out to the garden, bursting with apologies and excuses for her lateness, but the garbling words drained harmlessly away as she saw him sitting on the steps leading to the garden with two tiny patients, all of them giggling.

He was lifting his leg up and waggling his foot and they were trying to do the same with little success. Juliet stopped to watch. The girls' legs were incredibly thin with the ankle joints pointing down unnaturally. Jan was making them laugh as they wiggled their toes. He then sat on the grass in front of them and held his hand on the sole of one of their feet, bending the ankle up.

'Push!' he said before apparently falling back, sprawling on the grass at her birdlike tiny push. The girls burst out laughing, Juliet smiling too. He got up off the grass, pretended to roll up his non-existent sleeves and flexed his biceps.

'Again!' he cried. 'This time I will be strong!'

The girls took some time to stop laughing and try again, at which he managed an even more dramatic fall, plus a couple of backwards somersaults, inciting their complete collapse into helpless mirth. He sat up, held his head as if screwing it back into place and grinned at them, taking in his audience also with a little wink at Juliet.

'Hey, the mzungu is here. Time to go.'

He waited for the girls to recover, then clasped his hands together and nodded at them like a yogi. 'I go,' he said, faux serious. 'Good work!'

A chorus of goodbyes in English and Amharic.

'Good work to you, too!' smiled Juliet as they walked away across the grass. 'Physio and fun.'

'Some of the girls have such deformed legs – nerve damage from the childbirth, I suppose,' he frowned.

'Yes. And damage from so much time spent in the corner of a little hut, not walking anywhere.'

He cocked his head to the side. 'Like a dog in a . . . not pen. What's the word?'

'Kennel,' supplied Juliet, grimacing.

'Kennel. Okay, I'm learning it, thank you.' He paused. 'Very bad situation.'

Juliet knew it. Such misery, torture really, to come from the supposedly natural and beautiful experience of having a baby. She turned to him, as something occurred to her.

'By the way, should I be pleased to be a mzungu? Something for the resumé maybe?'

Jan's face lightened as he laughed. 'Perhaps not . . . it means

39

a white person. Buzzing like a mosquito all the time, not relaxed, not always exactly welcome, you know?'

'Oh. Yes. Mmmmm zzzzz. Okay, it's fair enough. Noisome plague element to us too, I guess. Old Testament-ish. And colonialism,' she added, before he could.

'That gives me a good idea,' he said, brightening up. 'Have you met Lucy yet? We should go see her before we start our journey north. I'll tell Jeff that you're insisting on it, otherwise he will ignore me.' He turned to Jeff. 'Oi! Special request from the Surgeon to meet Lucy, we had better keep her sweet, very dangerous with a knife probably . . . although Dr Valentine likes her. Good hands, she said.'

Juliet was about to splutter about the knife comment, but the Dr Val praise filled her with delight. She beamed at a slightly nonplussed Jeff and got into the car.

Chapter 5

Juliet

In the Museum of Ethiopia

'AH, I LOVE LUCY!' Jan opened his arms wide. 'And welcome to your ancestral home – did you know you were actually African?'

Juliet read the inscription:

3.2-million-year-old remains of a small-bodied early human, on the lineage that gave rise to Homo sapiens, named Australopithecus afarensis, but known to the world as Lucy.

'Oh, my God! Is she the start of all of us? She looks so small and innocent. And so real.' Juliet placed her hand on the glass case as though they might reach each other through all the years.

There was something utterly mesmerising about her. Somehow, through all these centuries and millennia, there was a link between them. Juliet felt herself standing at the end of a physical chain of motherhood, viscerally connecting her all the way back to this woman, this actual person. She searched for the right word, for the feeling the little skeleton provoked in her: belonging? Yes. She belonged to this first woman, on this earth.

An epiphany swept through her – a realisation that there was another story alongside the usual noisy tale which passed for history – war after war, men and their deaths. So many treated as mere bricks for the edifice of some would-be king, young lives squandered before they had a chance to fulfil their potential, as if they hardly counted. They counted to their mothers though – and each and every one was some mother's son or daughter. The mothers held the threads of this quieter but strong and lasting story of life and lives. And this little woman, little Lucy, was right at chapter one.

She felt it all more intensely than she could have imagined, was slightly embarrassed at her reaction, aware of Jan watching her.

She covered it with a little laugh. 'Hello Granny! I feel like holding her hand and saying, "Don't worry, there's some bad, some good, happening now, but you did well!"'

'Trying to be the favourite child, eh? Should have guessed.' He tutted and rolled his eyes, but he had seen the connection she made.

She was still staring at the little body.

'All those women and births between her and us,' she murmured. 'All the women, coming and going, keeping it all going.'

'Mmm.' Jan was gazing too, his mind full of his own thoughts.

'Why Lucy, by the way? Not very African is it?'

'What? Oh, her name? They found her and dug her out of the mud of the Rift Valley near here the summer that "Lucy In the Sky With Diamonds" was playing everywhere. That's why she's Lucy.'

'Epic song title. It was always looking for a good story, I guess. Doesn't get better than hers, does it? From her, all the way to us, all belonging to her.'

She continued to muse: where did anyone belong anyway? Did your country of birth trump everything else, geography over philosophy – geography *was* really family though, blood. How far back did one go before blood loyalty was stretched too thin – as far as Lucy? Maybe that was the only valid thing: to go back all that way, encompass everyone under that one diamond-spangled starry sky, and see that you belonged as much as anyone else. And that any other identity was about you, was about your being true to your own self. Carry your niche within yourself.

'There's something there. She has something. Do you agree?' Jan was smiling, but it was a serious question – she met his eyes, answering without the need to speak.

He blinked, then turned to Jeff. 'Not for the Americans though – look at Jeff, entirely unmoved. I think Americans believe they were dropped down into the land of the free from outer space – no connection to the rest of us.'

'You brought me to this museum about five times the

last trip we made to Addis,' complained Jeff. 'I'm all out of emotion. And she seems very hairy on that picture, even more so than my great aunt Mildred . . . not sure my family would have that much hair in their background. We were never sure Aunt Mildred was truly one of us either.'

'Chemically right about outer space, I guess,' said Juliet, still focussed on Lucy, unwilling to look away. 'Go back a bit further and every atom of us was made in a star.'

'No! Really? That's so cool!' Jan seemed genuinely excited by this astrophysical revelation. 'We'll have to call you Stardust Surgeon.'

'Chemically stardust,' she corrected him.

'Not poetic,' he shook his head. 'But still, Stardust.'

Chapter 6

Sylvie

Before

SYLVIE SAT IN THE shade of the Odaa tree beside her family hut, enjoying the cooling of the afternoon as evening approached. The sky was changing – the azure blue of day going up in flames with glorious streaks of orange-red lightreflected in her glowing skin. A secret smile hovered around her, a special light in her rich bronze eyes. She was deep in communion with the child she was carrying, gently caressing her through her rounded belly, rocking ever so slightly from side to side. For some reason, she felt sure that this child was a daughter. She had so much to tell her about the days to come, about the wide sun-drenched valleys and immense rocky mountains of her home. About the family she would be joining: the children, the grandparents, and of course Ivan. About all the lovely life that awaited her.

She had a view of the potholed path to her village, a collection of homesteads similar to their own: small mud houses, sparse grass, red earth. A little tribe of kids was running wild from house to house, playing some exciting game. A huge fruit bat swooped out of a tree, startling her and interrupting her wandering thoughts. She smiled up at the branches, her lovely face lighting up.

She liked the bats: their unwieldy shape no barrier to graceful flight. They always seemed to have their own busy agenda, with no interest in the stupid flightless humans and other creatures who shared their space. She herself felt more akin to an owl though: she circled her territory, managing it, scanning her loved ones, trying to make things better. She loved knowing that her job at the hotel meant her younger brother and sisters could stay on at school, taking some of the strain out of her father's eyes. She thought of him and her quiet busy mother, her heart stirring with love and the desire to look after them in future years as she made her own family alongside them.

She looked around the yard, swept and tidy, awaiting the return of the school kids. The chickens were pecking industriously around the hut, the goats meehing grouchily, stretched at the end of their ropes. Her mother had gratefully disappeared for a nap, leaving Sylvie in charge. Time to start a fire, fry up the offcuts of meat Cook had sent home with her from the hotel.

Within a few minutes, a flurry of arguments and bags heralded the arrival of Gregory, Neela and Zena. Sylvie carried on calmly tending to the fire, giving them time to settle. Quite soon the girls arrived by her side, jostling just a little and fidgeting more, but eventually quietening down in the hope that a story would soon be coming. Sylvie waited until the meat was brown, adding vegetables and chilli to make stew. She let it simmer, sloshed in some water, then turned, smiling to the girls.

'Now my lovely girls, how was school today?'

'Oh, fine. Zena got in a fight and I was top in my class.' Neela could hardly wait to tell her news.

'Well done for being top, not so well done for telling tales on Zena—' Sylvie reached over to caress her little sister. 'All fine now, Zena? It's usually best to talk things through rather than fight it out, you know,' she added, mildly.

'Pah!' was Zena's somewhat recalcitrant reply.

'You always tell tales, Sylvie!' Neela burst out after a short pause while her crossness at being rebuked boiled up and over.

'True, my little fierce one.' said Sylvie, chucking that little sister under the chin, 'but hopefully not nasty stories about anyone. I like stories that let you fly away to somewhere different in your head.' She caught the eye of Gregory, her younger brother, sitting nearby whittling a stick. Gregory and she shared an insatiable appetite for books and stories. She flicked her eye towards her bag, and he grinned. There must be a new leftover hotel book there for him.

'I want to fly away somewhere!' cried Neela. 'Please Sylvie, tell us a story—'

'Please, please,' echoed Zena.

'Well, what I want to tell you about is the visitors we had to the hotel last week. The Alien family, from the planet Zog. They were very friendly, but they did have rather a terrible time with the mosquito nets – got in an awful tangle with their four legs each—'

'Why were they at the hotel?' interrupted Zena, eyes as round as flying saucers.

'Ah, you see, they were trying to get to Jupiter, but they turned left instead of right at the moon and ended up here. Shall I tell you about the planet Zog? You should lie back and stare at our blue sky, see if you can imagine or even see that planet out there beyond the blue . . . It's quite different from here. They told me that their sun is pink, so everything looks pink. Light pink or dark pink, but pink nevertheless, and with very weird rocks that you can actually eat . . . '

They meandered off around the cosmos chasing aliens, as the sun sank behind the trees and their own world took on a reddish glow.

It was now the last few days of Sylvie's pregnancy. The months had passed in a whirl of excitement, with many stolen special moments with her handsome Ivan. He had seemed wonderstruck at her growing belly, the moving baby within. He was also very enamoured of her swelling breasts, apparently finding her body even more irresistible than before. She was pleased about that, pleased that his desire was unquenched, particularly as she herself really loved her pregnant body. She loved the smooth shiny skin of the bump, the sheen of her cheeks, the readiness of her breasts. She loved Ivan's exploration of her changing shape, his excitement at her. She revelled in his insatiable want for her, paying him back like for like with lust.

Now that she had become too big to work at the hotel, she had moved back to her parents' hut in the village, missing him more than a little, and waiting for the great day to arrive, for the baby to come. Ivan was busy at his work, could not be in the village with her, but sent messages and little food parcels when he could.

Waiting and waiting. The neighbouring women would call to see her and her mother, would tut, feel her belly, pinch her cheek and tell stories of their own babies. They all had stories of their childbearing; all had advice to give and were offering to assist her when her time came. They had given birth in their huts in the village, the older ones helping the younger ones. There was no tradition of going to hospital – let alone the impossible costs involved, hospital seemed a frightening and alien place to go, especially for such a family event as having a baby. It was not even considered as an option. Sylvie had no desire to challenge the traditions described to her; rather, she eagerly anticipated continuing them in her own life. She wanted nothing more than to have her fledgling family welcomed into the community fold. She felt secure in the affections of all the well-known faces around her.

Sylvie's mother said little. Bathed in the pure joy which radiated from Sylvie whenever the baby was mentioned, she reflected a smile back, but could not banish a slightly anxious urgency from it. Only Amara, her oldest friend from the village, noticed and squeezed her arm as Eshe thanked her and the other village women for their help. Amara knew that there was danger in childbirth – she was well aware of the histories of the women of their village. And there were the other stories from further afield – Amara's son, Edmond, was a nurse in the town hospital and had shared some distressing tales with her during his training. He was quieter about it all now, processing things without her, but she had not forgotten.

Sylvie was taken aback when it started; it seemed so innocuous at first. Just a few flutters. Well, nothing too bad about this, she thought. Fine – nothing she couldn't handle. She almost welcomed it, knowing it brought the moment closer when she would meet her little baby, look into her eyes, know her.

Walking slowly around the yard, dreaming of holding her babe, she smiled at her mother. Word was sent to Ivan, but he was not to come yet – this was a time for the women. They filled it with song, ancient comforting lilting melodies, repeated over so many years to so many women at this crux in their lives. It was as though they were conjuring help from the spirits of the many who had trodden this path before: suffered and sweated, paid the price for the miracle of birth. Sylvie felt the beautiful age-old harmony of it; felt her own spirit lifted up. It was a wonderful thing she was part of now, increasingly painful, but wonderful just the same.

A few hours later, though, it was not so fine, not so fine at all. The pains were more and more intense, robbing her of breath, smiles and speech, making her double over, grip her mother's arm hard.

God in heaven, she thought, is this how it always is? How has Mama got through this five times already? She said it would be difficult though, so this must be right; I must be doing it right.

She fought to reassure herself in between the pains.

Three neighbouring women had come to be with her and her mother, full of chat, songs and jokes. Their sureness was heartening, their confidence cheering. They did not seem in the least surprised by the intensity and duration of her labour; instead, they seemed to be in for the long haul. But it was a longer and longer haul.

The sun set, rose again, set again. Sylvie continued to drag herself through the oh-so-regular pains, her mother valiantly trying to hold back her own distress, and make her suffering daughter drink a little water. By the end of the third day, only one neighbour, Amara, remained silently with her mother. All the confidence was drained away, all the jokes and birthing songs were finished. Different songs were waiting in the wings: the minor keys for weeping and loss.

Because now it was wrong. The scales had tipped. It had been too long; it should have been over well before now. Expectation had faded to hope which had now run out, leaving only silent desolation, interspersed with exhausted cries and moans from Sylvie. She knew herself that she was caught in an agonising limbo. Never-ending pain, with no sign of the baby.

Mama, please help me, she pleaded silently, looking at her mother, imploring her for help, for hope. She saw only the mirror of her own desperation: fear and helplessness. Eshe was holding one of her hands, Amara the other, their eyes full of anguish, no words of comfort coming now. They tried to support her when the pains came – mopped the sweat off her brow. They could no longer bring themselves to tell her to push, though. They could see that she was done.

None of them knew how to stop the horrible unfolding of this disaster. They knew though that Sylvie and the baby could not both survive this and perhaps neither would. They had seen this all before, just as their own mothers and grandmothers, aunts and great aunts had. Not everyone made it to the other side of childbirth.

Sylvie had not seen it before. She was clinging to threads of hope, unable to imagine that her lovely life was imploding all around her. Her life, her baby. Her baby, her baby . . . Please, God, please. Let this end. But how? How could it end?

The answer was too terrifying to voice, to think. And, really, thinking was now too hard in this black and painful blur.

Something deep within her was making her keep breathing, but her strength was almost gone now, ebbing steadily.

Death was by her side, waiting. The galaxies continued to shine above her, as glorious as ever. Silent witnesses: unflinching, unmoved.

She took another breath.

Chapter 7

Sylvie

After

IF SHE DIDN'T MOVE, maybe there would be no stinging. She would think hard about a different bit of her – about her face instead. Her eyes and what they could see out the door of the hut: the black sky, a sprinkling of glittering stars, shadowy palms. Lick her teeth and then her lips, form some words, remember some good words: moon, breeze, coolness, flowers.

Words to conjure some welcome ease in her mind. Private words just for her, thought, formed and whispered to keep a part of her pure, happy. A special place where good things could be left alone to flourish, a secret garden of the mind. She could walk into that sanctuary in her head and rest there. Remembered scents of jasmine and frangipani would drift around her; the very air a balm, caressing her, tending her fragile spirit.

Owww. The garden disappeared with a fiery shot of brutal pain. Sylvie had not moved a muscle, but a trickle of burning liquid had found its own way to the raw sores on her thighs. The daily torture had begun, the daily battle within and without herself. And now the repeating wail of her fully conscious self was winding up. Such a loud lament, howling through her all day, behind the silent façade she showed the world. Never breaking through but almost all encompassing for Sylvie.

Part of my soul was taken and is gone. Gone. I don't know where. Somewhere, elsewhere, not here, never to return. How I long for her. My empty arms ache.

She shook her head, tried to find clear thoughts above the fog of pain and grief. It would be morning soon, time to get up and get washed, try to be clean for a short time. For seconds only, not even a minute.

She stretched her head up, ran her hand over her damp, shorn head. She had never got used to that part of her yet, still felt naked without her lovely braids. They had become a nightmare though, soaked from the leaking urine every night, impossible to clean. Her mother had taken them off, silently crying along with Sylvie.

It was still night, but she could sense the darkness thinning, ready for the light to elbow its way in. Another day. Another whole long day of making herself live with all that pain in the most sensitive parts of her; continuously tormented with the unending stinking hot urine which ran uncontrollably from deep within her, burning its way like lava down her legs.

And all of it reminding her of her loss, her terrible loss. Her baby, her dreams, her life, her purpose. Her very self. The brutal tsunami of childbirth had borne it all relentlessly away on that day, leaving only poor trashed debris for her to clutch at. And now her damaged body and her aching soul had somehow to carry on, feeling as hope-drained as a prisoner given a life sentence without parole.

She shut her eyes, steadied her spirit to withstand these endless waves of anguish, as she had done every day now for three long years. Oh, for a rest from this life, her thought began again: no. No. She would not let that thought finish, she would not give up: *no*. She pressed her lips together, schooled her mind. After a few slow breaths, she opened her eyes again.

I won't think of the cursed thing, or of me at all. I will think about the good things I have, things which were not lost when it . . . when I . . . good things. Like this little brother, snoring here beside me. Yes, you, Jonny. You will talk and read and count and see the wonders of life for me. You will have my voice in your head and when you are old enough to see the thing that blights me, maybe you will reject me. But still my voice will be in your head. And I will tell you that you are loved, and that life can be beautiful.

She tried to shift position a little to divert the slow burning trickle, but she knew it was useless; she had to get up, find a dry rag and gently pad herself, try to clean up. The sooner she did it, the easier it would be, the less pain it would cause. She looked down at Jonny, her slightly grubby four-year old brother, open mouthed in sleep. She looked after him day and night, while also helping her heavily pregnant mother through the chores required to feed a family of seven. Trying to grow some roots, some greens, trying to keep order in the small crumbling hut of twigs and mud, in their patch of earth, over a kilometre from the nearest water pump.

Water. That was Sylvie's aim now, her task. She had to get up, get padded up, strap the empty jerry cans to her father's bicycle and walk it to the pump. Then push it back slowly, laden with full jerry cans, avoiding potholes, not causing any damage to the precious bike: essential to her father. And she had to go *very soon* – before dawn, before anyone else. Before anyone could see her, or worse, smell her.

When she had the water back at the hut, she could disappear for a few minutes into her own washing place, carefully constructed from bamboo at the back of the main hut. There she would wash herself properly, revel in those short precious moments of being truly clean before the hated urine started to seep out again, soaking her rags, filling the air with ammonia, keeping everyone out.

Everyone except Jonny. He never seemed to notice her smell. Maybe he was just used to her. Her other brother and two sisters certainly noticed, though. She had been such a goddess to them, a person to emulate. Now they shunned her, afraid of what had become of her, angry at her for letting it happen. They were also angry at the reduced life they too now had; with no hotel wage money from her, meaning no fees for high school after they completed primary school. Her brother was already through that, working alongside their father at just fourteen, shifting heavy sacks, brickmaking, digging. Hard labour for a boy who had loved books.

She had spent hours with him reading, all for what? Nothing for him, nothing for her. She shook her head to dispel the hateful thoughts, gritted her teeth, fought. It was not nothing. They had seen, understood and known more of life from these books. More than just the struggle to survive, more possibilities, more to think on besides the daily grind for food: ideas, beautiful words, understanding, visions of other times and worlds. They carried it all within them now; once seen, never could be unseen.

She must keep remembering the good parts of her, even if almost no one else could see her through the stink of her, the curse on her. Later, she would tell Jonny stories of heroes and heroines and their great struggles in distant lands. Her sisters would listen while pretending they weren't, the nearest she could get to them.

And for a few minutes now she would indulge herself with her own story – would open up the box of happy memories – of her and Ivan, before all this. She let herself remember. Remembered walking down the road to town with an easy grace, her footsteps light on the warm tarmac. The day almost done, the luminous air thrumming gently with the slowly building excitement of the coming night. Muffled beats of music gaining ground above the rumble and roar of traffic, while small plumes of smoke signalled the lighting of the roadside braziers.

She saw herself then. Her bright eyes, full of life, laughter lurking just below the surface. An open smile, expecting joy. Shining skin, slim waist, smooth limbs. Everything fitted perfectly, everything was grown and honed and polished in harmony to arrive at this fulfilled song of girlhood; everything called to the world to celebrate her wonderful being. She felt beautiful, blossoming, strong.

The older women had watched her silently as she passed, pausing in their cooking and chatting. Ah, they sighed a little, feeling the stirrings of memory, reminding them of how it felt when it had been their own time in the spotlight. Those beloved girls, lost now in the women they had become. And oh, the fearful danger of being her. They shook their heads ever so slightly to burst the bubbles welling up from the past, returning to their pots.

Two well-fed businessmen turned their eyes from the football on the TV of the Wild Rose bar to stare at her firm breasts and curves. There was a certain unpleasant ownership in their look – a claim of something due to a successful forty-year-old man. The motorcyclists and boda boda riders waiting for custom outside the bar whistled and revved at her, but only a little – giving precedence to the older, richer men.

Sylvie had walked on by. A corner of her mind registering the low level threats, but pushing them away into the background of raucous trucks and cars, horns blaring and people shouting. She wanted to keep her thoughts focussed internally, let them all race around the one nearly all-encompassing occupant of her consciousness: Ivan.

Just saying his name in her head gave her a rush. She would let her mind circle him, let him remain kinglike, enthroned in the centre of the swirling desires, building gradually with a zillion spin-offs, crazy hopes and imaginings, all the while wondering would she see him tonight? Would she?

He came to the hotel to ask if she was going out tonight. She was little flustered to see him; it was a busy time and she had not even had a chance to check her hair in a mirror. But she knew she looked good in her receptionist uniform: smooth and slightly untouchable.

'Hello,' he said with a nervous smile but a light in his eyes.

'Hello,' she replied, matching nerves for nerves. Nothing world shattering there, she had to admit. Ah, but the eyes. She caught something there – a recognition of something between them, which she reflected right back to him. A spark. She wasn't imagining it, was she?

No – she knew he admired her. And he had not even bothered to pretend he was just passing: he had clearly changed out of his mechanics' overalls into his good clothes and come over for the single reason of her, as if summoned by her.

Summoned, she repeated to herself. It was a heady feeling, but there was no doubt in it. She had felt that power, the power of her body, the possibilities in it. Surely he felt it, too, shared the breathless excitement of this awakening.

If she saw Ivan that evening (of course she would, of course he was gravitating towards her, wasn't he?), then more would be said, more would unfold. She knew it, felt the inevitability. Just as she had felt herself to be absolutely balanced, poised and ready to execute a perfect swallow dive . . . into what exactly she did not know. The waters were untested, the currents unknown, but there was no doubt that she would throw herself into them, take her chance.

Later, in the bar, she shifted her chair very slightly to the right in subtle invitation and in a breath, he was beside her, an arm slung over the back of her chair slightly brushing her shoulder. She felt a little tremor go through her at the touch, and the tacit understanding growing between them.

While the raucous laughter of the others crescendoed around them, Ivan murmured to Sylvie, 'So, the end of school and they are all leaving town – but not you?'

'Not me, no.'

She shot him another look sideways. His eyes were penetrating, seeking something, seeking her maybe. He was just touching the back of her arm, the tips of his fingertips making tiny strokes. She could feel her blood thrill under his touch, her whole body sensitised to it, like a perfectly honed as yet silent violin: yearning to make music.

'Good.' His somewhat intense expression melted into a slightly mischievous grin. 'Shall we go walking? When's your day off? I can meet you after work if that's better?'

'I didn't say *yes* yet!' She turned to him, her eyes open wide in mock admonishment, but a warmth in them which belied her words.

'But you will . . . when will you?' he returned, unabashed.

She cocked her head, considering him, pretending to be cool. She had no idea how to be cool. She hoped at least he could not tell how fast her heart was beating.

'Maybe on Sunday afternoon I would like to go for a walk. It would be good to get some air after work.' She pursed her lips, holding back the joyful laugh she could feel welling up inside her, ready to burst out.

'Yes, air is good. I am good too! You can have both. Sunday, then. I will come to the hotel.' He nodded, satisfied.

She gave way to a smile, her thoughts rushing away with her. Have both? Maybe, maybe. And what does he get? Me, clearly. I see in his face that it is he who means to have me. But for what?

It seemed something more than just fun. A serious beat accompanied his light banter, marching her towards him. She did not know where that journey ended, but it was a welcome wild card – unlike everything else in her rather constrained life. She was enthralled by his pursuit of her, enraptured by his desire for her. She was in.

Then there was the day he came to take her for a trip in the truck.

She was working on the accounts in the hotel office when Cook interrupted her, looking even sterner than usual, arms folded under her magnificent bosom, a formidable battleship ready to launch.

'Do you need me?' asked Sylvie, rather tentative. 'Is everything all right?'

'Hmph,' hmphed Cook. 'Well, we'll have to see if everything's all right, or not, won't we? What are his prospects, that's what I would like to know for a start!'

'Eh? Whose?' Sylvie was lost.

'Your young man. Very nice smile – is he relying on that? Is there anything behind it?' She glowered at Sylvie, who beamed at her.

'Thank you, Cook, for looking out for me. He works at Asefa's garage on Main Street. He's going to college, too, and will be a qualified mechanic and driver in a few years.' She added quickly, 'Ehm – is he here?'

'Hmph,' said Cook again, but slightly mollified. 'He's at the back door, with a message.'

'Thank you!' Sylvie skipped ahead of her protector to the kitchen, finding Ivan waiting on the back porch. She was closely followed by Cook, who took up a threatening position just behind Sylvie and glared continually at Ivan.

'Hello, Ivan,' smiled Sylvie, managing not to laugh at the spectacle she was making with Cook. She could not hide how pleased she was to see him, though.

'Ah, hi!' Ivan looked nervously between Sylvie and Cook, then obviously decided that it was best to just get his message out, since it didn't look as though any privacy was to be afforded.

'So, I have to make a delivery this afternoon with the garage vehicle. I wondered if you could come along for the ride?' He started to grin at her, glanced again at Cook, and straightened his face quickly. Cook sniffed malignantly.

'I'm sure I can,' replied Sylvie. 'So long as we're back in time for the dinner shift.' She smiled primly at Cook and darted past her before there could be an unleashing of the dire warnings and woeful predictions surely reaching bursting point within that redoubtable lady.

A few hours later, the delivery was complete, and Sylvie was watching Ivan drive back towards Adigrat. He was a good driver – relaxed and confident despite the potholes and cyclists, the animals and the unpredictable pedestrians who moved almost blindly under the impossibly towering loads of fruit, buckets and pots which they routinely carried on their heads. He didn't try to show off either, which immediately made her feel secure.

She was about to say something complimentary to that effect when the truck swung off the road onto a small track leading bumpily through the forest.

'Oh!' she exclaimed. 'Where are we . . . I mean, is this road okay?'

'Yes, Sylvie, don't worry. I'll keep you safe. I know this road, and it's a long way from where the army went. No mines here.'

'Okay . . . but can I ask where we're going?' She was nervous.

He smiled. 'Don't worry. We're just going to the next

village, then I have something to show you.'

After a few minutes, they reached the village. Ivan parked just out of sight of the last hut and turned off the engine. The heat inside the truck was immediately oppressive.

'On foot now!' he said, swinging out of the cab and coming around to help her out. 'Not far, though. This way.'

They followed a small path around the back of the village, then came out into a sizeable clearing in the woods. Ivan took her hand, and they walked through it almost to the other side, then stopped.

'Now turn around,' he said, 'and what do you see?'

Towering behind the village was a kind of a hill, surprisingly large and somewhat forbidding. Black clouds were gathering behind it, lending it even more dramatic severity. She was amazed that they had been driving around the foot of it without being aware of its rather threatening presence. She peered up at the cliff near the top and various old round huts and structures just visible on the summit.

'Oh!' she breathed. 'The monastery of Debre Damo. I've never seen it before.'

He smiled, pleased to see the awe on her face. 'It's very old, I think.'

'Fifteen hundred years,' she murmured, entranced by it, staring. 'All these years of men going up there to talk to God.'

He looked interested, but only slightly. He was watching her, rather than looking up at it.

She drank it in, still aware of him beside her. 'It's so . . .

so big and dark. I can imagine that God is actually up there today. Wow. Do you talk to God, Ivan?'

He shrugged. 'Oh, that kind of thing is for them, the monks, not for me. I'm busy here, with men's things down here. My work, cars, my woman . . . ' His eyes bored into her. 'You.'

She felt him pull her gaze away from the monastery down to him. Standing in the sunlight, rippling with youth and strength and sureness. He was everything alluring, his physical potency drawing a visceral response from her like a magnet. A force of nature she could not resist. She reached for him and in a second was enveloped in strong arms, intense eyes melting into hers. He carefully swept her braids behind her upturned face and slowly bent to kiss her. A deliberate, careful kiss, keeping her pressed against his muscled body, so alive. She let herself relax just a little into his chest, let him also feel the life pounding in her.

For a few minutes they were oblivious to everything bar each other; but the huge raindrops now falling and the growling thunder finally percolated through.

Sylvie pulled back and looked up at the dark sky. 'Oh, proper rain coming,' she said.

'Not yet.' Ivan was still holding her and was kissing her again, an urgency to him now. But the rain was truly coming now, torrential.

She pulled away again, laughing up at him. 'Ivan! Let's go!'

He grinned, grabbed her hand and they ran through the

pelting rain across the clearing into the trees to the truck, diving inside, both completely drenched. The rain was drumming on the roof and windows, obscuring everything outside. Sylvie was still giggling, slightly out of breath, eyes bright from the run and the adventure, her heart beating fast. She looked down at herself: her wet clothes were transparent as gauze, clinging to her glistening skin, showing every fulsome inch of her figure.

Ivan pulled her into his lap. 'Sylvie. You're all wet.' His fingers traced the contour of her neck and down to her breast, peeling back the thin soaked shirt as he kissed her, deeper than before, demanding more.

The kissing was burning her up and she moaned against him, wanting his touch all over her body, intoxicated by her own desire as well as his.

'Sylvie.' He was breathing heavily now. 'I want you, girl. Be mine? And I will be yours.'

Now she was touching him, pulling his top off, touching his broad chest, kissing him back, matching his demand and echoing his words. 'Yours, and you will be mine.'

And she had no fear, for this was what her body was for, this lovemaking. She wanted Ivan. She trusted his desire for her, that it would hold and sustain them. Nothing else mattered then, just the two of them, their glorious bodies together, safe from the storm in the truck, and hidden from the world by the teeming rain. She let everything else go.

*

Sylvie let the memory roll to a close, let it slowly sink back down into her mind. She took a breath, knowing it was time to face the present again.

Come on Sylvie, time to go, she thought. Don't be late, not when she might meet someone, feel their pity or censure, feel her shame. She could keep her little inner secret garden growing, keep some love of life somewhere if she didn't have to face that shame, that censure. That had to be avoided, every day.

Within a few minutes, she had the cans strapped onto the bike, and carefully made her way round to the front of the hut and onto the track leading to the road. The cicadas were done for the night, but there was chirping from various birds in the trees overhead. Two dogs were howling nearby, probably hungry. The cockerel from the hut next door was strutting around his deserted yard, puffed up and crowing to his snoozing hens.

There were intermittent roars of motorbikes from the main road, about a kilometre away, heading towards the town, ten kilometres off. It seemed such a long time since she had lived there, worked there, gone walking with Ivan . . .

Ivan. She had thought of him this morning for the first time in many days. Their romance almost seemed like one of her stories – as if it had happened to someone else entirely. Their wooing and courting had only lasted a few short months before that one fateful afternoon, sheltering from the sudden rainstorm at Debre Damo. They had been slightly crazy in the monsoon, unhinged. She had been enveloped in his kiss, and then it was much more than just kissing; she could no more have stopped it than stopped the rain from falling, or the sun going down that night. She hadn't wanted to stop it!

Sometimes she ached for him, and for herself when she had been with him. For their fine kisses, for the heat of their passion, his seeming worship of her then perfect body, for their murmured plans, for their shared hopes, for their bab . . . No. No.

That dream bubble had burst, and with such violence, such shocking violence, that it somehow extinguished the previous interlude. She and Ivan could not survive it.

Three years had passed since then. Three years of trying to crawl back from the hopeless hell she had found herself in, dealing with her impossible body, trying desperately to find the vestiges of Sylvie in the ruins: trying to step carefully around the terrible truth at the heart of the disaster; trying to avoid the whirlpool to everlasting torment over her lost child.

At first she had not understood her horrible fate. The realisation of what it meant had crashed over her that awful night early on when her friend Justine had taken her out 'to cheer her up'. Even now remembering it brought a horrific wave of nausea and shame. She shuddered as the events of the night fell into razor-sharp focus in her mind. She had been anything but sharp up to that night: stumbling along half blindly, not looking up, not wanting to confront and comprehend the awful calamity that had befallen her. After that night, there was no escaping it. It was seared across her mind, and visible to all, a shameful glaring brand.

Justine had come for her on her brother's boda boda, wanting to help.

'Come to town!' she said. 'You can't hide away forever. Come with me, we will just go in and see some guys at the poolroom. I'll bring you back whenever you want. It will be fun, like old times!'

Sylvie complied, her old please-everyone instincts kicking in. She didn't have the strength to resist anything. She cleaned herself, padded up as best she could, unthinking, almost trance like, believing poor Justine that all would be well.

All was well initially. They met a few of the guys, nobody she knew well. Some of the pretty girls from the hair salon, ex classmates, and a cousin of Justine's. They had exchanged some banter, some light gossip. Those girls were always slightly dangerous, aware of everyone else's business, competitive. Sylvie usually kept her distance, was careful around them, but this day, her defences were all shot to bits. Luckily, no one asked her what had happened to her, where she had been. No one even mentioned Ivan. One of them gave her newly shaved head a quizzical glance when they first arrived, but backed off at Justine's warning flash of the eyes.

They all had Cokes . . . a Coke! What an idiot she was, to actually drink something. Her brain was not functioning, that was for sure. Within about ten minutes of having the

Coke, she felt the leaking – her inadequate pad was filling up, relentlessly fast. She looked around for Justine who was deep in conversation with her cousin.

Starting to panic, Sylvie turned to the girl beside her, starting at the horrified look on her face, her scrunched up nose. A puddle was forming under Sylvie's plastic chair, the smell of urine unmistakeable.

'Excuse me,' she said, trying her best to sound normal.

She stood up, leaving another puddle on the chair, a dark patch spreading on her pink skirt. Conversation around her stopped; embarrassed silence hung in the air like poisonous gas. Justine, unaware, was still talking.

'Justine!' Sylvie gave a strangulated gasp. 'I need to go home . . . my mother . . . ' She ran out of words.

She bolted from the bar, into the blessed shadows outside by the boda boda, cold and shaking, desperate to escape. The silence around her departure filled quickly with low talk. She could hear Justine, apologising, saying farewell. The noise increased, some laughter.

Where was Justine? – she had to go!

Eventually, a quiet Justine appeared. 'Sorry Sylvie, I had to clean up . . . anyway, no matter, let's get you home.'

They journeyed in silence, Sylvie weeping freely into the slipstream they made.

The consequences of that night's disaster were laid bare. She had effectively declared to one and all the catastrophe of her body. How could she ever face any of them again? She could not. She was shamed and tainted, starting her exile.

She remembered the realisation hitting her, turning to face the wall, sobbing and sobbing. Her mother coming to comfort her, stroking her neck.

'Ah, daughter, my own girl. Stop your crying now, it's over now. Sylvie, Sylvie. You know, I thought we were going to lose you but here you are, my girl, here you are, thanks be to God.'

Sylvie's great wracking sobs eventually began to subside. Her skin wet with sweat, she turned to meet her mother's eyes, the tears still pouring from her.

'Mama. Everything is lost; everything is gone. What shall I do? Whatever shall I do?'

'Live, my sweet girl, just live please. I will look for help for you.' Eshe had leant her forehead on to Sylvie's and let it rest there.

But there was no help.

Her mother's tentative enquiries of the village women had confirmed the awful truth that there was no treatment for her. No one at the local or the regional hospital able to help, even if they could have somehow afforded to go, which they could not.

Sylvie had not forgotten the nightmare, a couple of years ago, when her brother, Gregory, had been ill. What had they called it in the end: *appendix* or something like that. He had got sicker and sicker, until they finally had to take him to the hospital. The doctor had said he needed an operation right away, but . . . No money; no operation. Thank God, then she had been able to get a loan from Kaleb, from the hotel, and pay it back over a number of months. Just in time for Gregory. There was no possibility of a loan or of paying anything back now. Not that there was anything to pay for, anyway.

She sighed quietly as she pushed the bike along. No way through there. And no point counting time. She had to find a different way to measure out her life. Find momentary pleasures and make them matter. Perhaps that was something. And of course, Jonny. She could help him have a good life: a happy life. She was trying.

She looked up from the path to the pump. The darkness was still dense enough to see some stars, the moon sinking now, beginning to bow out. She felt the hard cold brilliance of space resonate against her, inexplicably comforting in its majestic indifference. Her fleeting body could no more match up to the hugeness and power of these galaxies than her family hut could stand against strong rains.

What was there to hold up to the universe, to cling to? Nothing physical anyway. Maybe only love. A pretty thin cord to keep her secure. Would it be enough to hold her through this short and stormy life? Maybe she could make it enough, but . . .

The other face of the love looked not up to heaven but down to hell. She had killed the very being she loved. That was the hideous, terrible, inescapable truth. Any time she raised her head up to see the love, that dreadful truth crushed her.

Chapter 8

Sylvie and Edmond

SHE WAS NEARLY AT the pump. Edmond was watching her, unseen, as he did on many mornings. He hadn't approached her since that horrible time he had to tell her Ivan was gone. She'd been in such a state of shock that his message barely registered.

He thought that she must still be mourning Ivan, but so much else besides – her lovely life before all of this. And yet he could see the determination in her, heaving to get that overladen bike up the rise towards her family's rather miserable hut.

Sometimes when the moon was full, he caught sight of her heart-shaped face and was shocked to see her beauty undiminished, the soft nose, wide mouth, exquisite tilting eyes. No happiness, but also no anger in that face, still beauty, still love. He wondered how it was possible. He had no idea how she was managing to live, and how she could be so tenderly lovely in all her hardship.

He didn't know how to reach out to her either, so he

watched from the darkness of his porch, quiet always. He had to see her though. Whenever he was not on duty at the hospital, he would watch for her, clock her face, check she was still . . . still what? Suffering, toiling, surviving, being. What else could she do; what else could *he* do other than be her witness?

He had enquired for her, quietly trying to find out what was likely to be wrong, asking everyone he met if they knew how it could be fixed. Eshe, Sylvie's mother, had begged him to ask for help from anyone and everyone at the hospital. He asked everyone, all of his colleagues confirming the hopelessness of the situation.

There were plenty of stories of girls disappearing from the community, soiled and shamed, their names no longer spoken. Finally, he tried the regional surgeon – the most senior person available. He waited until the end of the monthly clinic they did together, before bringing a cold drink to his sweating boss and asking for a word of advice. 'Is there anything that could be done for a friend, wet and damaged after losing her baby in childbirth?'

The man downed his bottle of water, wiped his damp face and shook his head regretfully. 'These women,' he said with real sympathy in his eyes, 'fistula patients. They're lost and gone. Poor things. There's nothing for them. I can't help them – no one can. Although, I did hear a rumour of a place in Addis, but you know, people want to hear such rumours.

Personally, I've never known a fistula patient treated. So sad.'

He shook his head again, ready for his day to continue, the casualties of childbirth left behind.

'See you again in a month then, shall I, Edward was it? Bye!'

With a jingle of car keys, he was off, driving back to the regional capital three hours away. Edmond watched him go, disappointment hardening into a heavy stone in his stomach. How could he tell Sylvie and Eshe this terrible outcome, explain that hers was an inescapable fate?

Edmond could feel their gazes following him as he put-putted carefully behind the hut, a light film of dust covering him and his moped. He passed a hand over his hot face, bracing himself. He had nothing good to tell them, no morsel of hope to satisfy their hungry eyes.

His mother smiled at him as he emerged from the house onto the porch, standing to greet him and holding the hand of her friend, Eshe, Sylvie's mother. He felt the familiar lurch of his stomach as he saw that Sylvie was there, too, standing quietly outside the porch in the shade, head down.

'Edmond.' His mother prompted him gently. He caught her eyes, instantly communicating his lack of good news.

The light in her eyes darkened, but she nodded at him. 'Let me get you some water, son.'

He couldn't meet Sylvie's eyes. He had to say it to them though, could not lie; he had no choice but to break her last tiny straw of hope.

Sylvie noticed that his shoulders were down, his eyes avoiding hers. A dread chill started to grow in her heart.

Oh, Lord. He didn't have good news for her. Was it just too expensive? She would think of a way round that: maybe get a loan, a few loans, pay them back over years if need be. She tuned into his quiet words, hearing the sorrow, hearing the sickening truth but unable to grasp it. Unwilling to believe what he had just said. Was he really saying there was no treatment for her? Not now, not ever? Nothing to be done to stop this awful stinking leakage, following her through all her days?

She stared at him, tears falling fast, her fragile spirit collapsing, crushed. The flimsy hopes she held only this morning were now like extra burning whips, licking at her raw wounds, adding to the torture.

She stumbled down the steps and through the garden, not quite reaching the track, when she felt the light touch of a hand on her arm. She stopped, turned to face Edmond's soft eyes.

'Sylvie – I'm so sorry. Can I . . . I mean, I have a message from Ivan. He's sorry, he doesn't know what to do. He's gone to the capital to work.'

Sylvie was silent. Ivan was gone. He would not be back, she knew. She would have to accept this betrayal, too. There was nothing he could do, other than move on. She could not move on, not her, no. She was stuck. But he did not have to stay with her, in her dead-end life.

All of this was in her eyes as she looked back at Edmond.

She tried hard to keep her voice from breaking. 'Maybe you could tell him . . . Tell him not to worry, I understand.'

Then she fled. She did not see the sorrow in Edmond's eyes, his parted lips as he sought in vain for something to say for her, some help to give her. He had not managed to speak to her since that day.

And now, as so many mornings before, he watched her. He watched the clouds, saw they were moving. He waited, knowing the moon would light her up in just a moment.

She stopped just in front of his house, watching the clouds, waiting for the moment. Here it came: bright moonlight bathing her beautiful, upturned face for only a second or two. She drank it in, closed her eyes briefly and opened them to gaze upon it. He didn't breathe, mesmerised by her opening to the moon like a hidden night flower. And before he knew it, it was over. Her head was down, pushing up the hill. The clouds were back.

The morning was advancing, the heat increasing. The girls were dressed for school, waiting for their father and brother to walk them there. Sylvie's father was leaning on his bicycle, calling for Gregory, her brother, to hurry and join them. Gregory was not hurrying. His muscles ached and his head ached at the thought of another day of labour. He did not want to pass his old school friends on the road. Getting him out of the hut was a daily battle, and everyone was feeling it.

Sylvie filled a tub with some hot water from the pan she had taken off the little charcoal fire they used. She put the pan back, dousing the fire with sand. She then returned to the tub with a bottle of soap, ready to add a few drops.

'Dammit girl, washing again? How am I to afford the soap?'

Her father's roar stayed her hand. Jonny burst out crying; the girls shuffled quickly along the path away from the hut. They had learned that distance was best when he lost his temper. Gregory had been coming around from behind the hut, but stopped to look at Sylvie and their father.

'Well? How?' he yelled. 'Come on, Gregory, I am waiting, always waiting for you.' He spat angrily on the ground, then found himself facing the quiet face of his wife Eshe.

'You know she washes all of our clothes first, then her own, no extra soap.'

'Ha, some place you are running here. Let's go and leave these women, Gregory. Now! Neela, Zena, wait for me.'

He stormed off, Gregory following slowly, casting a regretful look back at his mother.

Eshe squatted down beside Sylvie, silently picking up the brush to share in the scrubbing. She saw tears falling silently from the bent head of her daughter.

'Sylvie,' she murmured, 'he's angry, but not at you. He loves you. He is afraid that he has failed somehow.'

Sylvie sniffed, trying to stop crying. 'I know, Mama. But I think I will never please him again, never make him happy.'

'None of us know what life will bring, child. We hate to

see your hurt. I pray to God that it will get better. That's all we can do.'

Sylvie nodded, her tears continuing to drop into the washing.

Chapter 9

Juliet

On the Road North

IT WAS LIKE A bad video game, thought Juliet, going through the levels. Every hour or so the road, which had started off being less than brilliant, became slightly worse. It was now only wide enough for one vehicle, causing many problems whenever they encountered anyone, was full of potholes, and seemed to be going deeper and deeper into uncharted territory. There were no signs. It was a mystery how Man-U knew where to go.

She decided not to think about the fact that further north there were landmines. Presumably Man-U knew where they were. He had stayed alive up to now at least, and (she peered at him) yes, he was beyond the first flush of youth – probably in his forties. Hopefully with some survival skills then.

The houses they passed had started off made of concrete, then slightly higgledy-piggledy brick, now mud – wattle and daub: the eponymous term for anything at all you could slap into a lattice of sticks – probably cow dung. Very useful stuff, she mused – remembering seeing cakes of it prepared for burning in the fire in India. Bit more pungent than Scottish peat, but same stuff really, only at a different stage of development.

She stared at the rickety ramshackle huts and dwellings they passed, all at varying angles, all propping up an illusion of civilisation. Each one a home for someone. It was amazing how people would manage to scramble something together from the most unlikely beginnings to get shelter for their families, to take care of everyone today and even to make plans for tomorrow. Digging and planting something, anything they could, trying to be ready.

Maybe that's what actually constituted civilisation – managing the immediate but also looking to the future. To focus on surviving only one day at a time would perhaps be rather a torment, denying that instinct for planning. Humans and squirrels, she thought.

'Hey boys, are there any squirrels in Ethiopia?' she asked, to the mild surprise of her companions.

'Never been asked that. No idea,' replied Jeff, turning back from his front seat. 'I would ask Man-U, but it seems a bit weird. Can't you ask about monkeys or lions like a normal person?'

She laughed. 'Don't worry. I'll look out for them and let you know if I see one.'

She turned her face back to the miles of sparse villages and dwellings, the land on either side of the road stretching out to faraway horizons – no other roads or towns to be seen. You could be days and days from a hospital out here. Surely there would be fistula patients in these vast expanses, hiding their shame in little huts. But lots of other women, too, happier women, she mustn't forget them. Women who had chosen or accepted, or at least not declined the chance to make a home, make a family with someone. Settled down, that's what they called it at home. Who knew what terms were used here?

She, Juliet, was unsettled, of course. She gazed at the ever-distant horizon. There were many miles to cover today – maybe this was the perfect time to finally think through that last weekend when she had definitively unsettled herself Jason-wise.

It had been yet another wedding from amongst the loose-knit group of ex public school twenty-something-year-olds Jason called his friends. Juliet had been more than a little relieved to see Caitlin just as she arrived.

'Hello there, fox of foxes, Queen of viruses and The Pill.' Juliet squeezed Caitlin's waist and kissed her cheek.

'Ah, thanks be, the human race sent a representative to join me in this alien throng!' Caitlin beamed at her.

'You went to Posh School with most of these aliens. Anyway, how the devil are you, my dear?'

Juliet deftly relieved a passing waiter of two glasses of champagne, and gave one to her friend, accompanied by an admiring nod at her appearance. Caitlin had the uncanny ability to look perfect almost always: immaculate bob of gleaming raven hair, white porcelain skin, shocking against her black eyes and deep red lips, and a very neat figure, encased in some designer dress. Snow White rocking Versace.

'Shit, unremittingly shit. I hate viruses and the pill (except my own ones, obviously) and I hate my job and my downtrodden dowdy life. And I particularly hate these Aliens. Oh, God. Talking of which, here come Camilla and Ange. Oh, hi! We're brilliant, thank you! Mwah mwah. And look at you, dressed to kill as ever—'

'Oh, darling, you are a tease. Who would we be killing in these Louboutins – they might get scratched!' Camilla's long lashed eyes flicked up and down Juliet's off-the-peg dress and her non-Louboutin heels, then turned back to Caitlin. 'So how are you? We've been hearing about all the ghastly junior doctors' strikes; you must be exhausted? She does look tired, doesn't she Ange?'

'No, no,' said Caitlin over-brightly. 'It's absolutely fine, vocation you know . . . ' Her voice trailed off, Camilla clearly not listening anyway.

'Such a shame for you, darling. And you used to be so clever! What would our old mistress Miss Holder say to you now?'

'Well, I'm sure she'd be pleased!' spluttered Caitlin, a pink flush of annoyance on each cheek. 'Anyway, Juliet here is a surgeon!' Her flush deepened at this hopeless sally.

Camilla's eyebrows lifted a little and started to smile sympathetically but was interrupted by a loud 'Yeeuck!' from her friend.

Ange had been standing beside them, like some magnificent bronze statue of Venus, her incredible body set off to perfection in her exquisitely cut long gown. Years ago, she had discovered that she didn't really need to converse at social events; people preferred to ogle her, their mouths slightly open, not enunciating any actual words. She, therefore, rarely bothered to join in any talk . . . however, the news that Juliet was involved in something so intrinsically nasty and fluid-y as surgery had shocked her into an utterance, accompanied by a wrinkling of her delicate long straight nose.

'Ange!' smiled Juliet. 'That's the first time I've heard you speak! Or at least, make a noise. With your mouth.' She turned her smile on Camilla, inviting her to share her pleasure.

Camilla frowned. This inexpensively dressed and irritatingly tall girl already knew Ange? She looked inquiringly at her friend.

'Ski. Jason.' Only two disparaging words from Ange, and yet so much more information flowing out. Juliet was (only) one of Jason's (many) girlfriends – as irrelevant as last year's jacket, and had met Ange on a ski holiday – nothing of any lasting importance.

Camilla sucked in her cheeks and turned back scornfully to Caitlin. 'Lovely. Well do try to get some rest won't you darling – those bags under the eyes! – we must carry on and mingle – mwah! Toodle-oo!'

Juliet snorted with laughter as they glided off. 'Fabulous! I do admire these girls. I love hearing them with each other

– truly vicious social chat. They're only warming up with us. Anyway, where were we? Oh, yeah, your shit life doing a job you're brilliant at, with patients who adore you and an uber-gorgeous love-of-your-life always near, ready to spring at your every whim—'

'I don't know about springing,' Caitlin said doubtfully. 'He's getting a bit porky these days. His new hobby is chess, and he thinks he has to stare at the board for at least forty minutes before he moves to be doing it properly. I can do four consultations before it's my turn again.'

'Aw, are you playing online with him? Very sweet. Have you let him win yet?'

'No, I think I will soon though, if he starts to get depressed.'

'Charlie is the least likely person I have ever met to get depressed,' refuted Juliet, firmly. 'He loves his life almost as much as he loves you. Mind you, he has quite a fun life and you are very lovable.'

'Yes, I am, aren't I?' Caitlin looked distinctly cheerier. Her angry flush had faded to leave her usual perfect ivory complexion. 'And it's good that one of us has got some sort of purpose in life. Some days the only useful thing Charlie does is bring me lunch.'

'The curse of being fabulously wealthy. I love the way you're seen as a rebel for going to uni and getting a proper job!'

'Hmph, Camilla and her lot see me as more of a saddo than a rebel.'

'Saddo my arse.' Juliet was having none of it. 'Think back

to those halcyon student days: snogging unsuitable people, inventing disgusting cocktails—'

'Smoking in the toilets before the exams,' interrupted Caitlin, giggling now.

'Hitching a lift home with the milkman—'

'He was so nice! And do you remember us and Lizzie turning the flat into a beach volleyball pitch for a party?' Caitlin laughed.

'My God, yes! So much sand – always in your knickers, for months afterwards. We had to leave that place and get another flat.' Juliet shook her head and blinked in pleasure at the memories.

'Worth it though – what a party! I met Charlie that weekend.' Caitlin patted her heart, closing her eyes, an irrepressible smile adding dimples to her lovely face.

'And you've been joined at the hip ever since. We had an amazing time, hon. I'll love you forever now. Have to – too many secrets!'

'Ah, yes, confessions in the wardrobe. I have it all on a microchip, you know . . . you're right, it was a lot more fun than continuous shopping and sparring with Camilla. Even despite the God-awful Krebs cycle and other biochemical tortures.' Caitlin swooped to grab two top-ups from another waiter.

'Yeah – and the anatomy of the forearm, and all of psychiatry: low points.' Juliet pondered as she tackled her champagne. 'Could do a pretty good essay on Personality Disorder now though, after all these years of surgical training.'

'Ha! How is the dear Professor?'

'God, same as,' drawled Juliet, downing her glass. 'Impossible, probably autistic, completely brilliant, utterly infuriating, my absolute hero – you know!'

'You will be just like him I'm sure, only much sexier in a tight dress.' Caitlin nodded encouragingly.

'Well, that's a bit unfair – he put on a pretty good show at the hospital play last year. An unusual Ophelia, but she left her mark . . .'

Caitlin gurgled a laugh 'Ha! I wish I'd seen that. Who were you?'

'Hamlet's dad/Scottish banshee. Channelled Kate Bush,' Juliet grinned.

'Perfect spot! You've been practising in the shower for years just for that! What is it this year?'

'*Sound of Music*. I'm gunning for chief Yowling Nun – probably Kate Bush again.'

'Love it. We'll come if you're dressed as a nun – never thought I'd live to see that. D'you think Jason will be turned on or off by it?' she mused.

Juliet gave a short laugh. 'Nothing really turns him off, other than my job of course. He kind of pretends it doesn't exist. Blanks it.'

Caitlin sniffed meaningfully, watching her friend over her glass. Juliet could look totally relaxed and content anywhere, apparently as at ease in her clinging dress and heels in the swanky ballroom of the hotel as she was amidst the chaos in the hospital, or pounding over hills in boots and waterproofs, wherever. Caitlin wasn't fooled though, and she hoped that her mate was not being taken for one.

'Where is Big Bucks anyway?' Caitlin almost always referred to Jason, Juliet's boyfriend of almost a year, with reference to his number one obsession. Juliet peered around the flower-decked room. Enormous vases of lilies everywhere, but no sign of Jason.

'He'll be off doing research, I expect.'

'Huh?'

'Suitable future wife material. You know – someone who will be self-sufficient enough not to mind him turning up for around ten per cent of dates, holidays etc., but yet, with no important agenda of her own that can't be entirely subsumed by his timetable. She'll need to make herself utterly subservient and adoring, yet without boring him shitless. It's a big ask!'

Caitlin widened her eyes at this speech. 'And I take it you don't fit that bill?'

'Oh, and also she'll need to have nymphomaniac tendencies,' added Juliet with a sideways smirk. 'Every cloud, you know!'

They chuckled in unison and Caitlin hugged her.

'Oh, can I join in?' Charlie lolloped up, beaming. A scion of a noble family, or at least minted and probably noble-ish if you went back far enough, Charlie was always a delight to see; enthusiastic and busy with his latest craze, full of admiration for any number of sportsmen, adventurers, collectors, unusually dressed people, countries, songs. He was supremely unconcerned about the crazy path his life took, following one interest after another, with absolutely no long-term plan or ambition. Amazingly, he very frequently fell into very lucky situations – just happening to meet a great guy who ran helicopter skiing trips and needed a man on the ground who knew the terrain, or a roadie in the pub beside Charlie's family estate wanting a place to let his world-famous band hang out etc., etc. The world was full of great guys and amazing strokes of luck. His amiable smiley manner, no doubt, attracted much of the luck.

The girls found themselves enveloped in a Charlie hug: long, warm, firm, heartfelt. Very bearish, thought Juliet as he released her but kept an arm around Caitlin, his preferred option being to always be in contact with her. Juliet took a step back to admire him, resplendent in full kilt regalia. He gave her a cheeky wink and twirl then lifted a corner of kilt to better show a hairy knee.

'Gorgeous!' pronounced Juliet. 'Authentic hairiness, and I'm loving the exhibitionism coming out too – are you sure there's no Highland blood in you after all?'

'He's pure Anglified gentry,' purred Caitlin, returning her boyfriend's caress, slipping her arm around his waist. 'Which means that his family shagged and slaughtered their way around the world for centuries and are in fact true Gypsies of all blood.'

'Absolutely!' nodded Charlie, 'but I don't think you're allowed to say "gypsy" anymore, poppet. Multi-ethnic . . . '

'Ah! So that's how you manage to pull off regional

costumes so well?' Juliet's eyebrows poseed the question; Charlie nodded solemnly.

'Talking of which, can you watch Jason at dinner today – see how many Hoots or Ochs he manages to slip in? I think it's a fiver for each. He's sure he can out-Scottish me – bit unfair with him having a proper teuchter in his camp.'

'Sure. And may I wish the best of British to you, and we'll see you after the torment of the speeches.' The teuchter waved them off, and headed for her own table.

After that, things went rather downhill. Juliet had found herself wedged in between two competitive second-homers. So much to say about the best way to furnish, staff, visit, entertain at the ski chalets . . . she considered herself now overly informed.

Jason, she could see, had spent the entire meal discussing the navigation of various quirks of the Hong Kong stock exchange with the husband of one of the chalet women, oblivious to Juliet's boredom. To be fair, he probably was truly interested in that, whereas furnishing ski chalets passed him by. For someone so fixated on making money, he was singularly uninterested in spending it. No passions for a football club, for art, for wine, for stuff.

His flat was strange, too: altogether too perfect, what with all the tasteful shades of grey, and the strategically positioned objets d'art. Almost nothing personal to Jason, though. The whole atmosphere was somehow austere. Perhaps it was just unlived in – a bit like him somehow: he flitted all over the world from office to hotel to office but seemed to keep separate from much of the teeming life around him. He stayed as unchanged as the unvarying Hiltons: the fitted wardrobes and shiny bathrooms reassuringly unaffected by whatever was outside the window – desert or jungle, shanty town or skyscraper city.

Her musings were interrupted by the sight of Charlie waltzing Caitlin off onto the dance floor, Caitlin's tiny feet completely off the ground even in her heels. Quite unperturbed, she called 'We're dancing!' to Juliet, as if an explanation were somehow required. Juliet lifted her glass in a toast and leaned back to watch, a smile in her eyes. Those two were unable to hide their besottedness. They moved in their own shared orbit, eyes locked, everything outside of that irrelevant and invisible. It had been that way between them ever since Charlie had walked into that party in their flat at uni. He had homed straight in on Caitlin, and she had welcomed him as though her long lost lover from a previous life. They had completely different personalities, outlook and ambitions and were inseparable from that night onwards. Juliet of course loved them both. She liked to see their love, too. Although, she couldn't see her own life following a similar route.

Talk of the devil, there was Jason, heading towards her. He skirted a group of excited pre-teens, saluted the father of the bride and then made an exaggerated bow to two remarkably curvy bridesmaids. Juliet watched as one of them said something which made him laugh and catch her hand up for a kiss. He looked up and found Juliet's cool blue eyes on him, let go of the hand, murmuring something evidently very pleasing to its owner, and walked to Juliet without dropping her gaze, as usual exuding a slight threat. He asked her to dance and that's what they did. That's what they always did: partied rather than paused or talked. Fun and sex, anything deeper sidestepped.

The next day was wet, rain battering against the big living-room window in the half-hearted Sunday-afternoon light. For once, outdone by rain and wind, there was no traffic to be heard – just an occasional muffled siren. Few of those though – it seemed all of London was indoors or hungover or both.

Juliet set her half-empty mug of tea on the coffee table and pulled her legs up and into the baggy folds of Jason's hoodie. She was not hungover, having danced off her champagne. No headache, but footache from all the dancing. She massaged the tender arches of each foot, rested her head on the arm of the settee.

The sound of the rain was drumming into her, her heartbeat slowing into its rhythm, while the white noise in her head was slowly washed away. A skein of thoughts was left, ready to be filled out. Truths to be seen, or willed into being? She wasn't sure of that. However, she was absolutely certain that she was on the brink of decisions; sitting in that quiet grey room, getting ready to burst out into the infinite light-filled vastness outside. Did she dare? She did.

She took a determined breath. Yes, yes. I am the narrator, and I will write my life properly. Time for a change.

'Penny for them? Must be nice, you're smiling.' Jason threw himself down into the opposite corner of his oversized settee. He was still wearing his kilt, but apparently nothing else.

Without waiting for a reply, he carried on thoughtfully. 'I think your lot were on to a good thing with kilts y'know. Nice and breezy, very convenient for pissing and other essential activities.' He gave her a lewd smirk. 'And very popular with the ladies. God, American women will be wild for it – I'd better keep this and take it to New York.'

'Lining them up over there, are you?' It was just a throwaway line, but, unexpectedly, Juliet caught a flash of guilt cross Jason's eyes before he started batting his eyelids at her and inching the kilt up his thigh, mock teasing. It wasn't worth pursuing, she decided. She already knew what lay at the end of that line, had always known. She would not be spending any more time ignoring it anyway – she had her own business to attend to today.

'You are indefatigable,' she told him, squeezing his knee.

'Is that good?'

'Well . . . like our old ladies on the ward at night mounting escape attempts: sometimes good; sometimes not so much.'

'Do they try to escape? Aw, don't you let them? How do you stop them though?'

'The nurses wheel them round to face the other way before they reach the doors – tell them the post office is this way, you know. Some of them have incredible energy – shuffle about all night.'

'But surely your patients have horrible tubes everywhere and nightmarish wounds dripping gore – they can't be wandering about?'

'I tend to favour sewing up the wounds to keep the gore in, much tidier. And there are lots of patients on our wards with nothing needing surgery – just waiting for some social worker to increase the carer visits, or up their meals-on-wheels order.'

Jason cocked his head at her, then shook it. 'The NHS is bonkers. I don't know how you can stand working in it.'

'Well.' Juliet sat up a bit, took a breath and looked squarely at him. *Now.* 'Actually, I'm going to have a bit of a break from it . . . You remember I told you I had applied to join Médecins Sans Frontières?'

He frowned. Of course he didn't. 'Is that the Foreign Legion? I would have thought I'd have noticed that—'

'You probably wouldn't, but anyway it's not – it's a big international charity, also called "Doctors Without Borders". They work in godforsaken holes all over the world – and they've offered me a job.'

'Okay, should I say that's lovely, honey? Do you know which hole they've offered?'

'Northern Ethiopia. A makeshift hospital for refugees. Starting in eight weeks, for one year. It's a magnificent country, not a hole. Although they haven't got around to clearing all the mines from the last war with Eritrea, which is partly why they need a surgeon. Wouldn't be a plus point on Zoopla, I guess.'

'Okay . . . okay.' He paused, scanning her face. Her big eyes were watching him carefully, her cheeks faintly flushed, that too kissable mouth slightly open. 'No more kisses then probably,' he thought. 'So – are you going to go for it?'

She turned away from his gaze, took another draught of rather cold tea, waited a minute, feeling the certainty that this was right, that she was getting off the merry-go-round of parties and dinners and London surgery. The whirlwind of activity hiding the vacuum at the centre.

'Yeah, I think so. Bit scary. But it's partly why I went into medicine in the first place – to do something like this . . . seems like the right time to do it . . . and I think maybe you're going to move to the US?'

She was speeding up now, beginning to babble. She hoped he would not bat this away with a joke. After nearly a year of being together, albeit loosely, she wanted to untangle openly and cleanly. To her surprise, he moved closer to her and took her hand.

'Ah, sweet Juliet. Playing it straight, as ever. Yes, my dear, I am going across the water. I don't think they need Big Bucks in Ethiopia.'

'Well, they need the bucks, but not you making them there.'

'And you, Juliet Macleod, you don't need me either, I think?' he said gently with a hand on her cheek. She felt her eyes swell. This was not what she had expected.

'Do you want . . . I mean, well, did you want to be needed?' she asked, all confused, not quite meeting his eyes.

He smiled crookedly. 'Maybe, maybe not . . . but we were

never going down that road, were we? I liked the road we did go down though – real fun.' He kissed her closed lips slowly, pulling back to say, 'So . . . friends?'

'Friends. Yes, friends.' Juliet gave a slightly watery smile and then blew her nose resoundingly on a tissue.

'Always the lady.'

She laughed and elbowed him in the ribs. He put his arm around her, pulling her into his shoulder. They stayed quiet in each others' arms for a full minute, then Jason mussed her hair and reached for the remote.

'Okay, let's watch a shoot-em-up film. This sort of emotional situation surely calls for some high-quality mindless violence.'

A short hour or two later the rain stopped. The world seemed surprised to find itself cleaner and fresher; leftover droplets glinting in the tentative sunshine, reminders that change had come and would again. Juliet and Jason walked to the tube station, neither of them sure how to say goodbye. She smiled at him a little lopsidedly when they arrived, saying nothing.

'Well, what to say – see you around?' he said, taking her hand and entwining his fingers through hers.

'What's more unlikely – me in Wall Street or you in Ethiopia? Not going to happen —'

'I guess. Well, I don't know what else to say – thanks for the mammaries?'

'No! You can't say that, that's too awful!'

'No, seriously, I do mean it, they were great, definitely in my top fi—'

'Right, enough! No more! You are completely awful! Don't change into some wholesome American type now, will you?' She leaned over and planted a kiss on his cheek, laughing despite this being goodbye.

And turned, and left, eyes firmly front, feeling him watching her disappear down the escalator. She was away. Stepping towards a new everything.

She wondered now if he had watched on as she left. Did he think she might run back up the escalator into his arms? Did he consider leaping the barrier to rush after her, stop her leaving? She would never know. And it didn't matter really, because that moment had gone for good. She could let it go, imagine it disappearing, shrinking into a tiny dot, no longer visible. She was in a new reality now. She would need all her mental energy to manage this one, no time to dwell anymore on what was past and gone.

She smiled to herself, looking out at the endless landscape and immense sky as the Land Rover rattled on down the dusty road. Africa.

Chapter 10

Juliet

Arrival

AFTER WHAT SEEMED AN interminable last few hours of jolts and bumps and dust, the jeep turned into a gateway – they had arrived at the hospital. Man-U blew the horn as he parked beside a low house to the right of the main drive up to the hospital building. They spilled gratefully out of the car, stretching and looking around. A guard emerged from the hut beside the gate and gave them a wave. Juliet was mildly disconcerted to see that he seemed to be fully armed and ready for combat. She decided it was probably mostly a peacock tail thing, designed to frighten marauders off rather than do battle.

She turned her attention to the house, following Jeff and Jan as they hauled the bags out of the car. All of the back of the house was taken up with a wide veranda, facing the grassy field between them and the hospital. There were two hammocks, ready supplied with cushions, and one straight-back chair on either side of French doors. She went through them into a bare room: computer in the corner, table in the middle and four doors leading off.

Jeff stopped and turned to face her. 'Home, y'all,' he smiled. 'Bedrooms left and right; kitchen and bathroom straight ahead. Want to choose your room?'

'Sure, thanks,' said Juliet, pulling the doors open one by one. Each bedroom was the same: one wooden bed complete with mosquito net, one wardrobe, one small table.

'Gosh, it's difficult to know which would suit me best in the face of such variety – how about this one?' She gestured to the first door she had opened.

'Well if you insist, I suppose it's okay. Jan, you taking this one again?' He winked at her.

'Yeah, yeah,' came a muffled call from the vicinity of the kitchen.

'I guess he's remembered where the fridge is, then.' Jeff slung his bag in one of the other rooms and went back out to unpack the rest of the stuff from the jeep.

Jan emerged from the kitchen with three beers and a plate of samosas. 'A homecoming party!' he grinned. 'Let's get some of this into us before we go up to inspect the hospital.'

An hour or so later, feeling much more human, Juliet found herself trotting to keep up with Jan as he bounded over to the hospital.

'How long have you worked here then?'

'Six weeks on and off. We were first checking out the

refugee camps. One of them is old, been here for years, practically a town now – that's the one just outside the gate. There's another newer camp about two hours east of here.'

'Are we here because of the new camp then?'

'I think so. Too far to Adigrat for the babies, and there will be a new batch of landmine injuries for you.'

'They said that at HQ in Amsterdam, yes. So have you done anything much here in the hospital yet?'

'Some cases, some medical patients, but mostly setting up, recruiting people. In theatre, you will have Sebastian: a nurse anaesthetist, and Chinua: a nurse-everything person. He scrubs, assists and runs the minor injuries every day. There's also Edmond, another nurse-everything person. He runs medical outpatients, the medical wards, and covers minor injuries at night, shared with Chinua. He comes to us for help sometimes for the medical cases, but the sick ones get transferred to Adigrat – just over two hours west of here by jeep. He's been managing the fractures and injuries on the surgical ward the last few weeks, too. Irene is the nurse in charge of the surgical ward. She won't like you—'

'What?' Juliet felt her stress levels rising. 'Why?'

'It's just her way . . . slow to warm up. She'll be very unsure of you, and distrustful, then when she knows you, she'll be your mother and bodyguard all at once.'

'Okay.' Juliet was wary. She wasn't convinced she wanted an extra mother or bodyguard, never mind a stroppy ward sister.

Before she had time to properly worry about that, though, they were walking through the trauma admissions department and Jan was pointing: wards, theatre, scrub room. She immediately recognised the ubiquitous hospital smells: pungent little tell-tales of infections, birth, death. An undercurrent of blood, which was never shifted by a bucket and mop, but which she had long ago become used to.

There were about twenty beds in each ward and a pile of mattresses in the corner. Jan saw her frowning at them.

'Overflow beds – very handy. They can go on the floor in here, or on the veranda, wherever. No such thing as a full hospital here!'

She nodded, slightly bemused, and turned her attention to the surgical ward. 'Better see what's what then,' she said determinedly.

Jan looked around. 'Maybe wait for Edmond . . . oh, there he is! And Chinua. Hi guys!' Much fist bumping and shoulder slapping. 'Right then, this is Dr Macleod, your new surgeon.'

Two incredibly wide smiles now dazzled Juliet. She smiled back.

'Hi! Please call me Juliet. Very nice to meet you.'

Jan grinned, then raised a hand in farewell.

'Labour ward,' he announced and disappeared.

Juliet surveyed her new team. Chinua was quite little, with a bushy moustache, restless eyes and jumpy legs, bouncing around the group. Edmond was very different: tall, calm and appraising. He raised one eyebrow very slightly at Chinua, then quietly spoke to Juliet.

'Would you like to meet the patients now?'

'Yes, please, thank you, Edmond. Is Sister Irene here tonight?'

'No, off duty. Back tomorrow.'

His voice was deep, quite hypnotic, thought Juliet. Need to focus on what he actually says, though, not just how he says it. She hid the thought behind an encouraging smile and followed them into the ward.

Email to Caitlin

Well, we have arrived. 13 hours on the road bumping from bump to bump to even bigger bump. 4x4 seemed like a good option in Addis, oh, the naivety! In fact, relatively it is, but the best option of all would be an actual road. Or a plane.

And now I am home for the next year – seems on the basic side, hospital-wise. Missing a few things I would have had down as essentials on my list, like walls on the ward (half tarpaulin instead), running water (large buckets instead with taps at the bottom. Some poor sod has to fill them from the borehole in the grounds. Actually I hope that poor sod is not me. Something to check tomorrow.)

Will write more soon when I have acclimatised and my back stops feeling like I have lugged those buckets halfway up Ben Nevis.

Love from Ethiop.

PS tarpaulin is no barrier to goats, bats, frogs, chickens, nasty bitey beasties . . . the ward is a shared environment!

PPS the entrance guards are kitted out with machine guns here — might be one way of stopping the front-door smokers at home — just a thought!

Chapter 11

Juliet and Jan

IT WAS A BEAUTIFUL morning. The sky was already business like, wispy clouds sent scuttling to the horizon as the sun started to rise high in the blue.

Juliet was up early, wanting to be working. There was much to do. She had noted all the current admissions the previous night: various children and adults with legs in traction, a burns victim and a couple of kids with undiagnosed vague abdominal pains. Worms, Edmond had thought.

Maybe, Juliet had thought. In the absence of any test other than blood counts and malaria, it seemed wise to adopt an expectant policy. That is, to wait and see what happened – did they get worse, in which case they went to theatre for surgery, or better, in which case they went home.

Hmm, she mused. Theatre. That was maybe quite the undertaking out here what with the lack of running water, lights and probably good equipment. Would everything get infected in these open wards too? It was worrying.

Well, one thing at a time. And the first thing was to look

at the *Primary Surgery for Rural Surgeons* book she had lugged out with her. It promised to be a bible for these situations, indeed for all situations – there was even a chapter on dealing with a nuclear holocaust. (Very short chapter, that one.) Anyway, she needed to look it up to check the weights and directions of the tractions the boys had set up for the various fracture patients on the ward. Too much weight or too little and the fractures would not heal properly.

She would bring the book with her and get them used to looking it up. It could live in minor injuries theatre – or no, even better, Sister Irene could be in charge of it and feel the responsibility and trust of that request. She had quite a bit of team-building work to do to get them to trust her, too, she knew.

Her head full of the things she wanted to check, adjust, improve, she emptied her mug of tea and called out cheerio to Jeff. Jan had had the usual baptism of labour-ward fire overnight and had not yet emerged from his room, so she headed up to the hospital herself.

The early morning sun was just warm and pleasant. A cluster of people bearing yellow jerry cans were gathered around the borehole, waiting their turn to pump. She could see two little kids on the pump at the moment. A dog slunk around the gate and was chased out by the guard on peacock duty. Swifts – or was it swallows – she always confused them, were swooping and soaring around the field, coming back to their new nest under the eaves of the staff house.

They were old friends from Scotland, frequent visitors to Africa. She smiled, warmed with encouragement by them – if they could be at home here, surely she could.

Around 6 p.m., Juliet lowered herself gingerly onto a chair, trying not to wince. Her back was properly hurting. She might even need to take a painkiller – a dangerous crossing of the line between doctor and patient, putting her on the wrong side.

Jan eyed her thoughtfully, completely unconvinced by her rictus smile.

'So, all this charitable surgery and travelling in poorly-sprung humanitarian jeeps is not so good for the back, huh?'

'You're telling me,' said Juliet with a slight gasp as she shifted in the chair, trying to get comfortable but sending off a red-hot rocket of pain into her shoulder instead. 'I've been pretending to be fine all day, too. I don't think Sister Irene would be impressed with a whiff of malingering from me.'

'You can't fool her, but she might be impressed at your trying. Maybe.' Jan stretched his arms out in front of him and flexed his fingers.

'I suppose I could give you one of my famous healing massages, reverently spoken of from here to the Sudan.' He gave her an apologetic smile. 'But sadly I don't think you can afford one.'

'What? Nonsense! Firstly, I doubt they're as good as you say—'

'Better, much better,' he interrupted..

' . . . and secondly, I'm a western capitalist type of humanitarian. I have assets, as well as three dollars-fifty left over from this week's per diem.'

'I don't want your filthy money,' said Jan grandly, 'at least not until beer time.'

'Fine, well, let me just consider my assets . . . ' Juliet's amused face darkened into a scowl. 'Well, it's trickier than I thought. I mean, I've been investing in myself, you know – training costs, culture, food. What do I have in the way of a tradeable asset though . . . No, wait, let me think . . . Okay. I have a good working coffee maker. It can do the frothy milk thing, you know?'

Jan wobbled his head in a noncommittal way.

'No? Okay, I have an almost complete set of Harry Potter books, as well as quite a lot of poetry by that guy who rejected capital letters and grammar, although I'd like to keep that really . . . No, it seems I have no assets. A wasted life in capitalist terms.'

'Oh, don't be downhearted. Everything's rubbish anyway, you must know that – only time is valuable.'

'Oh, good! I have time, I hope, unless yesterday's lunch was as poisonous as it tasted. God, I hate injera. Why would anyone want to eat a soggy sour pancake ever, let alone every day? Anyway, assuming I live a bit longer, how much time would one Jan-massage cost me?'

He started pulling at each knuckle joint of his fingers, one by one. 'Well, I'll make you a special offer. For a first massage, always cheaper. One weekend.'

'What?' spluttered Juliet. 'A whole weekend in return for one massage? Are you crazy?'

'Yes, it's generous of me, I know,' Jan nodded, apparently weighing it up in his mind, wondering whether to withdraw his offer. 'But I should be more specific – it's a weekend of *fun* – you understand?'

Juliet peered at him, trying to make him out. 'You want to see round London? Art and royalty? Drink and dancing?'

'London? Pah! All buildings. No, I mean proper fun: mountains, lakes, sky.'

'Ah.' Juliet's mind wandered to Scotland. Wild and windswept Glen Coe. Battling up the Buachaille Etive Mòr, king of all the hills around there, to drink in the beauty all around. Swimming in the ice-cold pools of the River Etive at the bottom, then beer and pies in the most excellent Clachaig Inn. Camping beside the pub and waking to ethereal misty dawn. Plenty of fun to be had in Scotland.

'Yes,' she agreed. 'Okay, deal. You'll enjoy a weekend up in Glen Coe – there are mountains, valleys, sea and islands. And very fine pubs.'

Jan rubbed his hands together in delight, clapped them a few times then leaped to his feet, crying 'Excellent!' before performing a number of star jumps. Juliet looked heavenwards.

'Nearly ready,' he called. 'More info first – what is the name of this paradise you describe?'

Juliet laughed. 'Scotland, you mean? Well, I was particularly thinking of Glen Coe and the west coast—'

'Glen Go? Yes, we must go. It's beautiful, yes?'

'Coe, not Go, Glen Coe,' corrected Juliet. 'Beautiful, yes, but maybe not in the way you expect . . . imagine a solitary long road in between forbidding dark mountains: no houses or farms for miles. The land is full of ghosts and history – lots of memories of slaughter. The air is wild, windy and wet; the sky is very . . . very *there*, if you know what I mean.'

'Just go back to the slaughter bit – is that all over now? No skewering of fine Viking tourists?'

'Ha! You're probably safe from skewering these days, although not from midges – evil. Oh, I know a good dirge about the seventeenth-century slaughter – I could wail it for you if you like? Quite a catchy chorus?'

'No thank you, I just ate. And back to the evil midgets – is this a Scottish tribe?'

'Yes, bloody billions of them. Ravenous insects. Pestilent plagues. Can be avoided to some degree by moving fast, making the sun shine, or dousing yourself in fragrant Avon Skin So Soft – they hate it.'

'Hmm,' mused Jan. 'I can see this Scotland is a place of many mysteries. One weekend may not be enough. But we start there, anyway.' He rubbed and clapped his hands again energetically, before stretching his arms over his head.

'Are you ready?'

'Oh, well, yes . . .' Juliet was slightly disconcerted.

'About the Ts & Cs . . . what happens if the kneading of my broken back with your strong and overlarge VOG hands leads to sexual arousal?' she quizzed him, narrowed eyes looking over the top of her sunglasses.

'Ha! This is very strictly verboten. No sex in the team, even the Dutch will disapprove and fire us. Sex is for holidays; holidays are for sex. Anyway, don't worry, you're like an old lady to me.'

'Only six months older than you, and I know what Europeans are like with their strange erotic practices,' she retorted, reaching for her bottle of Sprite and wincing as she moved.

'Oh, yes, well, sure if you were a goat or something – wait – do you have a hairy back?'

Juliet choked on her juice. 'No, I do not!'

'Excellent, well done,' beamed Jan. 'And if I see that you are getting too excited, I will ask Jeff to increase the amount of bromine in your tea.'

Juliet now snorted Sprite up her nose. After a spot of choking and spluttering, she blew her nose to recover.

'I knew it tasted funny. I said it did! Okay, well pre-nup is complete, let's get on with it!'

She lay down on the bench, dangling her arms off the sides.

Thirty minutes later, she was in a state of tension-free bliss. Her achy muscles now felt completely realigned, tingling with health. Jan was still carefully pressing and kneading and circling, all the while muttering the Latin names of each muscle as though he were calling them to him. A Pied Piper unknotting and defusing each fibre and making it follow his tune.

'Okay, Juliet's back, I think you're conquered. Stardust, you will stretch or it will knot right up again, okay? Maybe run?'

'Amazing job. God, I can actually move again – thank you so much. And yes to running – I love to run. Is it safe?' she added.

'Well, apart from the landmines, pretty much . . . why don't you run with me – I know where is safe. If we go early in the morning around dawn it's best.'

'Are the landmines still asleep then?'

'Ha! No, but it's a beautiful light in the morning, you know. Everything feels safe.'

'Okay. I'll take your word for it.'

Email to Caitlin
So re home: eat your heart out bathstore.com – it turns out a large bucket and a small bucket is functional, cool and quick. Not a scented candle in sight and nobody missing them.

Not much in the way of furniture – hammock rather than leather settee...but a proper princess bed! Well, a mosquito net really, but when inside, one can pretend . . .

Love as ever from Eth.

Chapter 12

Juliet

Landmine

IT WAS THE BEST time of day. The land was basking in the last rays of the setting sun; time loosening just a little as everything relaxed.

Juliet sat on the veranda step, resting her back against a post. She gazed out, enjoying the lulling dislocation of the traveller, feasting on the sights while remaining unanchored. The ancient huge crags, which flanked the valley, glowed gold in the gorgeous light: stony witnesses of more than a million years of humanity.

The gloaming, they called this light back home. The northern skies, so airy and high back home, were altogether different to this wide immensity. But in both Africa and Scotland, this was still the golden hour: a magic time just before the close of day; a rich promise that sunrise would come again. She drank in the warm reassurance, let her mind bathe in it.

But now a figure was running across the grass from the

hospital towards her, indistinct features sharpening into Chinua, her cheerful and eager surgical assistant. Only he did not look cheerful or eager. His face was sweaty, his eyes slightly wild.

She stood up as he shouted to her.

'Doctor! Landmine!'

In one split second, the shimmering beauty around her dissolved to leave a nasty nugget of reality. No more lulling. She felt her mouth go dry, her stomach clench. *Landmine.*

She started to run, then waved him on back to the hospital and slowed to a jog. Can't arrive out of breath. And need to marshal the thoughts.

'Go on, I'm coming. And get a tourniquet, please,' she called.

'Now then, steady girl,' she said to herself. 'You know what to do. This is why you travelled all those miles, left everything and everyone behind. Maybe we don't need to say ran away, but we do know . . . anyway. You came here because you can do this thing for these people – you can tidy up these godawful bloody, messy nightmares. So go do it. And don't let them die.'

She came to a halt at the door to the operating theatre, hearing the shouts and noise of an emergency within. She felt the familiar wave of cool calm wash over her, slowing everything down around her, leaving her poised, almost detached. This was usually a sign that things were bad, but she welcomed it nonetheless, her inverse panic reaction. She was ready. She opened the doors.

Chapter 13

Juliet

The Morning After

THE MORNING AFTER THE landmine was calm and clear, as if life had not just shattered for someone. It was so strange how things could look reassuringly the same, despite the universe having reset, as new things were known and understood: new love gained; lives lost.

Juliet had spent some time on her ward round, making sure she had done all that she could for the poor boy, not quite wanting to walk away too quickly onto something else. He was very withdrawn, though – a mixture of pain, shock and morphine keeping him from engaging with her. She didn't push it – no point. She could feel Sister Irene's patience wearing a bit thin. Perhaps Juliet was encroaching on areas of patient care she felt were for her to manage. Not that Sister would say anything, but she didn't exactly radiate approval. That might just be her way, of course. Juliet made herself focus on the other patients in the ward as they slowly went around.

After the round was finally done, she was a little surprised and a lot gratified to be invited to Sister Irene's office to take tea. Was she melting a bit, deciding that Juliet was an ally after all? Had she passed some sort of test? That would be a relief. She smiled slightly nervously and followed her out of the ward, taking one sweeping backward glance as she left.

Most of the patients had fallen asleep after the frenzy of the morning – ward round, dressings, drugs, new intravenous lines, etc. The various children were more than ready for a nap, having been up for hours. Taye, the poor landmine patient, was snoring in a restless morphine sleep, his stump bandaged heavily. He was still pale and they were waiting for a relative to come in to give blood. Juliet paused at the door to look back and survey him, then frowned and sighed. She turned to leave, catching Irene's eyes, waiting for her. She wondered suddenly if there was a lake of sympathy behind that rather impassive face.

'What will become of Taye, Sister? What happens to these guys after mine injuries? Does anyone help them?'

She pursed her lips, shook her head sadly, answering the staccato questions slowly, carefully. 'Most people here are farmers, you know. It's difficult even with a good body. I don't think he's had much education either.'

Juliet was quiet, thinking as she followed Irene into her office and sat in the visitor's chair, suppliant position to the throne.

Irene sat at her desk, a queen of all she surveyed, carefully keeping her crown and gown in order. She arranged the china tea cups, sugar and spoons with much deliberation and finally poured out milky spiced tea from an orange vacuum flask. She gestured elegantly to Juliet to take a cup, waited for her to have her first sip, then took the other cup herself.

'Lovely, thank you very much.' Juliet was more than a little grateful to be welcomed into this inner sanctum and let it show. Irene gave a satisfied little smile, and waited for Juliet to speak.

'There must be some ways of earning money sitting down. Tailoring?'

Irene nodded this time. 'Yes, doctor, but some equipment is needed to start: a sewing machine.'

A light came into Juliet's eyes: 'Do you use those lovely old Singer machines with the foot pump here? My grannie had one of them. I used to love to watch her sew with it. Even the Singer name on it was lovely – all fancy curly writing like a spell.'

Juliet put her cup back onto the tray, biting her nail as she pondered. 'I wonder if we could get the UN to set up a project for mine victims, sponsor them to set up a mending and tailoring business or something?'

Irene poured more tea and sipped her own, studying Juliet. Such energy in the girl. Would she be able to harness it a little, direct it, she wondered. 'No harm in trying,' she concurred. 'They might have ideas of other things for business, too. Knife sharpening maybe. Shoe repairs.'

'Brilliant, yes! I could go and talk to the UN – see if they can help.'

She petered out, thinking for a moment, wondering if help would come from there. She wasn't sure of their priorities – it had been difficult to pin down their man on the ground, Kris, about that when she had met him at the weekend. No one seemed to know exactly what the UN were actually doing here. Politics, probably, she thought, waving a metaphorical hand to bat that incomprehensible thing away. She came back to Irene, rediscovering some determination.

'If not, Oxfam are just down the road at the other camp, maybe they do this sort of thing. I'll try to find something for Taye, and the others like him. I guess he'll be the first of a number of mine victims for me to treat here.'

That was quite a thought. A vision of the vulnerable lad lying thin and drowsy in his bed nearby popped into her head.

'We won't be able to talk to him about the future for a while, I guess – he will still be in shock. And he hasn't finished his surgery yet. I'll need to close the wound tomorrow or the next day, when the swelling is down. After that, it's a long and difficult journey for him.'

'Yes, it's always hard. We should keep him busy, as much as we can.'

Irene's big eyes were full of compassion, Juliet was sure.

'Absolutely. Physio, and more physio.' It occurred to Juliet that there was no physiotherapist. 'I mean, we will need to teach him how to exercise – keep the knee joint moving and keep strength in the quads.'

Irene nodded, an actual smile hovering at the side of her mouth, softening her features. 'Nurse here means also physiotherapist, counsellor, many things!'

Juliet gave her a genuine smile back. 'You do all of these jobs rolled into one and do them so well! I'll leave all that to you, and see how far I get with the UN and Oxfam.'

It had been an excellent tea break. She was beginning to read Irene, and thought there was acceptance there, maybe even approval.

Email to Cait

Had my first landmine victim yesterday. What a bloody mess. Blank eyes and torn shreds of flesh instead of a foot. Poor guy – he was just looking for scrap metal, harming nobody. Screwed now forever in terms of work, money etc and with a long painful recovery ahead. I was thinking of all the different people who contributed to inventing, making, transporting, hiding that mine. Do you think they will be pleased with the fruit of their labours? This is their typical victim: seventeen-year-old lad, foot and prospects blown apart. Don't know how to understand it, what context to put it in.

Love anyway from Eth.

Chapter 14

Juliet

Daytime work

'NOW THEN, STARDUST, YOU might not know it, but today's your lucky day!' Jan announced as they sipped coffee on the veranda. The sun was just up and warming the land; the sky tinged with yellow over the still dusky grey plain.

Juliet turned her attention to Jan. 'Really? Let me guess: do we have a VIP dinner guest? Has someone found a way of enjoying injera? Have Abba reformed?'

'Even better than that! Today you're going to be learning and doing the best operation ever! The speediest, most necessary, most appreciated and the only one to end up with a baby! A new live person! It's going to be the best fun you've had all year. Maybe ever!'

Juliet found her eyes sparkling back at him, 'Okay – you sold it. I'm in! Can I ask why you're going to let me do these when you probably want to do them all yourself?'

'Will you believe that I am full of generosity and good will towards surgeons?' He gave a hopeful half smile.

'No.'

'Didn't think so.' His cheerfulness was undiminished by her bald reply. 'It's because you'll have to cover for me next week when I go up to the other refugee camp.'

'What? Why do you have to go there?'

'*Visiting* OG you see – the obstetrician gynaecologist goes visiting. Got to scan anyone who might be pregnant and make a plan for them. Jeff does good log-type plans for cars and radios, but he doesn't do babies. Midwives do babies but can't scan. That only leaves me.'

'Well thank God you're leaving me the midwives. Will they tell me what to do?' Juliet tried to keep the panic out of her voice, but she couldn't help but feel that this conversation was not going in a good direction.

'Hmm. Well, Annet can tell you everything you need to know, but you've to let her whisper it to you. It's how she works. Shy. Jamila will look as though she's swallowed a frog if she disapproves of what you're doing, and won't tell you what she thinks you should do – you just need to work it out from her grimaces. Manjit will say all sorts of things, and you must ignore all of it as she's mad. Just find Annet if you need help.' Jan sat back, highly satisfied with his summary of the situation.

'Oh, my God, this sounds very bad for the population of Ethiopia – how long will you be away for? And can you give me some lessons this week?' There was no point hiding the panic now.

'Sure! Tell you what, I'll come to your ops and you come

to mine – and if I have something exciting in the labour room I'll also call you. And you know I'm only to be gone for a few days.'

'A few days?! Oh, my God.'

'A few days every couple of weeks, I should say.'

Juliet gaped at him, no words coming.

'Aw Stardust, you'll miss me? After such a short time – so sweet. You shouldn't be so soft, though, and emotional. You need to learn how to resist the VOG. Protect your heart! Be strong against these normal and understandable desires. After all, surgery is a hard career for normal people.' He nodded sagely, as if he was making any sense, and got up ready to depart.

Juliet shut her mouth resolutely, tried to not be infuriated, breathed. 'Thank you, VOG. Consider yourself resisted. Are we going to theatre now or what?'

They headed off up the field. Jan was relaxed and smiley as ever; Juliet was slightly sweaty, heart pounding with the thought of this new responsibility.

Finally, the action-packed day ended. Juliet had got herself a cup of tea and was sitting on the veranda steps enjoying the vibrancy of the last flourish of the day's sunshine, feeling partly relaxed, partly exhausted. Jan emerged from the road having obviously been for a run, ripping off his top as he loped the last few yards toward her. She was surprised to see how muscled he was under the ill-fitting T-shirt, and hid her appraising look behind her mug of tea.

'Hey, Stardust, how was your day?' He stopped beside her on the steps.

'Good,' she replied.

He stopped, waiting.

'What?' she frowned.

'That's it? Nothing more? Surely there is more! Ask me how my day was!' he demanded.

'Okay – how was your day?' she asked in a sing-song voice for addressing a class of five-year-olds.

He beamed at her, oblivious to her sarcasm. 'It was first a bit fast, then a bit slow and steady again, then way too fast, then maybe too slow, then a bit fast again.'

'God's sake, is he always like this?' She turned to Jeff, ensconced in his hammock.

'Oh, yeah. Content varies but not the quality,' Jeff assured her.

'Right, surgeon,' said Jan, patiently. 'Your turn – try again. How was your day?'

'Hmm. Let me see. I would say discombobulating,' she finished smugly.

Jeff burst out laughing at the confusion replacing Jan's eager smile.

'What? Jeff, is that allowed? Is that even a word?'

'Yup, she won that one, try again tomorrow, man!'

'Goddamn typical surgeon,' grinned Jan. 'You'll need to write that word down for me. I must get it into my next report.'

Chapter 15

Juliet

Night-time work

12:45 A.M. NOT A good time to be woken up and told about a nasty knife injury. Or in fact to be woken up and told anything. Well, anything medical anyway, Juliet qualified her disgruntled muttering as she stumbled a little, following Edmond towards the hospital.

Why oh why, anywhere in the world, could people not be ill or injured during daylight hours? Was it really too much to ask, for God's sake? She grumbled on to herself, the usual mantra, while simultaneously running through her memories of the anatomy of the hand. It had been a while since she dredged those up, but since the patient had apparently warded off a knife attack with his bare hand at the expense, no doubt, of a number of tendons, it was time to retrieve those memories.

Within a few minutes, she was sitting beside a cleaned and draped hand, the patient having been zonked out by a sleepy Sebastian. She was looking at a little bunch of white tendons, as delicate as snowdrop stalks, all hoping to be joined back to their original other halves.

This was not going to be a quick job. Juliet wiggled her bottom on her seat to get comfortable and started pulling on the cut ends like a puppeteer, working out what did what. Once she had a pair, she carefully rejoined them, then moved on to the next. A couple of laborious hours later it looked like a hand again. It had been carefully encased in plaster, and she was wide awake, slightly high and pleased with herself, and wondering how she would get some sleep before tomorrow. She became aware of a tousled head hovering beside her own, peering at the hand.

'Looks just fine, there, Stardust. Will it work again d'you think?' asked Jan.

'Sure it will! Just need to wait, wait, wait – let it heal. Patience!' Juliet gave a sanctimonious nod.

He quirked an eyebrow at her. 'Got much of that, have you?'

She smiled somewhat ruefully at him. He'd got her there. 'None, no. But luckily it's him who has to wait it out, not me. Going back over?'

'Yup, all the new lives safely started for tonight.'

They walked to the house, but just as Juliet was about to go in, Jan caught her arm and gestured her to follow him.

'Shhh!' he stage-whispered, as if he were not the one making all the noise. 'Follow me!' He disappeared around the side of the house, some clattering noises, then he reappeared with a ladder and a couple of cushions.

'Come on!' He tossed the cushions onto the roof of the house, started to clamber up the ladder after them, paused, turned and grinned at her then whispered, 'Come on up!'

She shrugged and followed him up onto the flat roof of the house. Fussily, he arranged the cushions then lay down, switched his torch off and gazed upwards.

'Come and lie here, surgeon! Amazing stars tonight!'

What the hell, she thought, she wasn't ready to sleep yet anyway. She lay down, aware of his body close beside her, and looked up. There were no lights around, and just a sliver of moon, close to the horizon. As her eyes became accustomed to the dark, she could see more and more stars bejewelling the night. Countless galaxies and constellations beckoned her. The Milky Way shimmered across the sky, tantalisingly beautiful.

'Oh,' she breathed, and felt rather than saw Jan smile beside her. 'It's like looking back in time, isn't it? A kaleidoscope of time.'

'I don't know what you're talking about, surgeon, but it sounds nice. Looks nice. Pretty lucky to see this, huh? Thanks be to God for night-time emergencies!'

'Right . . . hey, look at the moon – seems to have fallen over backwards. Is this a job for the Logistician?' She squinted at the crescent moon, which was clearly on its side, quite different to the way it looked back home in the UK.

'No need to wake him, I can fix this – excuse me, won't you?' Jan reached over and gently turned her head to the side. 'There we are. Right way up now?'

'Much better,' she thanked him solemnly.

They lay quietly together, watching the universe, letting time pass. Juliet felt strangely disconnected from her life and yet connected to everything, all at once. Nothing hidden or even separate, all out there mixed together. And almost hypnotised, tricked into the weird position of being in her own galaxy while seemingly watching it from afar.

'I feel like I may well float off,' she said wonderingly.

Jan smiled again. 'Sail out into a sea of stars. Launch your mind!'

Juliet smiled now. She let herself just breathe, look, and float for more minutes.

Eventually, Jan let out a contented sigh. 'Well, surgeon,' he said quietly. 'Shall we leave before they start to fade? Only an hour till dawn.'

'Hmm. Let's come again, though. I like assignations with the universe.'

He turned suddenly from the light show above and she caught his eyes, felt a shocking jolt of connection. It was as if he was able to see deep into her bared self, past the barriers. She looked away hurriedly. Too much rawness, hurt and regret to be found down there, not for public viewing. She made for the ladder.

Chapter 16

Juliet

Bleeders

THERE WERE TOO MANY flies, Juliet thought. Too many flies and not enough lights.

As the power was out again a very distractible Chinua was dangling a kerosene lamp beside her. It was not effective.

And there's too much blood and not enough gynaecologists, she thought, peering up into the dark internal bits of the patient, some part of which was bleeding rather a lot after giving birth.

'Keep massaging the uterus,' she called to Manjit, the midwife, who looked alarmingly as though she might have fallen asleep, head on the patient's tummy.

'Chinua, please can you go to the MSF house and ask Jeff for a torch? One of his good ones! You can hang that lantern on a drip stand first, please.'

Right, come on, no finesse required for this sort of thing, she thought to herself. The cervix is ripped apart and bleeding, so let's just get some big stitches in and stop it.

Easy. Come on, Juliet. Call up all the reserves, focus and do it. She took another stitch and readjusted her left hand, trying to work out where to stitch by feel since the view was pretty much black and more black.

God damn children – shouldn't let them be born like this; surely there could be a better way.

She got a stitch in, and the bleeding seemed to reduce a bit.

No. Wishful thinking. It had not yet stopped.

'Manjit, wake up!' Juliet was just about to try for another stitch when a beam of light shone past her illuminating the exact spot she had been aiming at.

'Brilliant, thanks, Chinua. Thank God for light.' She knotted the stitch and mopped. Was anything still coming? 'Oh, I think she is still bleeding though, dammit.'

'I know you're admiring of me, Stardust, but really it was nothing – just holding the light – hardly godlike, especially compared to some of my other skills . . . ' He frowned up at the patient, clocking the bleeding.

'Oh boy, am I glad to see you!' Juliet turned her sweating face to give a somewhat forced smile to Jan, unexpectedly back from the other camp. 'Got three in labour versus me and Manjit there. Asleep again.'

'Probably safer for everyone.'

'Can you look at this one – do you think I've got it? And why are you back anyway?' She scrambled out of the way, peeling off her gloves and taking the torch from him.

'Got an emergency section to do – poor girl went into

labour early and will not be able to deliver – deformed pelvis. Chinua is getting theatre ready.' While talking he had got his gloves on and was inspecting Juliet's handiwork. 'Hmm, still a lot of blood . . . Placenta come out intact?'

'Oh, well I think so, yes, yes . . . actually I don't know for sure, I let Manjit check it . . . So maybe not then, highly unlikely in fact.' Juliet did a complete U-turn. 'Oh, God, has she been bleeding from that all along?'

'Maybe, maybe, can you get Sebastian – he can give her something nice and I will do a quick clean out of any placenta left behind.'

'Here? Now?'

'Well, yes, I think we need to stop this bleeding.' He was already rummaging around looking for instruments. Juliet ran to theatre to fetch Sebastian, cursing herself. All that stupid stitching while allowing the poor girl to nearly bleed to death . . . wait though, recriminations later, save the situation now. She was back in under a minute with Sebastian.

'Right, you can assist me? Thanks,' Jan went straight on, not waiting for a reply. As soon as he had seen Sebastian give the drug, he started cleaning and giving Juliet instruments to hold.

'Give her some fluid, Seb,' he called. 'Maybe get blood?'

'We will try,' came the unconvincing response. It was a walking blood bank situation – you had to find someone willing and take a pint from them on the spot. Finding donors was difficult and for women doubly so. Part of the problem was that nobody believed their own blood would automatically regenerate, that the donation was not harming them.

Ten minutes later, the troublesome residual piece of placenta was removed and the bleeding was stopped.

Jan called to Sebastian, 'She is okay this end.'

He found Juliet's eyes, caught the distress starting in them.

'She's fine,' he said firmly. 'No need or benefit from any What Ifs. Next time you will remember to check. And this girl is okay . . . no blood though, I see. Seb! Any chance of blood?' Sebastian opened his hands to gesture. 'No, and what can we do?'

'Hmm, what is she . . . A-positive. Okay, she can have some of mine after the section. It's been a month since I gave, so all good.'

Juliet started in surprise. 'You've been giving blood?'

'Sure, why not? I used to donate at home, until they banned surgeons and gynaecologists.'

'Me, too. I am B-positive, so no good for her. I haven't been much good for her, all told.'

'Not true, you did your best and you didn't let her die – you would have figured something out. It will benefit many more people that you have learned this, Juliet.'

His blue eyes bored into hers, insisting that she accept it, agree, stop the spiral of self-loathing before it really got going. She widened her eyes, slightly shocked that he had clearly spotted this in her, despite her efforts to internalise it, keep it out of sight and torture herself later when alone.

Of course, coming to Africa had not changed this habit, and had not magicked away any past disasters.

She paused, then nodded.

'Now, can you help me with this section? I need you. It's going to be very awkward – she can't lie flat because of the contraction of her hip—'

Juliet shook herself a little, knowing he was right, knowing she should accept it, just be grateful all had turned out okay, and that she didn't really need to punish herself. Also, she didn't have time – she paled at the sight of the girl for the section, very twisted back and bent hip. How on earth was this going to work out?

Email to Caitlin
Bad day. Fuckwit day and no safety net Prof to rescue me. Actually, that's not true. I have Jan, thank God for him. I can busk it in orthopaedics, ENT, urology etc but obstetrics is a car crash all day long. Don't know how he can take it and still be laid back and . . . was going to say normal, not normal definitely, but human nevertheless. As human as you can be when you are a lanky, scruffy, pseudo-hippy with no career plan and a penchant for slagging off surgeons.
Anyway, back to me . . .
LFE, over and out

Email to Caitlin
Jan? Totty? . . . to be clear I am continually sleep-deprived, stressed, hairy-legged and probably insufficiently washed. Totty

not likely, therefore. Also, no time, as on call 24/7, and also it's not allowed. Out of order even for the uber-liberal Dutch MSF Holland, apparently.

Email to Caitlin
Whadyamean I doth protest too much . . . I doth not! Well, I know, maybe a little. Just making sure I cerebrally override the pecs and abs reflex response . . .
LFE anyway.

Chapter 17

Sylvie

Flashback

SYLVIE WAS CURLED UP in a corner of her washing hut, drenched in sweat, her heart racing, her eyes seeing nothing. Another yell came from the main hut – her mother labouring. Sylvie whimpered, seemingly trying to disappear into the ground. The world had gone black; everything was lost. She was back there again, falling, falling, falling. Her stomach seared with pain; her heart was about to burst. She was back in the hut, back in that barrage of pain, the inescapable nightmare. She was losing her baby again and again, was killing her again and again; she was helpless in the tornado of it. So much pain, so black. If she could only die, too, this time, find her lost child . . .

Edmond passed his mother running down the lane. He turned to call after her. 'What is it? Is someone hurt?'

'Baby – Eshe,' she called back, not breaking stride.

Her friend Eshe, Sylvie's mother, having yet another baby. That could be a problem. Edmond turned his moped around, caught up with his mother and signalled to her to get on the back. They quickly made their way to the hut and Edmond's mother disappeared inside. He was wondering if he should go after her when a small and remarkably grubby boy took his hand. The child had a tear-streaked face.

'Can you save her?'

'Your mother? Don't worry, there is much noise, but it will be all right . . . '

However, the child was pulling him around the back of the hut and into a small bamboo shelter. As his eyes adjusted to the darkness, he saw a figure on the ground, shaking and moaning.

'This one, save this one,' commanded the boy, crying freely now.

Edmond gently but firmly rolled the figure over, gasping at the sight of Sylvie in terrible distress, some hair pulled out, her mouth slack, her eyes rolling with terror, sweat dripping off her. Another yell from Eshe sent a spasm shuddering through her and she started to close her eyes.

'No!' cried Edmond. 'Sylvie, no! It is not happening again, you are safe, you are safe. I have to take you away from here.' He picked her up carefully, saying to the little boy, 'I need to take her away for a while to get better. We will go into the forest by the cow field. You tell your father and then come with us.'

The boy disappeared immediately and was back before they had made it to the path. He took a hold of Sylvie's skirt and looked trustingly up at Edmond.

'You save her.'

He walked slowly into the forest, carrying her, her brother by her side, the trees soon silencing the noise behind them.

'It is all right, you're safe, it is only a memory. Come back to us, you are safe now,' Edmond kept repeating.

Finally, he found a place facing the field, just inside the forest, but well away from the hut and out of earshot. He gently sat against a tree, still holding her. The child curled into the space between his legs, clutching his sister's arm.

'Sylvie, Sylvie, Sylvie,' he chanted.

She started at her name and stared at him. Her eyes did not seem to be seeing yet and her forehead was still wet with sweat, but she had stopped shaking.

'Sylvie, Sylvie, Sylvie.'

'Jonny?' she said falteringly. 'How are we, where, ah, is she gone?'

'Your mother is going to be fine, Sylvie, don't worry. And you are fine, you are safe now,' soothed Edmond.

'My mother?' Sylvie looked up at him completely confused. 'But she. My own, my only, is she gone? She is. She is. I know it. Ahhh, I feel so empty. She's gone.'

She turned her head into Edmond's chest and sobbed and sobbed. Jonny looked up at him, worried.

'Don't worry, little man, she's back. She needs to cry it out now.'

Edmond felt the truth of it. She could have gone, drowned herself in her own trauma and sorrow, left them. She had not.

They sat quietly until the sun started to go down. Edmond

was just wondering whether it would be safe to return when Gregory appeared.

'There you are!' he pouted, somewhat cross at his trek to find them.

Edmond ignored the sulk, caught his eye in a piercing stare and asked the question, raising his eyebrows.

'Mother is fine. Another boy to feed.' Gregory looked down at Sylvie fast asleep beside Edmond, Jonny in her arms. He quickly looked away again, embarrassed by her.

'She is fighting hard. You must not make it worse for her,' said Edmond to him mildly. 'What happened to her was not her fault.'

Gregory looked at him, stricken. 'But I can do nothing.'

'A few smiles go a long way. Every day, Gregory, she needs a smile from you.'

Gregory stared at him for a long moment, then nodded.

'Now, let us wake them and return.'

The night was still and quiet. The world continued to turn, paying no heed to the dramas unfolding within its forests and plains and cities. Sylvie lay quietly, wondering if she could feel the spin, feel the world held in place by the planets, sun and stars around. Sometimes it was easier to understand that planetary balance than to make sense of her own life. She felt that some of the defences she had painstakingly built over the past three years had been revealed as rubbish – weak and crumbling with little foundation. The pretence that she had accepted her reduced and restricted life, that her wounds were healing. The horrible revisiting of her own labour yesterday while she witnessed her mother in childbirth had swept it all away like a house of twigs in the path of a river in spate.

There was something left behind, though. There was still a small flame there desiring life, somehow unextinguished by that river. The raw core of her, still there, still wanting to fight for herself, for her chance. She was almost ashamed to admit it – that she wanted life even with the yearning for her lost daughter. Should she not want to die, to join her little one wherever she was? But then the love she had for her child would be gone, and maybe that was all that was left to mark that little life, unlived outside of her mother.

And truthfully, she wanted life. She could feel the will to survive beating in her despite everything, despite all the suffering.

It was too early for the water pump. She lay beside Jonny, thinking about the events of yesterday, at least about some of them. She certainly did not want to revisit the terrible feelings she had while her mother was labouring. She could barely remember what had happened, other than the dreadful conviction that she was falling into a terrifying void, nothing to hold on to to stop the falling, an awful screaming in her ears. Perhaps she had been the one screaming; she really didn't know.

Edmond had been there. She did not want to ask him what had happened. He seemed to have found it all understandable in some way and to expect no explanation from her. That was a relief, since she could hardly explain it to herself, let alone him. She was not too sure how she had come to the forest, but she remembered waking up cuddling Jonny, beside Edmond. Had he carried her from her hut? She felt a pulse of anxiety – surely she would have been wet, would have made him wet . . . she shook her head slightly to dispel it. Nothing she could do about that.

Jonny grunted and turned over, a small arm swinging across her face. She gently removed it and stroked his head. He had been very upset yesterday, then seemed to forget all that in an instant. After they awoke, he had been climbing trees under Edmond's supervision, running in circles, trying to do handstands, the usual Jonny continuous activity.

When they returned home, all was calm. Her parents were sitting quietly together with the new baby, Adrian, who was sleeping contentedly. She didn't want to go too near in case her fragile state, currently held together like a newly glued plate, started to break up again. But actually she looked at little Adrian and felt only love. Her father looked past her to Edmond, satisfied with the nod he received and said nothing further.

She said nothing to Edmond either, had just given him a tiny shell-shocked half smile and a mini-nod. He had gone home quickly anyway, leaving no time for embarrassing thanks or explanations.

She wanted just to be alone and quiet in her hut but had gone to wash then forced herself to help clean up after the meal. She couldn't face food herself.

Edmond. Her mind came back to him. He lived by the water pump – perhaps she would see him there. She found to her surprise that this did not fill her with anxiety. He seemed to accept her with her problem rather than just see it and reject her. He was a nurse, of course, or rather a clinical officer, she thought they called it. Probably he saw her just as another patient. Even as she said this to herself though, she felt it to be untrue. He liked her a little, always had, she thought. No point thinking too much of that, although surely to have any kind of friend would be so welcome, so precious.

The next day, Edmond came out of his porch and waited for her at the pump. He wondered if she would come, if after such a trauma, such a terrible revisiting of the nightmare she had gone through, she would be up and going again. He spied her making her way slowly towards him, her head down a little, but the steps were determined. He mentally saluted her bravery.

'Sylvie. How are you?' His voice was low, soothing.

'Oh! Edmond, it's you.' She fidgeted awkwardly with the cans. 'I'm not quite well today, but better than I was . . . I need to say: thank you for yesterday. Jonny says you saved us. I am not quite sure what happened—'

'It doesn't matter, it's all over now, no problem.'

She lifted her face up to his, the pain in her eyes stark and raw, despondency dimming the light of her lovely face. He flinched from it.

'It is not over,' she countered. 'You saw me, you know. I failed her, she died. I have my punishment.'

'No!' he cried out, vehement. 'No, Sylvie.'

'You are kind,' she said, dropping her eyes and starting to fill her jerry cans. 'But I know.'

He waited, filled the cans with her, helped her strap them to the bicycle. She was about to go when he stayed her with a hand on her arm.

'Sylvie. You know I work at the hospital? I see a lot of things there. I see so much suffering, but I don't see justice. It's not sent fairly. I'm just trying to say . . . maybe you should consider that it's not your fault. Please say you will consider it.'

She looked at him for a long moment, searching his eyes for truth. She blinked eventually, maybe an almost imperceptible nod and started up the hill.

He watched her all the way up, then returned quietly to his house.

Chapter 18

Sylvie and Edmond

SYLVIE WORKED HER WAY through her chores, faster than usual. She then hoisted Jonny onto her shoulders and the two of them went off with the goats to the field. She had been keeping Jonny busy all morning and knew that soon he would keel over for a sleep. While he did that, hopefully in a nice shady place, then she could think.

The swifts were back, she noticed, when they reached the meadow. Full of energy and joy, whizzing about, diving and turning. They flew for the fun of it, she was sure. She pointed them out to her little brother, who squirmed out of her arms and was off, trying to copy them and pretend-fly after them. After charging around the field in this way for about half an hour, he arrived back at the tree she had chosen, ate the apple she had for him and promptly fell fast asleep. She shuffled back against the tree trunk and shut her eyes.

Edmond's words were waiting for her. Waiting for her to be ready to drink them in. She had taken some tiny delicious sips, circling the temptation cautiously. She was afraid to succumb fully, to let her desperate thirst be quenched, although something told her that she absolutely needed it, as a drying flower needs the rain.

'You should consider that maybe it is not your fault.'

Could she really? Was it really true? She could not bear to deceive herself with anything false. Could it be true, could she believe it? How she wished it were true, repeated it, wondering.

She carefully, deliberately thought of the many people in the village, the town, the world who had suffered illness and accident, war and misery. She knew it was almost always not their fault, and that they could not stop whatever it was happening to them, to their children. Maybe likewise, this wasn't her fault, and she could not have stopped it. She felt her mind testing this statement, weighing it for truth.

She made herself think back to the labour. She was sure she had done everything she physically could to deliver her baby, had pushed and pushed and pushed, all the while knowing deep in her heart that it was useless, that it would not happen. The baby was not moving, not coming out. Did that knowledge mean that she had prevented it somehow? This was key. She paused, waited while her mind searched for the answer to this. No, the answer was no, she had not prevented it. She had felt the impossibility of it grow inside her as she laboured, but she had started optimistically. Had imagined it and tried to let it happen, then desperately strived to make it happen. To no avail.

She tested the words again for truth. They seemed to hold.

She took another breath and made herself move to the difficult question which followed: if not her fault, then whose?

Impossible to answer, but not the babe . . . no, poor sweet darling, not *her*. They shared in the misfortune, both suffering the loss of her little life. Yes. Sharing it. And maybe sharing more – maybe having not been born alive, something of her spirit had returned to her mother, had joined with Sylvie's. Was that possible? Perhaps.

Sylvie had an overwhelming feeling that she needed to embrace her little baby. No more flinching with remorse and pain whenever she thought of her – only loving her and celebrating whatever she was, is. Let herself feel that love in every part of her being.

She let her head fall back, her face upturned, let the sun warm the gentle tears flowing from under her closed lashes. She gave a long shuddery breath out. She could almost feel a place in her heart where her baby's soul nestled, safe forever now in that love. She felt herself comforting her little daughter, telling her again how she loved her. She rested.

The next two mornings, there was no sign of Edmond. Sylvie felt her spark of hope flicker and fade a little. She must have revolted him of course – how could it be otherwise, despite his saying it wasn't her fault? Nevertheless, he had gifted her a powerful idea, sturdily planted in the midst of a barren garden of the soul, growing slowly, a patch of green hope. If she could just lose more of her guilt, only feel the love for her child . . . maybe she could bear this life.

★

More time went by. Sylvie was back at the pump. The sky was shadowy grey, hopeful signs of the coming dawn of yet another day. She found herself looking over at his house as she balanced the bike. No one was around.

He was watching, though, wondering if she would search for him. He only needed a hint of that to take him out of his dark porch.

'Morning, Sylvie,' he smiled shyly. 'Let me help you.' He held the can for her while she worked the pump, then took over the pumping.

'Boring job this. I tell you what – if I can tell you a story about my work at the hospital, will you tell me one of your stories? Jonny gave me a taster the other day, but I think you might be the master storyteller. I'll start,' he quickly added, seeing her slightly panicked look. 'Yesterday a boy came to hospital with a fly in his ear – it had just flown in there!'

He had caught her interest. 'Really?' she asked. 'What sort of fly? Did you get it out?'

'Yes! We had to use a big syringe and inject water into his ear for about five minutes and then finally it came out on a wave of liquid. One of those flying ants with long wings. I'm amazed it got in there at all! A swimming flying ant.'

She gave a satisfied *Ha!* – almost a laugh.

He felt his heart warm at the sound – such a little laugh, but so rare.

'Now you! Can you tell me the end of the story of the ostrich-riding king who was looking for the best mango in the world? And why was he doing such a thing?'

Sylvie gave a hesitant smile. 'Okay, I'll tell you while we fill the last can. It wasn't to catch a princess or anything like that. It was because his ostrich loved mangoes and he wanted to get the best possible one for it – there was to be a race, you see, against the next-door kingdom. He had to win it – to beat his annoying cousin who was king there, but his ostrich, although very fast, was quite naughty and would only run if it saw a really good mango at the finish line. So he came to this very town, as he had heard that the best mangoes were in a tree in the garden of a small boy called Jonny . . . '

She finished the story and he laughed properly. 'That's a great story. Lucky Jonny. Do you think I can earn another story if I come and help you with the cans next time I'm home? I'm on duty tomorrow night.'

She smiled shyly at him, waiting a moment and checking his sincerity, before saying, quietly, 'Yes. And . . . thank you Edmond, you're very kind. I must go now, though. Thank you, thank you Edmond.'

There was no doubt about it, Sylvia's heart was a little lighter. She did not know how to think about Edmond – was he her friend now? He was a nurse of course, and likely was wanting to help her, just as he helped other people all day long. And she knew that he had rescued her from the terrible flashback trauma she had while her mother was giving birth. But was he also her friend?

Well, she shrugged, if he wanted to be entertained with some silly stories for helping, was there really anything to worry about? What harm could it do? A few minutes of conversation with someone near her own age would be a precious thing. She should find a good story for the next time. Maybe the one about the treasure hidden in the old brick kiln – a favourite of Jonny's. She would practise it with him.

Chapter 19

Juliet and Abele

ALL WAS QUIET AT the breakfast table: companionable silence and coffee. Outside, the cockerel was taking a break, having been crowing since 4 a.m. Juliet watched him strut past the open door and narrowed her eyes at him murderously.

Jeff clocked the look with some alarm.

'No, Juliet, no killing of innocent cockerels.'

'He isn't innocent. He's wickedly nocturnal. His days are numbered. I have already told Goretti how much I like eating scrawny old cockerels and that it's my birthday next week.'

'It's not nice to lie to the cook.'

'It's not nice to bloody cock-a-doodle-do all bloody night either. A capital offence, he may find.' She turned away from the door, giving Jeff a bright smile. 'But not today, today is a special day.'

'Really? Why?' Jeff was wary.

'D-Day for little Abele.'

'Little strung-up Abele?' asked Jan, emerging briefly from his morning stupor.

'Is that one of the children you have tied to the roof, beds, walls, Dr Macleod?' Jeff went into formal mode.

'It is, Mr Jeff, and it is called Traction. Abele was the first one to be held up to the rafters. And the first to be set free. I have been feeling her thigh bone for the last week without her seeming to mind and I think it's mended. We're going to slowly loosen the rope today and see what happens.'

She smiled again, a tiny bit too determinedly, noted Jan. She was going to take any failure with this very badly, he thought. Then again, she had presumably been dealing with complications and failures from day one of practising medicine, just like everyone else. So why did he worry about her? Why indeed. He could feel somehow that she carried them all with her, those bad things that happened, lugging them from place to place, unable to share or put that burden down. And he did worry.

Jeff had caught some excitement but not the subtle tension behind Juliet's smile.

'Oh, my gosh. That's exciting. I might have to stop fiddling with my knobs and switches for a while and come over there.' He looked quite animated for once.

'You could even bring her some more of those sweeties you've been surreptitiously feeding her.' Juliet pretended to look stern, pursed lips belied by dancing eyes.

'I could! Just so long as no one finds out. I wouldn't want anyone to think this tough guy had a soft centre.'

'Of course not! Who would be afraid of you then – who would respect you?' Juliet looked over at him sorrowfully. 'No one, that's who.'

Jan raised his head from his coffee again. 'I'll respect you for a sweetie.'

'Ah, I bet you say that to all the girls. I'm not falling for it, even with your cute European accent.' Jeff gave Juliet a big wink.

The three of them walked relaxedly to the hospital. The ward was full of the morning bustle. Patients were being washed, beds changed, the floors swept, the nurses sailing from bed to bed.

'Morning, sister!' sang out Juliet. 'Rounds soon?'

'Eight o'clock, doctor. Yes,' came the calm reply. Irene glided out of the nursing office, her gaze taking in everything happening on the ward – patients, nurses, doctors.

'Okay. We're going to see Abele first – a big day for her!'

'Yes, doctor.' Irene gave a wide smile, turned and called to Abele's mother in their language, no doubt warning her.

Little Abele was lying quite comfortably on her bed, despite being on her back, legs carefully strapped together and held securely up towards the roof with a tightly knotted rope around her little ankles, holding her legs upright at ninety degrees to the rest of her, her pelvis just lifted off the bed. She had broken her left thigh bone falling off the crossbar of a bike, a traditional perch for three-year-olds, notwithstanding the terrible potholed roads.

Juliet could not pin her little leg, but keeping it still and in

149

position with the traction she had set up should have done the same job just fine. The bone just had to fuse together again, in the right line. As soon as they had got her straight and still and the leg not moving, her pain had vastly improved. She had been amazingly quick to adapt to lying on her back too, rarely moaning or crying. She was a little sweetheart – huge brown eyes, a throaty chuckle and a mad sprinkle of tiny curls of hair in her head. Juliet had bought coloured bobbles for them which had caused much excitement.

Juliet eyed Abele, then turned to Jeff. 'Now Jeff, how is your juggling? I do hope you have some sweets to juggle?'

'A1 top class from the US of A! Are you ready?'

'Oh, yeah, always ready.' Juliet had surreptitiously taken hold of the rope, while Abele tried to work out which one of them to watch.

'Jan, can you steady her ankles and I'll loosen the rope a little.'

She brought it down about ten degrees, Abele glancing at her with trepidation but very distracted by Jeff.

'Okay, well done, that's one sweetie for her. We'll do another ten to twenty degrees after the ward round.'

'Do you mean you need me all morning?' whined Jeff. 'Don't you know I'm very busy and important and have much to do?'

'We know – you have to have breakfast, check your emails, take a radio apart again . . . But if you could possibly do your sweetie round here first, that would be great.'

'The things I do; the sacrifices I make.' Jeff was in drama-queen mode. He pretended to take a sweet out of Abele's ear to her huge delight, then passed on to her neighbour, seven-year-old Salem, also in traction, but this time attached to a sandbag dangling over the end of the bed.

'Hey dude, are you going to try that trick I taught you? Try it on me and if it works, we can fool the doc with it.'

Juliet smiled. She was a bit nervous about Abele, but mostly confident that it was going to be all right. 'Are you off to labour ward?' she asked Jan.

'Where else? It's the beating heart of the hospital, the only place to be, a mecca for the coolest people—'

'Yes, yes. Off you go then, coolest person, come get me if you have a section. It's my turn.'

'It certainly is not,' expostulated Jan. 'You did the little bald one yesterday—'

'And you did the twins at midnight,' she returned, quick as a flash. 'In fact, does that count as two?'

'Oh, my god, I forgot the twins, I better go check them first. And that still counts as one section, although I suppose it's your turn, pah. Goddamn surgeons wanting to do my operations.' He carried on muttering as he sped off to his ward.

By lunchtime, Abele's legs were flat on the bed, with very little trauma and quite a number of sweets efficiently disposed of.

'Thank you, Jeff,' said Juliet, meaning it. 'We'll let her move around a bit by herself now, maybe try to get her on her feet later—'

A shout came from the direction of the labour room. 'Surgeon! If you want your turn, come now!'

Juliet went. She found Jan in the process of leaving the labour room in a most odd position, actually in between the legs of a groaning patient on a moving trolley.

'What on earth?' she started to ask.

'Cord prolapse,' he barked. 'I am holding the head in, trying not to touch the cord or it will go into spasm, then no oxygen for the babe. Can't let it come down either though or the babe is gone. No, Mama! No pushing, don't push! Breathe! That's it, breathe slowly! Sebastian, are you there? Can you give her something quick, quick . . . Juliet, I need to stay here, can you do the top end?'

'Already scrubbing up,' she called from the washing bucket.

'This has to be a speedy one – we have about two minutes max before damage will be done to the babe,' warned Jan, slightly muffled from his position down below. Sebastian had already given anaesthesia, looking as unhurried as ever, but getting it done.

'Okay. I'm on it. Knife!' Juliet was there.

A short hour later, drenched in sweat, coming down slowly from the crisis, they sat on the bench outside the theatre, enjoying the reassuring squalling of the latest Ethiopian, born with no little effort from all involved.

'Well, was I quick?' Juliet asked.

'Christ, yes. Terrifying. Thank God someone taught you how to sew it all up again.'

She laughed. 'Otherwise, I would just be yet another knife-wielding maniac, and we don't need any more of them, do we?'

He smiled at her. 'No we . . . oh my – what a heartwarming sight. Look now, six o'clock. You'll probably cry . . . and me, too.'

She looked where he was pointing, and sure enough felt her eyes swell. Little Abele, holding her mother's hand, carefully tottering down the corridor towards them.

'Oh, wow,' she beamed and clapped and thumbs-upped and beamed some more. 'You clever girl! Well done, well done! Just to the door then rest – okay, Mama?'

Juliet enjoyed the happiness of the mother's face more than she could say. She wiped her eyes. They both did.

Email to Caitlin
Newsflash: I am not giving up after all. There is a dearth of nutty surgically trained volunteers out here (and in fact of anyone surgically trained) so I have decided that they are not better off without me, despite my flaws and drawbacks. My post-empire issues, as Jan would say. What would he know though, closet communist that he probably is.
Pah.
And LFE

Chapter 20

Juliet

Party

'PUS-FILLED.'

'Stop it!'

'Sorry, Jeff. Jan asked me about my day, that's all. What is the adjective from pus anyway? Not pussy. Pusy? Pus hyphen Y?'

'Do stop it,' moaned Jeff. 'And I like the word pussy. Many happy memories. Don't spoil it for me.'

'Sorry. Let's just agree to go with the hyphen then, shall we?'

'Yes, yes, hyphen away, only change the subject for God's sake. And, in fact, let's change everything. We are cordially invited to sponge off the UN tonight – schmooze their visitors from Geneva, eat their food, drink their beer, chat up people from the other NGOs working in the camps—'

'Excellent! We're right behind you, Oh Logmost one, lead the way!'

A short walk along the main road, and they were in the UN

compound, joining the visitors from Geneva as well as the locals who worked for the UN and various volunteers from other Non-government Organisations in the area.

'Look at this display of capitalist filth. Thank God they ask us to share it with them, very generous.' Jan surveyed the table laden with bottles, crisps and even a very uprooted looking dish of olives.

'Very kind, I'm sure, and very chatty-uppy, which is also most appreciated. Especially the ones out here for a weekend UN jaunt. I wonder if that truck driver with the unfeasibly huge biceps is back—'

Juliet swept the room, contorting her head to look behind them. 'Aw, don't think so.'

Jan was not paying attention to her, but was grinning slightly stupidly and watching two slender, fresh-looking girls trying to open a beer bottle, as if it was the most earthy and poor-country thing they had had to face so far. They were half-heartedly flicking at the top with long red nails, and practically fell upon Jeff's neck when he produced an opener from his pocket. One took the opportunity to lay her long soft fingers on his arm and lead him to the side; the other had felt Jan's stare and looked straight at him, eyebrows up in a slightly subtle question.

'They just want to use your body for fleeting meaningless pleasure, you know. Back to Geneva on Monday.' warned Juliet.

'I know, isn't it great? Like an edible Christmas present.'

'Yuk, too much.' She frowned disapprovingly at him.

'I just mean not lasting,' he chortled quietly, suddenly turning and catching her eye with a dark blue flash of his own. 'Although . . .'

The edible present was bearing down on them, drink in hand, sleek black hair tumbling down one shoulder, a look of hunterish expectation on her face.

'Looks like you might be the one being eaten,' murmured Juliet, smiling somewhat fixedly and moving away towards Kris, their host, and possibly the only person in sub-saharan Africa more scruffy than Jan.

He was peering at a wine bottle label through his rather thick glasses, but looked up at her approach. She was aware of Geneva homing in on Jan to her left and gave a bright flash of teeth to Kris.

'Juliet! Do you think fourteen per cent sounds good? How's your palette?'

She laughed, genuinely. 'Out of practice! I don't usually choose based on percentage. . . ' He looked a little crestfallen.

She quickly resumed. 'But I'm sure fourteen per cent alcohol sounds absolutely right, probably excellent, in fact. Let's try it and then describe it properly – all the flavours now – summer rain or granny's out of date chocolates – be creative!'

Kris nodded eagerly, opened it, and knocked back a whole glass, then stared slightly manically at her.

'Ah. Beach sunset with first girlfriend, salty crackers and strawberries, trying to tempt her!'

Juliet burst out laughing. 'Top job! Let me try, too.' She took a sip rather than a glassful. 'Mmm yes. Sea air and fruit and first-date nerves definitely – you must be a natural sommelier?'

'A nose – that's what they say – you're a nose,' Kris nodded sagely, polishing off another tasting half pint and tweaking his own sizeable nose rather proudly.

'That's a very fine nose. Let's hear about the beach, then. Did your evil plans succeed?' she asked, smiling at him, while noticing that Jan and Geneva seemed to have disappeared.

'No, of course not, completely hopeless.' He downed one more taster, then held out his hand purposefully. 'Right, let's get the dancing going. Only you can match me.'

It was true – he was serious, bookish and somewhat awkward usually, but uninhibitedly exuberant on the dance floor, and she always responded, her inner wild child breaking out. They headed out to the concrete back yard that substituted for a dance floor and within a few minutes Florence and her 'Dog Days' had them wound up to a swirling twirling fever pitch.

Jan watched them while Geneva fussily found him a drink, unable to repress a small smile of pure enjoyment at Juliet's mesmerising swing and sway. Her arms were up, and she was fully absorbed in the music, almost drunk with it. Kris was cavorting madly around her, a satyr to her Aphrodite, never inside the force field though. He wondered if she was lost in it, or rather found. Something to think on. He turned back to Geneva.

★

The next morning dawned blue and sunny as usual. Juliet narrowed her eyes as Jan shuffled towards the kettle, giving her a blurry half smile, half grimace.

'Exhausted, are we? Looks like it.' She heard the slight sharpness in her voice and her irritation grew. Now she was cross at herself and at him. 'God, you look worse than a labour-ward night.'

'One forceps, one bleeder. One busy boy,' mumbled Jan hoarsely, stirring his coffee with a knife.

Juliet felt a surge of relief, was immediately annoyed about that, then contrite about being cross with Jan, then annoyed about that, too. None of which she allowed to show, aware of Jeff's rather carefully nonchalant observation of her. Jan was blearily slurping his coffee.

'Such a bad career choice,' she clipped, shaking her head. 'Despite which, let me help. I'll do your round and watch things this morning while you sleep.'

'Oh, yes. Thank you.' He abandoned his coffee, gave her a grateful thumbs up and disappeared back to bed.

Jeff now narrowed his eyes at Juliet. 'Softie,' he said accusingly.

'It'll go on the tab,' she quipped shortly, and took herself off to the hospital, feeling oddly joyful, and not quite wanting him to see that in her eyes.

Chapter 21

Juliet

Decisions

'CAN I CHECK MY emails please, Jeff, if you're not needing the computer?'

'Sure.' Jeff waved a hand in the air, but didn't look up from the science mag he was reading in his hammock.

Juliet disappeared into the living room / dining room / office to laboriously log on, waiting for the interminably slow internet to wake up, hoping that she could see what was happening in the other world, her old world.

Her mother was the same: sore knees, perfect grandchildren. And Caitlin – two short emails, each packing a punch. She sat looking at the screen for a while, went between the two messages a few times. Thought about country roads taking you home – to the place you belong. Did she though? Belong. Yes. Yes? Yes.

'Need me to crank it up a bit for you? Pedal faster on the dynamo?' Jan called through from the other hammock.

She smiled. 'You know me, I'm always all about the speed. I'm done now.'

She read the emails once more, then logged out.

'Are you anywhere near the fridge?'

'Our house is about ten feet square, everywhere is near the fridge.'

She collected three beers, knowing the request was coming, as Jan spoke to Jeff.

'Seriously, you know – whatever you say, you can't fault her logic.'

'What do you mean, whatever I say?' retorted Jeff. 'I don't say anything at all! I grunt admiringly – that's it.'

Juliet expertly uncapped the beers on the side of the table and handed them out.

'Even though she insists on taking chunks out of my table,' frowned Jeff.

'Now which of you boys is feeling lucky? I am here to hammock.'

'Well, you're very welcome in this one I'm sure, honey,' drawled Jeff, stirring up rather than clearing the papers and magazines strewn around him, sounding far from sure.

'No, no, come to me – this is the premium first-class hammock tonight, smoking one tonight,' insisted Jan.

Juliet clambered aboard. 'You don't smoke – are you starting tonight?'

'These are not normal cigarettes – these are very precious, difficult to find, clove flavoured wonders – each breath a delicious experience . . . And I am personally demonstrating the possible peaks of goodness one human can attain by giving you one – here you go – a Gudang Garam!'

'Is that their name? Very fancy. Mmm they smell really good. I think I'll just have a draw of yours, not a whole one, thank you.'

'Watch this, Jeff – this is real humanitarian action!' He solemnly handed her the cigarette and she wiggled into the hammock with him, taking an aromatic draw before handing it back.

'Good? Touching places other cigarettes do not?'

'Mmm, yes, actually. Weirdly lovely in a spicy kind of way.'

He nodded, satisfied, and took a draw himself. He peered at her through the smoke, feeling the churning of her spirit from her recent emailing.

'So, how is the other world?' he asked lightly.

'Well. Moving along without us. My best mate is rearranging her life.'

She cocked her head to the side a little, bit her lip gently. He could recognise these signs now. Something important. He waited.

'So maybe I need to think about mine. I normally trundle after her wherever she goes . . . or she follows after me.'

He raised his eyebrows, questioning, offering another drag.

Juliet studied the cigarette for a moment before declining.

'No thanks, I'm fine. She's found a place on the beach near Inverness – a nice old city in the north of Scotland, near all the mountains. Her boyfriend is going into business with a guide there and so they're moving. She has sent a job advert for me to apply to the local hospital!'

'Beach and mountains, eh? Sounds terrible.' Jan took a long, slow draw and blew out the smoke. 'Why would you want to go there instead of back to the middle of a huge, dirty, mean, nasty city?'

'Well, that's the question, I guess. Feels a bit like growing up though – am I ready to grow up yet? Only thirty-one, still very nubile.'

'Are you really asking him about growing up and settling down?' asked Jeff, putting down his magazine. 'You do know that he's practically a hobo?'

'Is he? Are you?' she asked mildly.

'Yup, no fixed abode. A stray,' Jeff answered for Jan.

'*Visiting* OG!' Jan defended himself, smiling relaxedly, completely without rancour.

'Yeah, yeah, always visiting – refugee camps in Africa, Asia. A cowboy moving from town to town, a broken-hearted cowgirl left in every one—'

'No cowgirls in Africa or Asia – verboten all,' interjected Jan.

'So, no ties, no roots.' Juliet surveyed him, trying to size him up. He was tricky to understand though, and seemed to be following a tune she didn't recognise. 'Where do you go in between missions then, Jan?'

'Ah, telling you my secrets. Secrets of a happy life! I make sure my missions finish in the summer, then I sail.' A light came into his eyes, sun-filled memories.

'Sail? In boats? Where?' She was surprised again – he was always surprising her.

'What else would you sail in? Boats, yes of course – lovely, long white boats around Greece – my friend has yachts he hires out. I can be crew or skipper, engineer, cook, whatever. Actually, not cook, not a popular cook anyway. But anything else.'

Jan sat up, turning his deep blue eyes on Juliet.

'You know, it's so good there, the sun on your back, swimming in the morning, all day and at night. Sleeping on deck, so many stars. Milky Way is there too! Only wearing shorts – bikinis for you.' He settled back down, enjoying the picture he had conjured.

'Right. I didn't realise your usual attire here was overly formal for you.' She pointedly looked at his perennially rumpled T-shirt and shorts. 'These flip-flops must really constrict your feet.'

He grinned, despite his reverie. 'Ah, it's so free there, Stardust, so blue and free and somehow ageless, you know?'

'Well, I guess people have sailed and swum there for centuries. Odysseus and the rest.'

'Was he the one who went off looking for a gold sheep? Maybe I share a sailor's gene with him. Not so interested in sheep, though, personally.'

'Not Odysseus. Jason was the sheep man, I'm sure,' Jeff chimed in.

Juliet started a little at the name of Jason, realising she hadn't given him a thought for many days. Weeks and months probably. He, and she when she was with him, felt like a finished story from another time. She knew she was not going back to that life.

Jan caught her start, flashed a curious look at her for a fraction of a second, then returned to the last of his cigarette.

'This is also an ancient taste – cloves and nutmeg, many centuries old. Chinese at the start, I think.'

Juliet breathed in some rich spice, felt new and old worlds opening around her. It felt good.

'Let's talk more about the cowgirls. One in every port?' Jeff was nearly through his beer and had livened up – never as energetic as the rest of humanity, but maybe approaching third gear now.

Juliet winked at him. 'A commitment-phobe, do you think?'

'Ah, you know the type.' Jeff sat back, down to second gear. He directed his questioning to Juliet now. 'Previous experience?'

'I do have, of course, yes. But I have no problem with them – I know what they want and what they offer – happy to shop there!'

Jan narrowed his eyes at her. 'Restless, huh? Like a different operation every day, new patient every day, is that it?'

'Sure, why not – I don't like to do the same easy thing every time. Some variety, some more difficult than others, more challenging, more satisfying. You know how difficult it is to stave off boredom,' she twinkled at him, teasing. His dimples deepened, his eyes amused. He lay back in the hammock.

'So, do we take it that you have not left a broken-hearted lover back home? I may have tried to wheedle this info out of you once or twice before,' Jeff was probing, for the nth time.

'No.' Juliet smiled, lips staying shut, nothing more forthcoming.

'I do love these heart-to-hearts, sharing together, deepening our friendships. My guess is you left a commitment-phobe behind.' He nodded, satisfied with his assessment.

'Actually, he's looking for a wife,' Juliet frowned, nettled into revealing more than she had intended and consequently annoyed with herself.

'Like you look for a house or a car?' asked Jan.

'Kind of.'

'Not you though?' Those blue eyes were upon her again.

'Being some guy's accessory is not one of my life ambitions.' She countered the sharpness with a lift of the eyebrows, pursed her mouth and blinked her eyes just a little. 'Even a super-hot rich one.'

'Oh, he was hot, at least? Thank God for small mercies.' Jeff's smile widened to a toothy grin. A perfect American one, always giving her a small jolt of surprise at its whiteness, natural or not.

'Okay, your turn, Jeff – spill! Are you actually an incurable romantic underneath the rest of the, well, you know, you?' Juliet turned purposefully to him. His grin changed to a scowl.

'Goddamn women! I'm here for some relief from them.'

'Ouch, sorry man,' winced Juliet. 'No need to say more. I'm sure she wasn't worth it.'

'Goddamn women,' muttered Jeff again. 'I'm turning to beer. You guys want another or will that cause wavy scars?'

'One is enough, thanks,' confirmed Juliet. 'No wavy scars tonight. And Jan is floating on a cloud of memory-laden spice, musing on his Mediterranean maidens – he doesn't need anything more.'

She wriggled back in the hammock, still sipping her beer, thinking. How much did your environment impact on you? If you spent thirty years surrounded by violent, unhappy liars, braggards and self-pitying bullies, you would not expect to turn out the same as a person living in peace, sailing in sunshine. She wondered if this issue had been adequately brought to the attention of the home secretary or whoever was in charge of prisons, traffic wardens, customer complaint phone lines. Of course, it wasn't a foregone conclusion that one would become different, but you could surely protect your soul better by alternating between working hard to help people and wandering around paradise islands . . .

And what about a career in surgery, in the NHS? What did that do to your soul? She wondered. Of course, mostly you were surrounded by people demonstrating their great love for their family and dealing heroically with disaster, calamity and death.

All of which should be highly impressive and laudable for a person to see and emulate. All of which does grind you down a bit . . . but then again, it's not just about fun, is it?

Set to work, endure. There's a deeper satisfaction in that.

'Have you solved your metaphysical problems?' Jan was watching the to and fro of emotions flitting across her face.

She looked up and locked into his gaze. It was a little unnerving, that deep blue demand for truth.

'Not exactly. Got to work out what to do long term. Got to have a plan before the next email goes!'

'What are the choices?'

'Let me see . . .' she counted off on her fingers. 'Become a consultant surgeon, get a pinstriped suit, get a bit fat and bolshy, get a posh car. Oh, no, that's not it. I remember. I'm a girl! So start again: meet a dashing stranger, maybe in a late-night deli; move to the south of France with him and have five children in a dilapidated château. No, shit, that's not it. I'm a girl surgeon. So, consultant job again, pin-striped skirt maybe, and spiky heels initially, then flatter and flatter heels, eventually lace ups and a cagoule and a committee habit . . . Hmm, not so appealing. I might have to get back to you on this, actually.'

'We have so many of the same fantasies,' he beamed. 'Your cagoule was a lovely purple in my one – how about in yours?'

'Always blue. Shall we chat about what you were wearing in my fantasy?'

'Ha! Yes, please! Something very macho, I am sure of it. Irresistible and good for showing my amazing physique. Maybe made of leather?' He looked hopefully at her. She frowned and shook her head disapprovingly.

'I think we're back in your fantasy again. Let's talk more reality – what are you going to do while I take up a respectable job again? Hmm?'

'Hmm ... ' He frowned back at her, mimicking the hmm, then raised his arms and hands to gesture 'what?'

'I already have a respectable job! Visiting OG is top of the medical food chain, did you forget?'

'I did forget, sorry,' she retorted sarcastically. 'And did you forget that you're a mzungu, not an African? And are you going to be forever visiting?'

He grinned maddeningly at her. 'We're all visitors, aren't we? Permanent – pah! What does that mean – how can anyone so fleeting, compared to the life of a planet, actually think they can even own part of it? Nonsense. Short-term everything. Rent always.'

Jeff looked over, winked at Juliet, didn't bother to challenge.

'A hippy and a hobo,' he pronounced. Jan was on a roll, however. 'Also, I'm a child, I mean a man, a proper hunky man, of the liberal free world. My roots are in the causes of freedom and equality everywhere!'

Juliet rolled her eyes. 'Also, you get paid more in dollars as a volunteer here than as a training doctor in Slovakia. But you are of course still a noble and admirable humanitarian. Is that the plan for now, then?'

'Ah well – someone has to run around refugee camps getting the babies out – why not me?' He leaned back into his end of the hammock and peered at her, apparently expecting an answer to this ridiculous question.

'You're right – it should be you, no one else will do, for sure. Whereas many people will seem to be much more suited to the jobs I want. They will be better at rugby, have published more obscure research papers than me and look better in a suit.' She concluded as if nothing more could be said.

He ignored the dismissal in her voice. 'Your logic is fundamentally flawed,' he said calmly.

'How so?'

'You don't know what job you want, so how do you know other people will be more suited to it? You need to work out the perfect job for a strong-willed, adventurous, strong-willed, opinionated, strong-willed, general surgeon. With philanthropic tendencies. And nice hair,' he added, thoughtfully.

'I feel you're trying to tell me something. I can't quite get it, though – you're maybe too subtle?'

She tried to suppress the pleased feeling she had that he liked her hair, irritated with herself. I mean, for God's sake, it's hardly a window to the soul.

Jan was apprising her critically. 'Also, I suspect you might have some hidden wildness. I am not sure how to get to it, but I'm looking into that.' He smiled beatifically – psychological profiling ended.

She was somewhat nonplussed and forgot about the hair. 'Well, let me know if you find where my wildness is lurking. I'll be interested.'

He smiled, noting the closing of her face as she withdrew into herself to ponder, while he enjoyed the ripples he had provoked.

Email to Caitlin

Cait – Inverness sounds perfect for you guys. Maybe for me too – why not? I wonder if they would let me have extra weeks off to come back here . . . I will apply, I promise. Not sure what else to say – it's difficult to imagine normal life at the moment, so please forgive me for being brief. Let me know how it is working out for the two of you there!

Chapter 22

Juliet

More Decisions

THE WARD WAS QUIET, other than snoring from the appendix patient in the first bed. Even the skinny old man with the rotting foot had stopped his high-pitched whiney murmuring. Which was maybe a bad sign. Juliet turned her head sharply to check he was still alive and caught a little shiver and a shake from him, propped up in bed with his foot all wrapped up. Alive then, good. Maybe good, anyway, she wasn't completely sure about that.

She turned back to the child on the bed in front of her. He was awake, lying still, looking at his mother, saying nothing. Ominously quiet. He was breathing quickly and sweating slightly. His eyes were sunken and there was a smell of vomit. She looked at his little body, his tummy swollen and firm under her hand. Not obviously tender anywhere, though. She had seen lots of similar kids with malaria, with dysentery, with worms.

Was there something different here though? He had been on

the ward since yesterday and was worse than when he arrived. Was there something in that tummy driving the illness, killing him? Could she stop it? Maybe. That was the torture of it – maybe. Or maybe not. There were no useful tests that she could do. He did not look strong enough to withstand much. Would an operation be the last straw for him? Maybe.

We could get him better a bit first then try, she thought. Give him some fluid, get Sebastian, who had been here forever and seen everything many times over to see what he thought – could he get him through an op? Just in case there was something. She sped up the intravenous fluid drip, smiled at the mum in a worried 'I'm not actually happy at all' kind of way and went in search of the In-Charge.

Next morning, deja vu. The mother stared at her beyond begging for reassurance now. The child was still breathing too fast, still sweaty, still too quiet. When he looked at her, he seemed to look through her to something else. Now he had a scar down the middle of his abdomen where she had cut him open. She had found something there – an infected portion of his intestine and she had removed it. He wasn't better though. Maybe it was too early. Or maybe he still had the infection, typhoid maybe, and she had done nothing to alter its course, only cut him, defiled his perfect skin.

Maybe, bloody maybe, always bloody maybe.

She breathed out. Explore the possibilities, she thought, let them exist, weigh them up, decide. But keep your eyes and your mind open. Make sure you have done everything that you can: fluid, painkillers, antibiotics, even when it seems futile.

Is that to treat him or me, she thought, then shook her head slightly to be rid of the depressing thought. Keep sane, keep able to make the calls. No one else here can decide or can act. You don't have the right to grieve here, at this moment. Do the job. Do your job. Keep doing it.

The sun was beating down as relentlessly as ever, welcomed by the singing washerwoman at least. She was busy with sheets, towels and clothes, draped carefully on the ground to dry. No washing lines here, Juliet wasn't sure why. Spreading washing on the ground seemed to her like getting it dirty again, but whatever. There probably was a good reason for it, albeit obscure to her. The lady waved as usual at Juliet, as she crossed over the grass from the hospital to the MSF house. Juliet smiled automatically and waved back.

Her face was a perfect mask belying the turmoil of the thoughts behind. She could feel a rising tide of self-loathing, threatening to engulf her. To let her be caught again by the black spectre which had followed her from dank UK to this sun-bleached land, chaining her to the dismal dungeon deep within.

This was the price you paid for the job, for sticking your head above the parapet, howling your battle cry and entering the fray. The secret shame of failure. Not secret in terms of the reality, but in terms of the effect it had on you: the slow erosive effect. All compounded by the façade of perfect competence that everyone still wanted to see; the belief they needed to have that you knew best, that every decision would be right, and no mistakes made.

Only rarely could she share with anyone the struggle back from the sinking marshes of failure and insecurity. It was her struggle, undertaken internally, unwitnessed. She knew also that the wave of self-hatred would be temporary, that she would break out of her prison again. After some unpleasant hours, or even a few days, she would emerge again, shaken but still with her feet on the ground, still walking the walk.

And how could you ever complain, given that the precipitant for this horrible process was someone else's suffering or even demise, not anything that would be overcome in hours or days? You just had to suck it up. Everyone involved in medicine and surgery understood that.

But. But everyone did not have an unmanageable unfathomable tragedy from when they were ten years old sitting deep inside like a stick of uranium. Everyone did not have to tiptoe around that toxic memory, to desperately try to avoid revisiting the hellish scene of destruction and loss and be faced with the same awful questions again and again: *why couldn't I have saved him?*

One day maybe the poisonous radiation would have spread through all of her, and there would not be enough left to carry on.

★

She had reached the house by now and was making herself a coffee; her face closed, little more than a nod and a bland smile exchanged with Jeff, who had commandeered the table and surrounded himself and his laptop in papers.

Jan came out of his room, hair all over the place, bags under his eyes, heading for the coffee.

'Morning, princess,' said Jeff, handing him his coffee and going to make another. 'You look like shit. Another top night in the labour ward?'

'Mmmf,' was the somewhat ambiguous reply. 'Coffee.'

Juliet gave him a short smile, then took a seat at the other end of the veranda, grabbing a decoy book as she went, not up for banter. A quiet ten minutes passed, her sipping her coffee and staring at the horizon, the dusty grey stony crags which surrounded the valley. She felt pretty grey and stony herself, was starting to really feel the hurt, when she was interrupted.

'Hey, surgeon, you got any ops planned today?' Jan had awoken.

'One debridement, one hernia. You?'

She gave him her blank, nothing-wrong-that face. He caught it, despite his labour-night hangover. He narrowed his eyes slightly but spoke quite normally to her.

'Nothing planned, but you know how it is. There are a few in labour still. Always.'

True to form, just as he spoke, they saw Chinua walking towards them. They let him make his way to them, each of them downing the rest of their coffees, knowing it would be time to go. Again.

Sure enough. 'Doctor! Caesar!'

Jan looked over at Juliet. 'I don't miss the rambling tales leading up to the list of possible diagnoses and begging for help, do you? Doctor, Caesar! Much better. Coming Chinua!'

He put down his cup and started to head for theatre, still looking at Juliet. Maybe this would soothe whatever turbulence was going on there, just a bit.

'You coming to help? Let's go get a baby! Did I ever tell you this is the best operation invented?'

She pushed her gloom down deeper, and determinedly got up to join him on the march back to the hospital.

'You mentioned it once or twice in passing I think.'

'You never know what you're going to get, you see!'

'Girl or boy?' Juliet cocked her head at him.

'Tut tut! Open up! So many possibilities all encased in that tiny bundle. Maybe a runner, a singer . . .'

She gave a weak smile despite her low spirits, then joined in, as they walked. 'A cook, a DJ . . .' She made the squeak and jerk of an Ibiza DJ on the discs.

'A boy who truly loves his dog.'

'A future mother of ten!'

'Maybe even the pinnacle of human achievement: a VOG.' Big smile as Jan contemplated this.

Juliet burst the bubble a little. 'Of course, you might get a bad one every so often.'

'No, no! None of them are bad! And all of them will be a bit bad and a bit good. Yes, both.' He nodded sagely.

They were at the hospital now; he was checking the sweating, moaning mother.

'All right, Mama, don't worry. It will all be fine. Hi, Annet, show me the chart. Yup, everything going in the wrong direction, and you checked her below? Of course you did. Okay – Caesar it is, let's go!'

They helped position the lady, ready for her spinal anaesthetic, then started to wash their hands.

'So, I have a question,' asked Juliet while she scrubbed. 'How do you decide what they are? The babies?'

'You want to know all my secrets?'

'Yes.' She stared straight at him, serious eyes but twitchy lips.

'Very demanding, Stardust, very demanding. Chinua, tie my gown please.'

'Why be anything else? We'll discuss that another time, though. Back to the babies. How do you know which is which?'

He looked behind him as if for spies and leaned in to her. 'The secret is they can all be anything!'

She broke into a grin. 'Okay. And they'll all be something. Nice. Pluripotential operation, I like it!'

'Good word! New one for me – teach me later, okay? For now, let's get Elvis here out . . . Hold this, thank you.'

Elvis successfully extracted and given to his exhausted mother, now all sewn up, Jan and Juliet removed their sweat-soaked gowns. They washed their hands again, but afterwards he grasped her wrist gently.

'Has your little boy passed on? He looked as though he had a foot in the next world.'

She stilled for a moment, then met his eyes, saw her own sorrow reflected in them.

'I'm going back now to see. Probably.'

They went together, not speaking. The mother was sitting outside the ward, cradling the body of her son, crying silently.

Juliet sighed. She placed her hand on the mother's shoulder. 'I'm sorry, Mama. Sorry.'

Annet, the midwife, was behind them, translated for her. The mother looked up at Juliet and murmured a few words to Annet.

'She says she knows, and thank you. God's will.'

They walked slowly back to the operating room still in silence. There was nothing to say to make it better.

Juliet felt her heart dropping stonelike into the poisonous swamp of despond, stirring up the evil vapours. *Can't outrun your failures*, they whispered as they swept sulphurously through her. Failed again, another in the long series which started with your brother, your own flesh and blood, dead in your arms. Jan caught her arm and pulled her round to him before she could disappear into theatre, away from the rest of the world. She tried to give him a tight smile, her eyes wide with the stress of trying to contain the fight raging within.

'Juliet,' he began.

'It's okay, I can deal—'

'Just don't, okay? Don't do that.' His voice was low, but intense.

'Don't what?' She stared deliberately past him, the attempted false smile long gone.

'Don't hide it. You don't need to. Not from me, I know the road you're on. Look at me!'

'I can't. You don't know . . . there's something. I can't . . . Rotten.' She shut her eyes, willed herself to shut it all back inside. 'No. And I'm busy, sorry – I really need to dash. I'll see you later.'

She slipped out of Jan's grasp, wriggling away from him, but he found her hand, stopped her for a moment, gently.

'Juliet. After the operations today, let's run. Five o'clock.' He dropped her fingers and let her go, her words echoing around his head as he tried to understand what it was that she could not share with him.

She made herself not look after him, the expected bleakness now oozing horribly everywhere, blackening everything. She could run with him, but she could not talk to him, could not watch him realise that she was bad news, poison, a girl with wreckage in her past and again now in her present. The guilty survivor. He would step back, withdraw to a happier place, a land of the fortunate and victorious, away from the taint of her. Of course he would, and quite right; leave her in her accursed bog, not sink with her.

★

It was the precious hour before dark; the heat had receded. Jan had come to look for Juliet, silently insisting that she come and run.

They ran unhurriedly through the dusty town and onto the dustier main road, avoiding any off-road potentially land-mined paths. There were few cars in this much fought over corner of the land, more bikes and carts and animals, easier to avoid. They did not talk – running was for thinking, indeed almost nonverbal thinking, reordering of the mind. Juliet was desperate for a rest from her thoughts. She let her body take over, enjoying the mild punishment of having to work hard, feeling the exertion needed to keep going as the road headed uphill.

Jan bounded beside her like a big hare, not seeming to notice the slope they were climbing. At the top, they stopped to catch their breath and gaze over the valley. A moonscape of rocks, surrounded by the unyielding craggy cliffs. There were only occasional patches of green where teff was tentatively trying to grow in its weedy half-hearted fashion, apparently as unenthusiastic about its final injera destination as Juliet. She looked up at the timeless stone and was astonished to see a multicoloured church implausibly perched on top of one of the crags, surprise cracking open a fissure in her gloom.

'Tough gig, trying to survive here,' said Jan, scanning the rocky valley, following her gaze. 'Even without wars, AIDS, all of it. Yet look at that church. It's hard enough just to eat, and yet someone, some people have built a church way up there. Crazy.'

He risked a glance at her, willing her to come back from her dark dungeon of self-chastisement.

Juliet rested her eyes on it for a few minutes, glowing in the light, a colourful beacon looking over the valley. Might it give up its secrets, explain these mysteries of people and history and God? Not to her. The blackness flowed around her mind. She could not reach those answers, touch that understanding. She was a long way from the light, separated by ever more impassable doors.

They ran on.

Chapter 23

Juliet

The Camp

THEY HAD BEEN GATHERING for the past three days. There was something strange about the feel of the ward with them around – so many women and girls, brightly dressed in their amazing African wraps. Some were very young, with smooth beautiful features and delicate childlike frames. That was often the pattern with fistula of course: part of the problem was girls being married and impregnated when they were too small and too young to manage a successful delivery. There should have been the usual sounds of girls gathered together anywhere in the world: a loud hum of chatter, interspersed with happy cackles and cries of laughter, not this oppressive silence. The whole group was hushed, subdued, in complete contrast to their vivid dresses. A fugue of weary woe hung over them all, inseparable from the sickly malodorous cloud of ammonia oozing around them, invading every inch of any space they entered, assaulting everyone who came near. They kept their eyes down, avoiding the revulsion they expected to see in people's eyes.

Juliet studied them from behind a sheaf of papers. She had been almost constantly in the hospital for the past week. The desolation from the loss of the little boy last week had not lifted. She felt it adding its own burden to the heavy weight deep in her soul, pulling her down, pulling her togetherness apart. She was working hard to hold firm, straining to stop the tectonic plates ripping apart, to stop the terrifying molten lava beneath from roaring up to engulf her. Socialising and fun were beyond her at present. She had been avoiding Jan and Jeff.

Except for running – Jan insisted quietly that they run together each day at dusk. He said nothing to her, did not try to pry into the emotional battle she was waging.

He must be avoiding talking to her because he could see she was a disaster, she thought. A fraud, a liability. Stop it, she rebuked herself. It doesn't matter what he thinks, you are nothing to him. You just have to keep trying to do your best. There's no one else here to do it instead of you.

Nothing to him, she repeated in her head. Yet, she was perfectly well aware that despite being unable to banter and chat, she couldn't help look for him, and felt a sense of relief whenever he was around. Pointless, she thought, swinging back again. Look to your own walls; this house has to stand by itself.

And it was true that she had far too much to do for the

camp, was far too busy to be thinking about Jan. Lucky that she was an A-grade compartmentaliser.

She focussed herself on the camp, surveyed the women around her. The radio announcement Edmond had written for her had advertised free treatment for women made incontinent by childbirth. She had no idea how he had worded it in the local language, but it seemed to have done the trick. Thirty-two of these cowed and nearly broken little creatures had crept out from their hiding places and come to the hospital. A few dragged a foot and used a staff to walk, but she did not see the awful deformities which had horrified her in Addis. Either these did not occur up here – nice thought but unlikely – or they had not been able to reach those patients. Maybe she needed to send transport to some of the more remote villages, try to persuade the people there to let her take and treat the girls secreted out of sight behind the huts and shacks, locked away by their own shame.

That was for another day, though. For now, she had to organise the notes she had made on them all, ready for Dr Val arriving tomorrow. She had carefully examined each one, Jan helping, as they tried to understand the degree of severity of their injuries and what could be done to help. A few seemed minor, easily fixed. Most were more severe but with a solution possible, and one or two just dreadful: no obvious way to treat them that she could imagine. Dr Val would need to check those ones and they would see. She knew that there was provision in Addis for 'the incurables' as they were termed. She did not know who fitted that description, and whether it would only be coined after one, two or many failed attempts at repair. Also, transplanting them to Addis, so far from their families, might well make their lives even worse – she was getting ahead of herself.

Back to the present, Juliet, she admonished in her head. Lots to do in the present. She had an appendix to remove, a fractured wrist to reset and a lot of preparations to make for the fistula camp starting tomorrow.

She thought of the NHS, how she had always assumed there was a magic refilling cupboard of supplies giving her whatever she could think that would help. Here the cupboard was less magic and often empty. Each stitch was precious, used fully, nothing wasted. Compromises were made all the time. It had been quite an effort to gather together the supplies she thought they would need for the camp – and working out the requirements was her job; no such thing as a store manager or procurement officer.

She would just run through her list one more time before tomorrow. She wanted to do as much as possible to lift the load from Dr Val, who she knew spent many exhausting weeks each year touring the country treating fistula patients who were unable to get to Addis and had no local surgeon to help them. There simply weren't enough surgeons around.

Juliet looked around the ward. She could feel that something was pulling at her here, something not right which she had to understand and sort out. She looked carefully at the patients. They seemed closed off from her, inaccessible. Maybe over the coming week she would get to know them more, reach them somehow. She hoped hard that the awakening to life she had witnessed in Addis would occur here, too – that miraculous transformation to vivacious, happy girls again. Maybe it would just happen, as they started to feel dry again after their operations.

There was something bothering her, though, gnawing at her. She breathed quietly, taking in the downbeat atmosphere around the girls. They seemed to be behind a glass barrier, cut off by something. What? Sadness, shame probably. It felt so different on the ward in Addis . . . the incredible healing loving atmosphere which flowered there – so different to this.

What was she to do about that – how on earth could she manufacture loving healing? She visualised her own scrawny battle-scarred soul. Not much succour likely to flow from that. She needed help; she needed Irene. Maybe they could work together to battle the shame, to banish it in place of faith and hope and acceptance. But how?

She thought slowly of her own life, remembered many afternoons holed up with Caitlin as they tried to deal with hopeless boys, too difficult exams, nagging mothers . . . all the slings and arrows, minor really compared to the things these girls faced. But hard enough – so how did they get through it all? They used vodka for some of these problems, yes, but not just that. Abba, dancing, nail painting. What could she take from that here? Definitely not the vodka. Dancing was tough, Abba maybe not loved the same . . . but singing, maybe. Nails maybe. Friendship absolutely.

Encouragement to share their burdens, talk, recognise each other's problems, empathise, sympathise.

Right. She needed one of Jeff's radios for music and some nail varnish. And a better place to hang out and make a noise – the veranda with mats, or a gazebo in the grounds. Jeff for that too. But first and foremost, Irene. She nodded to herself and went off on her mission.

Only six long, full and life-changing days later and everything was much better in Juliet's eyes. There was noise, music, even laughing and chatting. Nearly all the operations had been done, and there was just one day left. Dr Val had been wonderful, radiating strength and optimism for everyone. Juliet had operated with her all week, doing more and more of the cases and fitting her own surgical cases in before and after normal working hours.

Jan had done all his cases in the minors' theatre with Edmond and Chinua helping. He had popped in and out of the fistula operations, watching carefully, learning. He had helped at a few of Juliet's and done two himself with Dr Val. He was a quick learner and would soon be doing them himself. Just as she had been, Juliet could feel him being drawn into the enticing challenges of the surgery as well as to the irresistible girls, slaying everyone's hearts with their shy smiles as they opened up like daisies in the sun.

The ward was calm with newly operated patients dozing, Sister Irene always around them, always comforting and tending them, listening, reassuring, explaining. Outside there was a low-key party tent, laughing and music going on, not too loud though – volume set by Sister Irene: no arguments. She had been incredible, had mothered everyone. She had even managed to produce a pastor who had got everyone singing for an hour on the Sunday afternoon. The heady combination of the rich young voices and the vivid reds, yellows and greens of their wraps against the huge blue sky had been almost overwhelming. Juliet had to blow her nose several times, claiming allergies to a sceptical Jan.

One evening, Juliet had set up nail painting, making sure to gently touch the girls' hands, to breach the walls they had set up around themselves. Even Genet had come, accompanied by Irene. Genet was much older than the other girls, probably in her fifties, although she was not sure herself. She was still a little shell-shocked by everything. It would take some time for her to adjust; after all, she had told Irene that she had been wet and essentially completely alone for over thirty years. Who knew what had triggered her decision to come to the camp after so long – maybe Edmond's radio announcement was the first inkling she had that she could be helped. Her fistula was surprisingly small and easily fixed. One hour of work to alter a lifetime of misery. Juliet smiled at her encouragingly as she sat with Irene at the edge of the giggling group, watching the fun.

There were gales of laughter when Jan had joined the queue, insisting on having one finger painted. Juliet had given him and herself one blue nail only, saying more was not allowed for the surgeons. He had then tried to paint one of the girl's nails himself and that occasioned even more laughing and shaking of heads at the uneven edges. It was a lovely time, sitting on the grass under the gazebo as the sun went down, just being with the girls.

Juliet could feel excitement in the air around them now, even happiness. It had burrowed its way into her as well, jostling with the self-loathing which had burgeoned so much in the week before the camp. There was a pressure building inside her which was becoming difficult to contain, despite the years of practice in closing off her inner self. She sensed some danger, was not sure how to avert it.

Jan was watching her carefully, aware of the storm in her eyes, wondering when or if it would break. He saw how she left it to one side when working, understood that this was how she coped. He did wonder at the origin of the great wave of emotion he thought might be unleashed, perhaps sooner rather than later. How much of her would be washed away with it? That was the other question. It frightened him. Perhaps he should help her to keep it all bottled up in case the release destroyed some precious part of her? He had no idea what to do, could only vow to keep close by, be ready to help her if there seemed to be something he could do.

Chapter 24

Sylvie and Edmond

EDMOND HAD WATCHED THE awakening transformation of the girls with great interest. He had helped Juliet with the arrangements for the camp, had studied the book she had brought from Addis on fistula surgery, and had assisted at some of the operations himself. He was desperate to convey all of this to Sylvie, to see if she could be helped too. During the lead up to the camp he had told her about it at the waterpump, had described the radio announcement, tried to talk about the book.

She had not wanted to talk about it at all, had shut him out and run away, before he could press her. He could not understand it, but had not had enough time to pursue the matter, what with all his busy work of preparation, then helping with the extra surgery as well as managing all of his usual responsibilities on top.

He had just one more opportunity to try to see Sylvie during the week of the camp. Chinua was covering the night. Edmond was desperate to persuade her to come.

He could get back in time for the next day's operating if he left at first light. He got back to the village late – after dark, and decided not to go to her house, but rather to see her in the morning.

He was out waiting for her by 4 a.m. Surely nothing had changed; she would still be coming. He waited for a long ten minutes, becoming more nervous with every minute, ran back inside to check the time and came back out to find her already at the pump filling her cans.

'Sylvie!' he called, coming out to join her.

She raised her head to face him, a smile coming to her tired eyes. 'Hello, Edmond! You've been working hard this week, I think?'

He smiled back. 'I have, yes! And I want to tell you all about it – can I tell you while we fill your cans?'

She looked slightly wary but nodded. He launched into it, telling her all about Dr Val coming from Addis, about the patients coming after hearing the radio announcements, about the operations to make them clean and dry again. He wanted to explain how the girls were beginning to change, blossoming again, how they had made friendships, how they looked up more, met your eyes, smiled even . . . He couldn't put it all into words. And he could sense Sylvie recoiling from him before he got to that part, even when he described Dr Val and more obviously when he talked about the operations.

She raised her hand, stopping him. 'Please, Edmond, no. Please. You have to understand: hope hurts more than anything. I cannot go; how can I go? We have no money, none. I'm in rags. I cannot ask my father.'

'But Sylvie, I could—'

She interrupted him, turning to go. 'No. I cannot afford to hope; it will break me. I'm sorry.'

He watched her toil up the hill with the jerry cans sloshing heavily against the bike. He was angry at himself, sure he had messed this up. The opportunity was slipping through her fingers. He sighed. Maybe there would be another camp. Maybe Dr Juliet would come back, maybe Dr Val. People didn't often come back, though – they had their own lives to take up again, far from here. It was better to seize a chance now than hope for a future one.

He tutted, shook his head sadly. There was no way to persuade her, he knew. And she was right about her father. He could see how brittle the man had become: worn out from worry and anger, unable to see beyond the rigid confines of his family's reduced existence, certainly unable to imagine a cure for Sylvie, a release for them all.

Sylvie pushed up the hill, weeping freely, hoping he didn't come after her. She could not bear to talk to him about it; could not bear to glimpse the possibility of an end to her torment and then to accept it could not be. She could not go with him to the hospital. She had not been out in public for almost four years! She would die of shame before the first hour was out. She broke into a cold sweat at the thought of anyone seeing her dirty and ragged, let alone smelling her . . .

And she had no money for treatment or even for food at

the hospital. Edmond had said it was all free, but was that really true? Everything? Surely not. And how could she leave Jonny? The problems seemed insurmountable.

And another thing: what if they told her no, that there was no hope for treatment for her? How could she leave and make herself come back to this? This never-ending cycle of pain and wetness, of worry and hunger. Each day so difficult, each little pocket of fun or happiness she could conjure up for Jonny so dearly bought. Always seeing the resentment of her other brother at his lot, the growing realisation of her sisters that their lives were not headed for bright city jobs and prosperity, but something much closer to home, poorer and less fun. She knew she was not responsible for them, but she also knew she could have changed these paths for them if she were still working at the hotel. If Ivan had not happened, and the baby had not . . . if things had been different.

She wept and raged at it all, eventually calming and turning inwardly to the only thing that kept her alive at all: her still abundant store of love. Love for her baby most of all, not regretting her existence, only her end. Love for all of them. She let herself feel it, let the gentle waves of it cool the fires of anger which had been stoked up. Let it flow through her, strengthen her to face the day, another like so many before, like so many to come.

Chapter 25

Juliet

Trauma Call

'BEEP BEEP!' THE HORN on the jeep kept blowing as it pulled out of the hospital gate, bearing Dr Val away to the airport at Mekele and back to Addis Ababa. Juliet and the crowd of girls around her waved until long after it had gone.

There were about thirty girls, mostly short – maybe too small to have managed to deliver a baby – all clutching a bucket with urine draining into it; all desperately hoping that their operation was going to prove successful and that life could begin again. They were just beginning to wake up to that possibility and their youthful optimism was breaking through again, no longer squashed down by pain and shame. There was continual talking and laughing, the noise level rising daily.

Juliet sat down on the step of the ward beside the girls, ready to join with them in their basket weaving and knitting. It had been a very busy week, alternately assisting Dr Val and operating herself with that esteemed lady watching over, and she was relieved to be having a quiet day. The girls would stay on the ward for another week or two, then they would take out the catheters and see if they could stay dry. Dr Val had warned her that most would be okay, but usually one or two were not. They would need much counselling and encouragement to come again to the next camp in six months for another try.

Six months. Juliet should be back home then, entrenched in the NHS once again. Although, everyone seemed to expect that she would be there for the next camp, particularly Dr Val. Could she just take leave, pop back for a couple of weeks for a fistula camp? she wondered. Why not? She answered herself. Set your terms at the beginning and this could be a way of keeping fistula surgery part of your life. And Africa. She had just settled down to try some knitting alongside the patients, companionably sharing her step with Ruthie, one of the first patients to have their operation in this camp, when loud beeping was heard again.

'Are they back?' Juliet raised her head to look.

A goods truck was pulling into the yard, beeping all the while, with men hanging onto the bars at the sides of the truck and seemingly a load of bodies draped over the sacks. She had seen many such trucks lurching along the dreadful roads, completely overloaded with bags of charcoal or sticks or whatever and a scattering of workers on top like birds on a wire. Unfortunately, these human birds could not fly off to escape, crashing to earth if the truck toppled over on a too-tight corner.

Juliet was already up and running to it, calling for Sebastian, Chinua, Edmond and Jeff as she ran. Oh, God, it was some sort of awful accident. There seemed to be about twenty severely injured patients. The others were running to the truck too, the awareness of a disaster having spread almost instantly through the compound.

'Don't move them out yet!' she yelled, switching automatically into trauma mode: cool, in control and in charge, her pulse beating faster but fuelling purposeful energy.

'Help me into the truck; I'll triage from there. Everyone who can walk should go into the Outpatients waiting room. No, sir, not now, we will be with you as soon as we can. Chinua, have you got your tape in your pocket? Give them all a number and take notes about who is to go where. Jeff, can you get Jan to turn back – I need help, then get some blood donors. Edmond, can you put drips up on the ones I tell you and give them painkillers then try to get them off the truck slowly and into the ward? Sebastian, can you get theatre ready: two tables, two sets of instruments and get the midwives to scrub and assist me. Chinua is going to be busy here . . .'

She continued to bark out instructions as they surveyed the boys in the truck, finding the sickest ones who needed surgery first. There was one who had already passed on, and another who was surely about to: unresponsive with a bad head injury; nothing she could do about that one. She took just a few minutes to check and number the others, then ran to theatre, praying Jan would be back soon to help.

He saw her jump out of the truck and disappear into theatre, Jeff having radioed to him to come back immediately. Jan hurried after her, clocking the lads working on the other groaning patients in the truck and the crowd of agitated guys milling around the doorway to outpatients. The least sick patients were always the noisiest and most demanding.

'Irene!' Jan called towards the fistula ward. She appeared quickly at the door. 'Can you keep these guys in the outpatients' hall and start cleaning wounds. Chinua and Edmond will join you when they can!'

He ran into theatre. Juliet was already scrubbed and starting to open one young very pale looking teenage boy's abdomen, and there was another one looking similarly unwell lying on the table beside her.

'Oh, you came back, thank God – got a ruptured spleen here I think – hope so anyway, quick to fix at least. Can you open that guy and pack whatever is bleeding – I'll be there in a jiffy, I hope . . . Yes, this is a spleen, right you go, matey, you are for the bucket. Clamps please. Sebastian, lots of blood here, can you make sure we know what groups they are and just give them blood when we get some? Maybe the guys waiting in OPD can donate.'

Jan scrubbed and got started, calling for instructions as he went. Juliet was everywhere it seemed, finishing her case, helping with his, running back to the truck to get the next one and check she had made the right decisions at the first triage.

So it went on, all day, all night. Five people had to have abdominal surgery, a further two had drains inserted in their chests and their ribs strapped, and four had terrible open fractures which needed to be cleaned and set. There were patients with head injuries, dislocations, arm fractures, scrapes and sores. Chinua and Edmond dealt with most of these, checking their plans with Juliet. The whole team was there, Jeff getting the blood donations from volunteers in the camp and then going to Adigrat two hours away for more supplies.

The two young men with head injuries had died early on, but so far everyone else was holding on, a major effort for all of them.

Chapter 26

Sylvie and Jonny

UNLIKE THE FULL-ON ACTION in the hospital, in Sylvie's village it was another sleepy Sunday. Sylvie could hear gentle snoring from the main hut: her father and possibly Gregory also, a little duet going on. They generally slept late on a Sunday, no school or work. Even her mother got up a little later than usual, although there was no rest day for her, no change in the chores to be done, animals and humans to be tended and fed.

Sylvie felt Jonny squirming at her side and sighed a little. Jonny had no concept of a lie-in; he was up and at it shortly after dawn each day. She would let him wake then spirit him away so that he didn't disturb the others. They would go to the woods and bring the goats with them. She would invent a new game for him, make him laugh. She fell to thinking about that, trying to ignore the slow burn of the sores on her thighs.

An hour later, the goats were tethered by a patch of scrub and Sylvie was explaining the game to Jonny. It was a race around the world, or rather the wood. He was to race against time itself and she would count. There would be many obstacles on the way: rivers to ford, crocodiles to fight, mountains to climb. She would be most surprised if he got back within the year, but would keep counting in case. Most importantly, he was not to leave the wood, and whenever he got thirsty, he should come to her for water.

Jonny sped off, calling out the obstacles as he overcame them, a diminutive but ebullient Hercules. He did two laps then stopped for a rest and to tell her outlandish tales of the monsters he had met. Jonny's life was well populated with monsters which he regularly vanquished with sticks.

Sylvie was about to suggest a different game when he jumped back up, crying 'Around the world again!' and was off – but in the wrong direction.

Sylvie called after him. 'Jonny, not that way! Stay in the wood!'

He paid no attention, indeed could likely hear nothing over his own war whoops. Drat it, she thought, I need to go after him, in case he goes out of the woods. The road lay close by the wood in this direction. It was difficult to catch him, though; he was small and speedy, and she was padded, wet and uncomfortable.

'Jonny!' she called. 'Not that way! Come back!'

She could hear the road now, and the intermittent roars of motorbikes and trucks. She felt sweat breaking out on her back, a premonition of some terrible thing building in her stomach, making her nauseous. She tried to run faster, still calling for him.

Then she heard it: a scream of brakes, a thump, shouting. She flew now, her heart beating so hard she thought it would burst out of her chest. She reached the road to find a little crowd of people around a very still small body, a motorbike on its side nearby and a truck halted beside them all.

'No, no, no, Jonny!' she screamed, pushing through the people, never giving a thought to them seeing or smelling her for once – all her focus on her brother.

Was he alive, dear God, was he alive? She dived for him, lying unconscious on the dusty road, looking for all the world as though he had fallen into a beautiful sleep. There was a graze on his forehead, and his leg, oh dear, his leg was at a horrible angle. She took his head, washing his silent little face with her tears.

'Oh, God, Jonny, no, don't die, no Jonny,' she moaned. Someone was talking to her, shaking her shoulder. Finally, she looked up. It was Amara, Edmond's mother.

'Sylvie!' she was saying, a little sharp, trying to reach her. 'He is alive, but he must be taken to hospital, now, right away. This man whose truck hit him will take him to Edmond's hospital. It's only an hour away. You will need to go with him. I will tell your parents.'

Sylvie could not think. She nodded, holding on to Jonny's head. She helped Amara and the driver as they carefully lifted the little body onto the passenger seats, some moans coming from Jonny as they moved his leg, ensuring it was

Mhairi Collie

tucked against the back of the seat. Sylvie sat holding him, mute with terror, praying incoherently in her head, weeping silently. The driver was talking but she could hear nothing, see nothing other than the beloved boy in her arms, hanging on to life by his fingernails.

The truck lurched around the potholes, and slowly trundled towards the hospital.

Chapter 27

Sylvie and Juliet

JAN LOOKED AROUND THE now densely packed male ward. It seemed that finally, everyone was patched up. Juliet was finishing off with the last standing patient, suturing a nasty lip laceration which needed repair of the muscle underneath.

She must be exhausted, he thought. A week of intense fistula surgery, then no time for a breath before this major trauma call. She had been amazing, though, a whirlwind of activity blowing organisation, energy and confidence into every corner, and making everyone feel that they could also do this: could save these patients, look after them all.

Surely she was about to crash though – a person could only keep that level of adrenalin-fueled activity up for so long. He started back towards theatre, meaning to take her back to the house to rest, when his name was called by Edmond.

Edmond had been his usual incredibly helpful, calm self throughout the trauma – sorting out the patients pre- and post-surgery, setting fractures with Chinua once that was done, always quietly smiling and working away. In fact, Jan thought he had never known him anything other than calm. Until now.

Now his voice was raw with anxiety, breaking with emotion as he called to Jan from the entrance hall. Jan ran to him and saw that he was standing over a young boy: pale and still, his little leg at a terrible angle, a girl bent over his face exhorting him to breathe in between her sobs.

'Where is the surgeon?' rasped Edmond, his eyes wide with distress.

'I'll get her, you get an IV into this boy. Sebastian!'

Jan was off at a run, almost colliding with Juliet as she emerged from theatre, the first signs of weariness showing in her somewhat disco-ordinated turn at the door.

'Juliet! A child. Come quick! Someone of Edmond's I think.' Jan grabbed her hand and they ran to the entrance.

Then everything fell apart.

Juliet gasped as she took in the unconscious boy: his arms flung out on the floor, his right leg at a terrible angle, clearly broken.

She lurched backwards into Jan.

'No, no, no, Drewie, no,' she moaned, white as a sheet, shaking violently.

Jan caught her. 'What the?' he started. 'Juliet! What's the matter? This boy needs you. Come on.'

Sweat was pouring down Juliet's face: all drained of blood. She shook and trembled and backed away from Jan into the wall as she stared horror-struck at the child.

'No, no, Drewie, no!' she repeated, in a strange, distracted voice, sobbing now, slipping down the wall, still shaking, her eyes not connecting with them, rather looking at some internal horrific scene.

This was it. The bomb had finally gone off. Rearing up into her mind, the memory of her eleven-year-old self sitting numb on a pavement clutching the cold white hand of her little brother. She could hear again the creaking of the wheel of his upturned bike, the blaring horn of the stalled van in the hedge. Could feel again the scream *Nooooo* reverberate through her as she sat helpless, unable to make time go backwards – to change it. The horrible clunking irreversible resetting of the universe, so that everything was re-understood as before or after this moment.

A black spectre was now alongside her, a hellhound breathing acrid death. A yawning terrifying hole had opened up, her brother disappearing into it. Gone. But she could follow him, go after him into the silent darkness. Be with him there, if she couldn't bring him back. Just slip down into the black shadow.

Something, someone, was pulling her back. A strong voice, a strong spirit that could see her teetering on the brink of oblivion, and insisted that she turn away, come back.

She blinked, tore her gaze away from the internal nightmare and looked instead into beautiful warm eyes, the reassuring bronze glow of the oldest stars, light and life.

The girl who was bent over the child had turned and straightened, looking directly at Juliet. Her face was dirty and tear-streaked, but her gorgeous eyes were rich with intelligence and understanding. She stared at Juliet, seeing all too clearly the sweat and trembling, the horror in her face, the traumatic revisiting of something awful showing in her tortured eyes. She knew that feeling, that helpless toppling into the black hole of despair. She also knew that she, Sylvie, had to pull this girl back from the abyss, bring her to the present.

Her voice came out steady and compelling as she took Juliet's hand, forcing her to meet her eyes.

'No!' she said. 'No! This is now, and this is my little brother, Jonny, nobody else. You come back here right now. He needs you. Don't go back to that other place, no! You are not there now; you are here with us. You can help him. You are the one. Come back to me now!"

Juliet's eyes were wild, but her shaking reduced to a quiver only. She stared at the girl for a full minute, breathing hard.

'Jonny?' she finally croaked. 'Your brother?'

'Yes,' said the girl, now starting to cry again.

She waited though, holding Juliet's eyes, insisting on having the reassurance that Juliet was back in the here and now. 'Please, I need you to save him if you can.'

Jan gently pulled Juliet back onto her feet and Sylvie took her other hand.

'Jonny,' she repeated firmly. 'No one else. Now.'

Jan was still supporting Juliet, and staring at the encounter between the two girls.

'Juliet?' he faltered, then, out of the corner of his eye, saw

Sebastian quietly setting up a drip on the little patient. He turned to him, relief in his voice.

'Sebastian, well done for getting the IV. Can you carry him into theatre when he has had the ketamine? Juliet, I'm here with you; tell me how to help you. This boy has a big abrasion on his right side – maybe he's injured his—'

Juliet focussed on the little boy at her feet. Jonny. Not Dewie, Jonny. Jonny needed her. She could help him, could save this one. In a trice she was down on her knees examining him. He remained unconscious but gave a little moan as she touched the right side of his belly.

'—liver,' she finished Jan's sentence. 'And leg. Let's get him to theatre, guys.'

She wiped her face, looked back at the girl, grasping her arm. She was still white and sweaty, but her eyes were back.

'Wait here, I . . . I . . . ' She ran out of words, nodded fiercely and followed Sebastian and the child into theatre.

Jan shook his head, wondering what had just happened. He gave the girl and Edmond as reassuring a smile as he could manage, noting the reek of ammonia around her with surprise – she smelled just like a fistula patient. He made a mental note to ask Edmond about that later, and hurried after Juliet.

Things were pretty ropey for the boy until Jeff appeared like Merlin with blood for him, and, after that, the operation went fairly smoothly. Juliet seemed like an automaton: concentrated and careful, repairing the liver, tying off the bleeders, calling out instructions. No chat. And Jan was careful to avoid talking to her, in case she lost her ability to do it all. They worked quietly together, stopped the bleeding, set the leg, and finally it was over.

Jan stripped off his gown and went to wash his hands again at the bucket, watching Juliet all the time. She was pale but composed and met his eyes now. Hers were red-rimmed, exhausted and slightly rueful.

'I—' she began, then stopped. 'I need to go see her,' and she disappeared.

Jan followed, slowly. She had her hand on the girl's shoulder, both looking at the still, pale sleeping child.

'I think he will be okay,' Juliet murmured.

She waited for the girl to look at her, then continued in a breaking voice, 'I'm sorry about . . . I'm sorry . . . I have, that is, I mean, I had a brother—'

And she started to sob. The girl gathered her into her arms, letting their foreheads meet and their tears pool together in her lap.

'I had a daughter,' she whispered to Juliet, weeping along with her. Jan leaned against the doorway, waiting and wondering.

After a long time, all the grief seemed to shudder slowly to a stop. Juliet raised her head to look at Sylvie, the girl. She was so beautiful, her eyes so kind, still wet with emotion. She seemed to be able to see fully into Juliet's soul, nothing hidden from her. The miserable wasted desert of regret at Juliet's core was laid bare for her, all the defences Juliet had created to shield it over the years swept away.

Sylvie knew; Sylvie could see it all, understand it all. She gently touched Juliet's forehead, still holding on firmly to her hand.

'Flashback,' she whispered. 'Terrible thing. I know, I've had it, too.'

They were quiet for a few minutes, feeling each other's pain alongside their own.

Sylvie eventually raised her head, determinedly saying the words, knowing Juliet needed to hear them.

'Guilt is the other terrible thing – it stands in the way of the love.' She paused. 'You have to let it go to feel the love again.'

Juliet could say nothing. She had nothing left: no fight; no resilience. She let the beauty of Sylvie and her words wash through her, bathing the ravages within. There was such understanding in those eyes. Reassurance from one who had faced the demons. Sylvie thanked her with her eyes, and let her go, turning back to tend her brother, drowsy but restless as he woke from the anaesthetic.

'Juliet.' Jan was there. 'Come, my girl, you need to sleep.'

She was stumbling against him now, absolutely exhausted. His arm was around her, half lifting her across the field back to the house. The sky was brightening up again; he wasn't even sure what day it was now. He helped her carefully onto the top of her bed, replaced the mosquito net and then collapsed onto his own bed to sleep finally, at last.

Chapter 28

Juliet and Jan

AFTER WHAT FELT LIKE only five minutes, but was actually four hours, he woke, his mind clear and his heart troubled. Was Juliet all right? What sort of horror had she lived through way back when, and revisited last night? Had she lost her mind? He needed to check on her.

He was about to enter her room when he saw her, sitting in her favourite place on the stoop, mug of tea in hand. He slowly went over and sat by her, saying nothing.

She kept looking straight ahead, and took a slow drink of tea. After a longish time, she started to talk, her sentences stilted and forced, her face stony, all the while looking into the distance, into the past.

'It was my brother. I was ten years old and he was five. He was my pet, my play pal. I adored him. We were always together. He was trying to ride his new bike. Got it for his birthday. Our road was usually so quiet, out in the country, no traffic. But then that day, a truck. Fast round the bend. Couldn't stop. Caught him. Leg gone just like Jonny there.

But something else, something sucking the life out of him. Maybe his head, I don't know. He wouldn't wake up. Got colder and colder. I sat holding his hand, but I couldn't stop it. Couldn't save him. The driver was unconscious. My mum was at the shops. I was to look after him. And I couldn't save him. Couldn't. I was useless. Failed. So he died.'

The hatred in her voice as she called herself useless was almost palpable, the desolation as she said the final words immeasurable.

Jan sat quietly by her, feeling her pain, the burning rawness of it still, after so many years. Did she really feel such loathing towards herself? Oh, yes. Yes she did.

He began to understand why she had withdrawn from him over the past couple of weeks. He had been a little rejected initially, but had quickly realised she was battling something, had decided to wait it out. Now he realised she had been ashamed. Ashamed of failing to save that little child, of being defeated by death. Ashamed and full of self-hatred.

She had run from him, expecting him to be disappointed, even disgusted with her, just as she was disgusted with herself. And what about now – did she think he would be repulsed by her now that he had seen that secret years-old shame, understood what she had been hiding since she was a child herself? Yes again. He knew her, he knew that would be exactly her thought. He had to break that thought, move her past it.

He glanced at her. Her eyes were dry now. He could almost see her starting painstakingly to wall it all up again, to let the noxious fire smoulder on, deep within her. She was getting ready to shut him out again.

He stood, reached out a hand to her. 'Come with me, show me the patients from last night.'

She nodded, a disturbing blankness competing with the pain in her eyes. He didn't know which was worse.

Methodically, they went around all of the patients: checking dressings, adjusting fluids, ensuring the pain was being treated. Jonny and Sylvie were fast asleep, but some of the others needed attention.

He could feel the comfort she took in running through the checks again and again, resetting her own brain with the routines and systems she had learned and absorbed over the years. All now part of her inner clockwork: her cogs and wheels. They came to the end of the ward and walked through the cleaned and scrubbed theatre. He leaned against the door, watching her looking around carefully as if reading the recent events by this arena, checking again through the procedures in her head.

'Juliet, I have to tell you something.' He interrupted her mental machinations, and waited for her attention.

'Yeah?' She wasn't listening. He waited a bit longer, until she noticed and turned to him, focussed on him. 'Sorry, with you now.'

'I have to tell you this, my stardust surgeon.' His deep blue eyes seemed to circle all around her like the tide coming in.

She was listening now.

'All of those patients, saved or helped by you, add to the list of the many who have gone before . . . and it will never be enough.'

She started, surprised, not understanding. He looked down, touched her wrist, then held her wondering gaze again.

'Never enough. I'm saying this to you because I have . . . I have also tried to ransom a ghost. And I know now that it's impossible. But you keep trying, keep doing it and it does make you feel a little better, but only for a little while. Like a sugar sweetie when you're starving: only a little better, never enough.'

His eyes slipped past hers now, to the reddening sky out of the window.

She had stopped in her tracks. What ghost?

'What ghost, Jan?' she whispered.

He was silent for a moment, as if deciding whether or not to open that door any wider. Eventually he seemed to decide that having shown her a swift peek, the wall was in effect breached and the inner courtyard already surrendered. He cleared his throat and went on.

'You know – my mother – I told you about her and her hippy ways: bicycling everywhere in her big straw hat, making friends everywhere, completely open to everyone – you know, so completely embarrassing that you actually couldn't be embarrassed and had to just go along and enjoy the ride. My father pretending to try to escape one or two of the many projects she dreamed up for us all but, how do you say it – strange breakfast phrase with eggs?'

Juliet frowned, then smiled: 'I have it: he eggs her on!'

Jan gave a half-smile back, pain still in his face.

'Yeah, he was egging her on really. Save the whales, the library, the language, always something going on. Anyway, she was, and is, very wonderful – a perfect mother really. Full of care for the world, and she loves me.'

He stopped. Juliet waited, slightly confused as to where this was going. He took another breath.

'So, in the big cities, in Germany and Czech and Slovakia, they have these special . . . they have these strange kind of post boxes at the hospitals. You can wrap a baby up in his blanket and leave him in the post box without anyone seeing you do it. The baby goes into the box, an alarm goes off and staff rush down to the post box to get the baby. They check it over, give it some food, you know. Look after it. Because some of the mothers are too poor or too young, and don't know how to manage. So they help them by taking the babies without making a big fuss. Not to let the babies be left in the park or something bad like that.'

He stopped again.

Juliet tried to imagine this. She saw a frightened girl in a dark street, distressed and unsure, looking at the post box and thinking it would be a safer warmer place for the heavy, hungry secret but unhideable babe in her skinny arms.

'My mother worked as a nurse in one of these hospitals,' Jan continued, 'and took the babies to the ward to look after. She explained it to me. Irresistible, she said. Me. You see?' His voice was light, but the air was heavy with the many unsaid things.

Juliet was quiet, processing this. All these little mothers he chased around day and night, in the camps, in the villages, in the bush. Trying to make them safe, to be cared for and to feel it too. With his wide 'you can do it' smile and crazy bark of a laugh and his big gentle hands. She had seen him with them, thought of him talking earnestly to them in his mayhem of an outpatient clinic. People everywhere, no apparent order, the desk covered with papers, serious jostling going on all around him to get his attention, but he always intent on the girl in front of him, fixing her with his blue, blue eyes, hypnotic. Or him, sitting on a little stool beside them for hours in the labour room, muttering Slovakian swear words as Manjit crashed about doing God knows what, other than getting everyone in a muddle.

And all the while knowing that his own little mother had probably been alone, scared and somewhat in torment. Surely there was a ghost who would never be laid to rest, a hurt never assuaged.

Juliet took his hand, traced the tendons on the back of it, turned it over and followed the lines, circled the muscle pad at the base of his thumb.

'Why do you keep doing it if you know it's impossible?' she asked, finally.

'Habit maybe . . . Actually no, not that.' He looked behind her, seeing something away back.

'I think the ghost and I have an understanding now. I will keep chasing around, knowing time goes forward, not back, and she will let me. Let me give them a little of all that I had for her, that she could not take.'

Juliet squeezed his hand, then spontaneously dropped a kiss onto it.

'Such riches you have, that you give away,' she said quietly, after a moment.

He wiped a stray tear from her cheek. 'And you, too. Toil and trouble.'

She gave a little unsure laugh. 'You think I'm toil and trouble?'

'I think you embrace it, take it on. A warrior, ready to fight, willing to suffer. Maybe you're paying a debt, chasing like me. Maybe it's enough now; maybe it never will be. I don't know. Maybe you don't have to feel you do it alone, though, or in secret.'

She let her pale blue fiery eyes bore into him fully now. He was there, opened up for her, letting her in: an Icelandic volcano meeting the depths of the cooling ocean. They seemed to breathe in time together. She felt something shift in her, and a rush of relief as she realised he did not despise her. Rather, he felt it all with her, did not shy away from regret and sorrow but took it in, lived with it. Laughed and loved alongside it.

Jan tilted his head slightly and blinked slowly.

'Come,' he said. 'This day really needs to end soon. Let's watch the sun go down and wish it farewell.

They walked quietly back to the house to sit together on the veranda, tired to their fingertips, watching the last light of the day. It always seemed more desperately vibrant at this time – one more mad swirl on the dancefloor before the inevitable fade into night. The background noise reassuringly present, clatter of pots, muted roars of motorbikes on the main road, always chickens, children calling, someone shouting.

She leant against his shoulder. He let his weight rest onto hers just a little, just enough that she could feel him there. His hand picked up hers to loosely hold, his thumb making slow strokes across her fingers.

Her hand was tanned, slim but powerful, with little rippling tendons and sinewy muscles, full of history and the future – of the work already done and the potential operations still to come. His also carried that story and that future, was similarly strong, but big, comforting and gentle. He felt her fingers relax in his, and gradually her weight against him increased as she let go of the day's burdens. She was spent: physically and emotionally. He waited for sleep to finally claim her, then before she could fall forwards, he wound her arm around his neck and picked her up, carried her to her bed in the house and laid her down. She curled over onto her side, sighing gratefully, but caught his hand as he straightened up to let go of her.

'Please stay,' she murmured drowsily, tucking his hand into her own and clasping it to her, without opening her eyes. 'Spoons . . . '

He looked down at her: her golden hair falling over the clear skin of her face, her loved face. He arranged himself beside her, letting her nestle into him. He stayed propped up enough to watch her sleep, thinking of the traumas they had both revealed today, of the blinding exposure to her locked-away secrets, now all spilled out. Surely she would be able to be herself with more confidence now.

Her wonderful self, thought Jan. There she was, there she'd been, trying and trying to make up for a tragedy she could not undo, could not repair. How many years of driving herself onwards towards that impossible goal. He had seen her moved, happy, sad – all of the little hurts and also joys felt in her vulnerable heart and showing in her eyes. He had also seen her strive to cover and defend that easily wounded heart with her sardonic wit and 'doctor' mien. He wondered what would happen now – would she rebuild more and more defences or let herself be?

'Time will tell, *moja krasna laska*, my beautiful love,' he murmured.

He turned to thinking of his own inner shrine to loss, shown to her. The loved space where his mother should have been, giving and receiving his love. All the real and true love he felt for his adoptive parents had never been able to fill that space – it was sacred, for that one woman connected to him invisibly. He lived with the space comfortably enough though, the emptiness of it almost a companion following him through life. He did not expect it to change, however full his heart became with love for others.

He gently stroked Juliet's forehead, sweeping her hair away from her sleeping face. Her eyes resting from their usual seeking and searching. He was sure they were irresistibly drawn northwards, wondered if they could pull him there with them, and knew immediately that of course they could. He was ready to follow her dance wherever it took her, was just waiting for her to want him.

The dark skies were beginning to lighten in the hour before dawn. She stirred, felt his firm chest under her head and opened her eyes to him, the fiery light of life there shocking after the quiet night. He felt his heart beat faster.

'Oh, you're here . . . mmm, good.' She wiggled a little to feel the length of him pressed against her. 'Welcome to my personal space.'

He smiled into her eyes, his dark blue gaze a caress.

'Why, thank you! It's very nice – I think I prefer it to my own. In fact, I may move in. To be very honest, my mind has been here for a long time, just my body to join now.'

'I . . .' Juliet's voice dwindled away as she saw the intensity in his eyes and met them, full on. His look was diving deep into her, unafraid, seeing everything, wanting everything, ready to bare everything of his own to her. She trembled a little, but held his gaze, let the communion unfold for a minute, two minutes, maybe more . . . Until it was done and all was silently said.

There was a warmth beginning deep down in her soul, down where there had been the hidden wasteland, now blown open by Sylvie. New shoots of life? Yes, unstoppable life, reclaiming her.

She lightly brushed her fingertips over his tanned shoulders and the hard muscles of his chest.

'Moving in here might be fine,' she mused. 'I think there's room for you. You know, also while you're here, I think we should undertake some important scientific research.' She reached up to gently touch his lower lip.

'Oh, yes?' He gave her finger a tiny lick, stroking her back, then entwined his fingers through her hair, holding her head.

'Mmm, yes.' Her fingers were now feathery on his cheek, his jaw, his neck. 'Firstly, we need to establish if your goatee tickles when I kiss you.'

'I wish you would establish that.' His mouth was nearly on hers now. 'I've been thinking about it almost constantly since I grew it.'

He gently brushed her lips with his own, then pulled her to him for a deeper kiss. A full, long kiss, gentle but insistent, as if forcing open the dam to the emotions he knew lurked behind.

She was the one for him, he knew, and was almost sure she would know it soon, if she didn't already. He told her with his kiss, told her that he wanted all of her, every single perfect and imperfect bit. She felt somewhat stunned at the fierceness of it, the seriousness she could detect. She wanted it like that though, and was suddenly aware that she was desperate for this not to be frivolous, or – even worse – regretted. Every fibre of her being was telling her that this was as far from a shallow time-filler as could ever be. She felt the joy of it, felt that she was exposed and defenceless to him but was excited to be so, to let him in.

'You know,' he said conversationally, after quite some

time, 'I think I need to expand the study – just hold on up there . . .' and he trailed a line of kisses down her neck to her collar bone, down onto her chest, his hand now stroking her leg.

'I do hope we're not straying into *verboten* territory?' Juliet took a sharp intake of breath as his hand wandered over her from thigh to thigh.

'Well, as my hero Gandhi would say, fuck it.'

She gurgled with delicious laughter, and he returned to her mouth to enjoy it.

'Gandhi is an excellent role model,' she acknowledged when able to speak again. 'Although I didn't know that was one of his sayings.'

'Very excellent, yes. The old rascal, he would've had your top off a long time before now. I try to be more like him, yes?'

She laughed again then turned her attention completely to him, to his firm body, his strong arms, his gently smiling beautiful face and deep sea-blue eyes.

Chapter 29

Sylvie and Juliet

JULIET WAS SITTING WITH Sylvie, the two of them watching Jonny sleep.

'He's had a bad night, quite a lot of pain,' said Sylvie, stroking his little hand.

Juliet grimaced. 'Sorry. It will get better soon, really. Kids heal so quickly, you'll be amazed. He'll have to stay with us here for over a month though, maybe six weeks, to wait for his leg to knit together.'

'Six weeks! That's quite a long time.' Sylvie sat back, surprise on her face, followed by a pushing crowd of thoughts. 'I'll need to stay here with him.'

'You will,' agreed Juliet. She said nothing more, waiting for Sylvie to tidy out the thoughts, think through the possibilities and consequences. They were quiet together, both still a bit raw from the exposure yesterday.

God, was that only yesterday, or had she lost a day somewhere? thought Juliet. She let herself dwell on Sylvie's words to her again, for the nth time that day. What had she said exactly? '*Drop the guilt and all that's left is love.*'

She gave a small gulp – it did feel as though she hadn't been able to love Drewie properly for all these years, to feel again how she had adored him. Her guilt and sorrow had submerged her love for him. She should let herself feel that love again, weep maybe when she did, but feel it all the same. She would do it if she could – but could she? Was it all waiting inside her? Yes, she thought, yes, it will all be there, to be let out, in my own time.

Sylvie turned to her, her eyes warm and inviting.

'You know, Jonny's normally the most active boy you could imagine. He has two speeds: maximum and stop, stop usually being when he is asleep.'

Juliet smiled. 'I'm sure he'll get back to that. Might need to add a slightly slower recovery speed for a little time.'

Her eyes roamed over Jonny. Really his similarity to Drewie was surprising – same size, same cute little nose and determined chin. She realised Sylvie had asked her a question, and turned back to her.

'I'm sorry, what was that?'

Sylvie took her hand, met her eyes. 'I asked the name of your brother.'

Juliet breathed in and out before managing to say the precious name.

'Drewie,' she whispered. Then again, louder, 'Drewie. His proper name was Andrew, but we all called him Drewie.'

Her voice broke a little, but she went on. 'He was the same size as Jonny when we lost him.'

Sylvie squeezed her hand. 'Was he a runner, too?' she asked gently.

Juliet thought and smiled. Maybe the first time she had thought of Drewie with a smile for many years.

'No, he was a builder. And a destroyer, it must be said. He would construct castles and towers of earth, twigs and stones, then wreck them all – that part seemed to be as much fun as building them.'

She let her mind wander down some old and fusty corridors of memories, at the end of which she could see her younger self and her brother playing in a garden in the sunshine – laughing at each other. She basked in it for a while, before coming back to the present.

Sylvie was smiling at her, waiting for her to come back from her memories. Juliet felt her hand in hers. Sylvie understood this thing in Juliet, this unmanageable loss, because she had lost her baby, she thought. Her baby. Because surely Sylvie was a fistula patient, with her lost baby and the aroma of ammonia all around her. And if she did have a fistula, if she belonged to this group of patients, would she figure out her own course over the next six weeks? Would she let Juliet help her? She let all these unspoken thoughts travel through their clasped hands. She didn't want to broach the subject yet.

'By the way, Sylvie, you have very good English,' she said instead.

'Oh, yes, I learned it in the hotel.' Sylvie smiled shyly.

'Ah, the hotel – that was quite a good job then?'

'It was, yes. But then, well, then I got sick.'

There was a pause. Juliet bit her tongue to stop herself from rushing Sylvie – she needed to make her conclusions herself, however impatient Juliet was for her to realise she needed surgery. And hopefully could have it, depending on how bad things were – would it be a fistula needing Dr Val, or could Juliet repair it? She would need to examine her to know the answer, and Sylvie would need to want that.

Sylvie was thinking hard. She was looking at the girls on the ward, Ruthie and the others. She was looking at Genet. She knew her story – over thirty years alone, a lifetime. She knew perfectly well that they all had had the same problem as her, had suffered the same disaster, loss and curse.

But they had taken a step towards normal life again, had tried to break out of the prison. Would she, also? What if it were impossible? What if she had to face that? No, she couldn't do that. Then again, didn't she already face that every single day, drag her smelly, sore self through each long day, one after the other?

'I'm afraid,' she whispered, finally. 'Edmond told me about the camp before. Free treatment, he said, although I couldn't believe that was true. But . . . but I'm so afraid. What if it isn't successful? What if I am like this forever? I can't face that. I can't know there is no chance left.'

Juliet looked into her big shiny eyes, seeing the tears pooling.

'I didn't think of it like that.' She pondered for a minute, and then continued, 'For a good reason – it's not a one chance only thing. Sometimes it does take more than one operation to be cured, but that's not a reason to reject it. You wouldn't be losing your hope by trying it.'

They were silent for some minutes, still holding hands. Juliet felt very connected to this lovely girl. As though she recognised something there – a resilience forcing oneself onwards, the effort of keeping oneself intact when some of your points of reference have disappeared – your body, your family. The beloved landmarks which give you your place in time and space, your co-ordinates. They had both had to find new ways of understanding their place in the world, and of accepting it.

'What about the girls around the ward?' she said. 'Have you talked to them?'

Sylvie nodded, tears falling silently.

Juliet went on, gentle but insistent. 'They are up and walking and hoping. Hoping their operation was successful. What else can we do, Sylvie? Hope and try our best.'

They sat quietly for some time, watching the other girls, watching Jonny. After a while, she turned to Sylvie.

'If I come back later, maybe you could let me examine you? Then I should know what we can do to get you right again.'

She squeezed Sylvie's hand and was hugely relieved to receive a squeeze back.

Juliet spent the rest of the afternoon doing battle in the minors' theatre, suturing lacerations, setting fractures, cleaning wounds, draining infections. Finally, the stream of walking, or rather hobbling, wounded dried up, and she returned to the ward, wondering about the gales of laughter she could hear coming from it.

She found all the fistula patients seated on the floor around Jan, who had his back to her. She leaned against the doorway to watch and listen. Manjit, who was a phenomenal actress and clown, despite her slight deficiencies as a midwife, was beside him translating and acting out his sage medical advice. Since this advice was all about if and when to return to 'intimate relations' after surgery and what to do if they got pregnant, she was having a ball, reaching well into pantomime dame territory.

The girls were howling with laughter at her, and Jan was pretending to catch her being rude and to disapprove. There was a serious purpose to their joking around – the girls needed to hear that they could have a baby someday, but that they must come for help in plenty of time. They should have a caesarean section next time, otherwise they risked another fistula and losing another baby.

Juliet was very pleased to spy Sylvie at the back of the group, sitting near the lovely Ruthie, on whom Juliet had operated on the first day of the camp. She could see that Sylvie was sitting on a piece of plastic, a little apart from the others, but the two girls' heads were close to each other, and they looked comfortable together. That was a big thing in itself – Juliet knew just how isolated Sylvie must have been since her injury, and how much she must need a friend.

After a moment, she must have felt Juliet's gaze on her. She looked up and caught her eye. Juliet raised an eyebrow, and Sylvie inclined her head slightly. It was enough of a yes. Juliet smiled and blinked at her, then headed off to hammock quietly all by herself and think. There was so much to think about from the last few days and nearly all good for once – a sunnier reordering of her mind, with room for Drewie again. And for Sylvie, and of course, the explosion of Jan . . . Joy was bubbling back up.

Juliet was tying her trainers as Jan came in from the hospital, eyes brightening as he spotted her.

'Stardust! Oh.' His voice fell. 'Are you going for a run?'

'Yes – my brain is scrambled today. I need to run. Stuff to process. I was hoping it might happen all on its own while I jog up that hill again. You coming?'

'Oh, I suppose so, yes. I had thought we might exercise in a different way, you know?' He leered at her suggestively.

'Wait a minute, are you sleeping with me as part of your keep-fit routine?' He could surely sense the danger in this question.

'Not sure *sleeping* works too well in terms of fitness and tone – got to think of these things at your age, you know.' He grabbed at make-believe love handles around his hips, started laughing at the fury on her face.

'Maybe this is a good time for me to run?' he said, legging it out of the house.

Juliet followed, muttering, 'Cheeky bastard, I'll make you pay for that,' as she ran after him.

She caught up with him finally at the top of the hill. He had obviously giggled to himself the whole way up, and delightedly pulled her into his arms.

'Am I in trouble?' he asked, gleefully.

'You know you are. Punishment will be forthcoming,' she replied, her eyes belying the apparent crossness of her voice.

'I don't know why you're upset. Your body's fine, you know: all the right bits in more or less the right places . . . '

'MORE OR LESS?'

'Yes! And you have the other stuff too – your big smile and just now your big frown, and your scary eyes and your weirdo warped surgeon brain . . . you are perfect, Stardust!'

He chortled then kissed her to emphasise the point. 'Do I still get punished?'

'Definitely deserve to be . . . have you seen the *Lysistrata*?'

'Is it a type of rash?'

'Not quite – it's an ancient Greek play about women keeping their men in line using a sex strike—'

'Good God, no wonder that civilisation failed.'

'It's hardly a failure to invent democracy, medicine, philosophy and all the rest of it, is it?'

'Sure – they were doing pretty well – until the sex strike! That was probably what did it for them. Best not to take the risk, Stardust. Let's run back while puzzling over the mysteries of the ancient universe.'

Email to Caitlin
Hey you. Hope you are well and honing up your BFF listening

skills — will need to have a good long talk going up some hill by Inverness when I get back . . . it's been a busy few days here physically and psychologically. This Juliet has been turned inside out, forcing some spring-cleaning and a new direction. Will be with you soon in your new kingdom and tell you all about it . . . well, not all, will spare you the X-rated bits! We'll find out if I am there to stay after my interview on Wednesday.

LFE

Chapter 30

Sylvie

Operation

THEY HAD WAITED A few days to let everyone settle. Today was the day for it though. Sylvie watched the light coming into the ward as the night faded. Jonny was fast asleep, she beside him on the floor. She signed to the nurse that she was out to wash and get herself ready, and tiptoed out of the ward. The sky was orangey pink and welcoming. The air was still, no breeze but no heat yet. Few people were up and about, only the odd nurse crossing from ward to ward and one other patient, an old man, shuffling past her to the toilets as she emerged from them.

Before going back to the ward, she sat on the step to watch the sun come up. What would today hold for her? Would it be a good day, a turning point in her life? Would anything go wrong? She opened her mind, let the worries fly free, hoping they might fly off. Too late to back down now. She would trust fate and Juliet, and hope to God it worked.

She could not let herself think what might happen if it

worked. Or if it didn't. She would just take one step at a time, assimilate it one bit at a time. It was enough today to deal with the small steps she had to take.

Not all that small, she thought with some trepidation, listing them in her head. To go into the theatre, only wearing the little gown thing they had given her. To have injections, not something she had really had before. And to lie still while they worked on her. Would it hurt? They had said it would not. She would need to believe that. And what would she think of while it was going on? A story, yes, that's what she needed. A story for Jonny tonight, inventing where she had been this morning. Abducted by an eagle, taken to meet his friend with a broken wing, help to set it? Maybe – she would work on that idea anyway.

She looked up to see Edmond coming towards her. He gave her his slow smile and gestured to ask if he could sit with her. He must have come in early to see her. His shift didn't start for another hour at least. He sat and she smiled, enjoying the reassurance of his presence beside her.

He waited a few minutes before speaking.

'Sylvie, how are you? Today, huh?'

'Yes, today. Quite a thought. I'm okay, I think,' she replied quietly. 'How are you, Edmond?'

'I'm happy for you actually. I'd hoped so much that this was possible.' He paused. 'And I have something for you.' He delved into his pocket, brought out a small wooden string of beads.

'My grandmother was Catholic, these were hers. They are

a prayer to Mary, mother of Jesus. Anyway, it helps to roll them in your fingers when you are worried about something, you know.'

He looked somewhat anxious as he offered them, but soon relaxed into a smile when her pleasure in his gift became apparent. The light of her lovely eyes bathed him in warmth making him sigh inwardly with joy at her.

She was busily thanking him now, while winding the beads round her little wrist.

'You're so kind, thank you Edmond. Can I hold them during it, do you think? It will help, I know.'

He smiled into the rising sun, sitting comfortably alongside her, waiting.

Juliet was also watching the day begin. On her usual step, looking towards the hospital, quietly drinking her tea. Such a big day for Sylvie. So many of her normal workdays were such big days for her patients. She was always aware of it, but made sure to keep herself a little separate from their emotional journeys. She had to stay calm and focussed, make all the right surgical decisions.

She could feel her fingers tingling, the joyful anticipation of operating. Supple fingers and a clear mind – she had all she needed. She let herself imagine the operation, made a sure plan to follow. It would soon be time.

A short hour later, they were all set. Sebastian was at the top end, calm and knowing as ever. Sylvie was numbed from waist down after a spinal injection, a little sweaty with nerves, keeping her eyes on Sebastian, since she could not see the others – she was unable to see anything below her waist for the sheet barrier they had erected there. She held Edmond's beads in her hand, slowly turning them around.

Juliet and Jan were scrubbed and gowned, Juliet in the hot seat and Jan assisting. He peered over the sheet and winked at her before disappearing again.

Methodically, carefully, Juliet again went through all the steps she had been taught. She felt her spirit settle as she studied the fistula, imagined how it could be repaired. It was quite big but looked as though it would be fixable. She had done worse ones with Dr Val, knew what that redoubtable lady would say if she was peering over Juliet's shoulder.

Go on then, she instructed herself in her head. Go into operating mode, ignore everything else, all the distractions and worries and potential outcomes. Focus on this fistula, do unto it what you know Dr Val would do. Okay. So, first let's expose it better, cut around to free up the scars . . .

Her hands were steady, teasing and cajoling the tissues till they were soft, mobile and would come together again. She let herself be patient, not rush, cut it free without damaging anything: control the bleeding. Finally, she was ready to sew it up. Good strong stitches to mend the hole, each one confident, accurate. Every one needed to be a winner.

At last, it was complete. She left a catheter in the bladder and a dressing on the outside. She pushed her stool back, giving a fingers crossed sign then a thumbs up to Jan, and trotted round to the head end to speak to Sylvie, keen to give some encouragement.

'Looks good, Sylvie, all done. We will watch you carefully, and it should heal.'

Please God that it does, thought Juliet, fixing the view of the repaired fistula in her mind and allowing herself to acknowledge that it was well repaired, that she had given Sylvie every chance. No guarantees, but a good chance.

Sylvie nodded with a tentative smile, whispered a thank you – her heart too full of hope for her to be able to say more.

She slept much of the remaining day, tucked into the bed next to Jonny's. Her catheter drained her urine and her bed was dry – probably, therefore, the deepest sleep she had had for years.

Jeff was the hero of the hour, entertaining Jonny with drawings and a Rubik's cube, which fairly blew his mind. He loved it instantly, spent hours turning and twirling it, making random and very pleasing patterns.

Chapter 31

Sylvie and Juliet

THE NEXT DAY, SYLVIE was up and about by the time Juliet came for a ward round, her catheter draining the urine into a small bucket which she carried around with her. Her clothes were dry.

'Why have you got a bucket, Sylvie?' asked Jonny, raising himself up on his elbows to peer over his traction at her.

'This isn't a real bucket, Jonny,' she replied solemnly, leaning in to whisper loudly to him. 'This is a type of magic dog. A special magic dog, disguised as a bucket, to go everywhere with me, guard me and report back to the magic master.'

'Who is the magic master?' Jonny's eyes were wide with excitement. Sylvie pointed to Juliet, just entering the ward.

'Don't say anything though – she is in disguise. Magic people usually have to hide their magic, you know.' She put her fingers against her lips and Jonny copied her with a bright smile.

Juliet came over. 'How is my favourite patient?' she asked Jonny.

'Can I have a magic bucket too?' he burst out. 'Please?'

Sylvie rolled her eyes. 'My fault, sorry.'

'Well as it happens, yes you can,' said Juliet. 'What do you know about magic buckets, Jonny?'

'They guard me and tell the master!'

'Absolutely right, well done. I'll just go to the special place and conjure one up for you, wait there—'

She disappeared into the storeroom and returned triumphant with a new blue bucket.

'There you are. You can put whatever you like in it, and it will be guarded too, okay? Sylvie, how are you?'

Sylvie was enjoying watching Jonny putting his treasures, number one being the Rubik's cube, into the bucket. She turned back to Juliet slightly anxiously.

'I think I'm all right – am I?'

Juliet smiled reassuringly. 'You look great! And your bed is dry and your clothes, and your catheter is dripping away, draining well. So all good; good, so far, Sylvie. Take it easy today, okay?'

Juliet had her reassured-for-today-but-still-worried look about her. It was about to get a bit stressy in the ward: most of the other fistula patients were due to have their catheters removed today. This was the main test of success of the operation – would they stay dry without the catheters doing the draining? One, Miriam, was already a little leaky, and Juliet went to talk to her now with Irene translating and comforting.

'Irene, can you tell her we should keep trying with the

catheter for another week. If she is still wet, she may need another operation. Some people do, that's just the way it is. We will help her to come back for that in six months.'

Irene was a mother of eight and a grandmother of more, and it showed in these situations. She was firm, true, and reassuring. Miriam hung on her every word, nodding but crying too. It was impossible not to be upset for her.

Juliet felt the pain of her disappointed hopes. This was the worst part of these camps – always there would be a couple of patients who didn't have the happy ending this time, and they could really break your heart. No showing that though – it was up to her and Irene to give Miriam hope, to help her keep going, keep hoping.

'Sorry, sweetheart, sorry if it needs more work, but that does happen quite a lot. It doesn't mean we can't get you dry eventually – just not in one go. Let's try leaving the catheter in for another week, anyway, and I promise we will try again if it doesn't work. We can't do it for six months though, until your body is fully recovered from this operation.'

Miriam nodded. Irene squeezed her hand.

'We will talk more later,' she said.

They moved slowly round the ward, talking to everyone.

'Okay, good luck with the catheters, Irene.' Juliet gave her a worried look and Irene patted her arm.

'God willing, it will be all right. And if not, I think you have made a promise to come back?'

Juliet surveyed her ward, the chaos of the tractions, the dressings and the girls with buckets roaming around. The precious girls, beginning to blossom now like glorious orchids, the beauty of it filling her heart.

'Yes, I did, didn't I? I can't imagine leaving. I do have to go home sometime, though. But really, I also have to come back! I'll speak again to the MSF boss about a follow-up camp.'

Irene laughed. 'Yes, a follow-up, then another one to follow that one up, then another—'

Juliet grinned. 'I think I'm properly caught now, isn't that right? Hooked like a fish!'

Irene loved that, went off repeating it and chuckling to herself.

'There are no better witnesses than your eyes.'

Sylvie had been watching the tiny frown on Juliet's forehead deepen as she surreptitiously eyed Jan through the maternity ward window. 'My grandmother used to say that to me all the time – it's an old Ethiopian proverb.'

Juliet turned back to Sylvie with a slightly guilty look. 'Oh, yes? Why did she say it to you?'

'Well, I suppose. I had a bit of a difficult time when I had to leave school to go to work. I accepted that it had to be, but I worried that I was losing my friends.'

'Did you not see them anymore?'

'I still saw them sometimes – it was more that I thought maybe they weren't interested in me anymore, or worse, that they were talking about me when I wasn't there. I think my grandmother wanted me to trust my feelings when I was with them, not worry and maybe spoil things.'

'Wise woman, your grandmother.'

'Yes, I'm very like her!' Sylvie grinned and Juliet broke into a chuckle.

The girls wandered off around the hospital grounds, enjoying their daily break together while, at eleven o'clock, Jeff ran the Jonny's-Bed Grand Prix – a new and very popular event for all the kids on the ward.

'So, who won?' Sylvie laughed at Jonny as they came back into the ward. He was so eager to tell her, he was almost moving his bed towards the door to anticipate her. His eyes were sparkling, his smile huge.

'Me, me, Sylvie! And I did a big skid, and I'm the winner!'

'You're my winner, every day, lovely boy.' She stroked his forehead. 'Let's do something quieter for a little while, huh?'

'See you later, guys,' Juliet said as she went off to check what was happening in Minors.

She chewed her lip a little as she thought about her chat with Sylvie. They had mostly been talking about Drewie and Jonny. Juliet had been finding more and more memories crowding her mind, which entertained Sylvie. It seemed, though, that she could still see past the funny stories to some unspoken worries Juliet was carrying about Jan. She hadn't actually voiced them to Sylvie, but it was true that she had a niggling dread that this was just another holiday-type romance for him, that he wasn't troubled by all the revelations of her years-long inner turmoil because it just didn't really matter, none of it did.

When she was with him, her worries evaporated; everything seemed completely natural and easy. But could it really be so straightforward? Maybe it seemed easy just because they were in the bubble of MSF and Ethiopia, and when they got back to normal it would disintegrate. But then again, what was normal anyway and why would it spoil this? She was going round in stupid circles.

'Trust your eyes,' Sylvie had said to her, pointedly. Well, she could try.

Relax, trust, enjoy. Maybe even stop worrying. She smiled to herself at the thought of it, her smile broadening as she spotted Jan walking out of maternity now.

She took a minute to study him unseen: was he any different? Was he happy? He was usually pretty cheerful, but he did seem *more* happy, she thought.

As for Juliet, she felt a warm joy diffusing all through her whenever Jan was near. It was difficult covering it up – for once she didn't want to. She had spent so long hiding herself – hiding the depressing shameful secret at the heart of her, not allowing anyone to see her vulnerable core, because they would see that. See the rotten bit and reject her then, of course. She had tried to hide herself from him, too.

And now all was exposed in the glaring light of day, with no possibility of her readopting any kind of cool detached persona . . . but instead of this making her curl up with mortification, she felt weirdly relaxed. He had not rejected her, so far anyway. Really, he did not seem to be about to do that. She felt that she could let him see these wounds as they began to heal. It was all so surprising, really.

And as for the nights, oh, my lord – how could he be so tender and yet so relentlessly demanding – taking everything she had. Giving everything, too . . . she felt as if they were truly making love.

She made a wry smile – God, she had gone all corny. Love, eh? Well maybe they could 'make it'. Somehow the possibility seemed to be there in her now, as if opening up that dark chamber of despair at Drewie's death had unbarred the way.

Relax, trust, enjoy.

Ten days later, Juliet was doing her rounds, checking Jonny's leg. She was weighing up whether there had been enough time in traction so that she could release him, or whether that release would allow him to go a bit crazy, maybe set the healing back . . . Hmm. Not yet, she thought. Perhaps she could put him in a cast to slow him down a bit? So long as it didn't affect the strengthening of his muscles and ligaments . . . She would consult the book, see if there was a chapter on overly-adventurous four-year-old boys. Probably there was.

'Not long now, Jonny my boy.'

She gently replaced his leg on the bed, pausing in mid-air for a second as Jan came into her field of vision, heading for the labour ward. She caught Sylvie smiling sideways at her, reading her again. They had spent some time with each other over the past couple of weeks, escaping for slow walks around the grounds and shady rests under the trees, sometimes sharing stories of their families, but mostly just being in the same space, content.

Sylvie occasionally mentioned her baby, stroking her tummy absentmindedly when she did, as if conjuring up the physical memory of her. It seemed to soothe her, Juliet thought. Juliet felt soothed in Sylvie's presence somehow, too, felt the discordant waves in her brain coming together to flow in synchrony under Sylvie's understanding gaze.

Sylvie slowly let her eyes roll to Jan and back, then gave a conspiratorial wink, teasing Juliet.

'Oh, is that Jan? I hadn't noticed – I was just looking to see if the car was back yet.' She grinned at Sylvie, knowing she wasn't fooled. 'Anyway, let's talk about you. Just a few more days I think.'

They both gave a little shiver of nervy anticipation. Very soon they would know if Sylvie's operation had worked, and as the time drew closer, they grew a little quieter, shoring their strength up against possible bad news.

Email to Cait
Well, my love, it looks like I will be joining you in Inverness in an official capacity! Had a very different interview from the London one. They actually seemed to be interested in what I was doing here, rather than embarrassed by my deviation from the straight and narrow path . . . I think I might even like them! So, do you think there might be a little corner for me in your

beachfront mansion, just until I can dig my own grass-roofed eco-burrow to fit in with the other rural hippies up there? Hope so, will be coming back very soon now . . .
Still sending L from E

Chapter 32

Sylvie

Crunch time

IT WAS SYLVIE'S DAY to get the catheter out. Juliet's heart was in her mouth. Both she and Sylvie gave each other their 'brave' smiles. Irene stood beside them, waiting to do it, gloves on.

'Right, you should go to pass urine every couple of hours, okay? Don't over stress your bladder yet – build it up gradually.' Juliet covered her nerves with instructions.

Sylvie smiled at her, only a little fear in her eyes. 'Okay so far. Can I go for a little walk with Jonny?'

Jonny was whizzing round the ward with his crutches, Chaplin-esque carnage following him, with toppling buckets and belongings only just saved by their owners or passing nurses. Irene caught Juliet's eyes, signalling clearly that she was about to police this. Juliet blinked reassuringly at her and turned back to Sylvie.

'Definitely you can, excellent idea in fact. Jonny, can you go and find the best place on the veranda for your sister to rest

after your walk? I'll look for you in an hour or so out there.'
They parted at the ward door, Juliet heading for the labour
room in search of Jan.

He was writing at the desk, long limbs all bent uncomfortably
around it like a daddy-long-legs. He was really not suited to
office work, she thought. Or anything very conventional.
Which did not diminish his irresistibility one jot. She leaned
her forehead against his shoulder.

'God, I can't bear to watch and wait and worry. Shall I go
for a run?'

He ruffled her hair. 'Could do. It is forty degrees in the
shade, but you like a bit of heat, don't you? Turns out you're
not such an ice queen after all—'

'Stop that, and get your hand out of my scrubs! What a
reprobate!'

'Whatever that is. Alternatively, you could help me with a
section?'

'Oh, yes, perfect, take my mind off Sylvie, ideal. Come on
then!'

Sylvie was also finding the waiting almost impossible. She
was see-sawing between dread and horror that she might still
be wet, and overwhelming happiness that this awful chapter
of her life might be about to close. Which was it? And if it
really was ok, if she had finally stopped leaking, would it last?

Jonny had quickly burned himself out and they found a
shady spot to rest on the ward veranda.

He dozed against her, clutching his bucket all the while. The sun was hot but there was a slight breeze coming from the east. Sylvie leaned back against the wall of the hospital, shut her eyes and tried to let her emotions settle. She gave a little wiggle, checking all still felt dry. The sores on her thighs had started to heal now, but she was sure there would still be telltale pain there if the urine began to leak again. She waited. No pain. She would count to . . . what? A hundred? Not enough, no – five hundred would be better. Then wake Jonny and go to the toilets, see if her bladder had filled up a bit.

It was pretty weird going for a pee again. But there it was, a little stream of urine coming from her own bladder. She stared at it. It was definitely real, proper pee in the right place. And no leaking, nothing to make her wet and smelly and sore.

She felt her self-control slide a bit as the hope threatened to engulf her. Wait! her careful brain cried. Give it a few days before you start to think about the changes you may have in your life now. A few days, and do what Juliet said – don't stress yourself or your bladder. Must get up once in the night to empty.

She tried to be calm and sensible and not get over-excited, but she could not help laughing when Juliet came tearing out of theatre an hour later to find her dry, and whooped and jigged with delight.

Edmond was just behind her. He beamed at Juliet and gave Sylvie's hand a squeeze but then rather quickly disappeared back into the hospital, as though he were busy.

Sylvie felt a little disquiet – was something the matter? She put it to one side to listen to Juliet chattering on about her staying around for a few more days, being careful with her wounds and her bladder. Sylvie did feel as though someone was switching the lights on again slowly, that parts of her which had been shut down were stirring – cranking up and clunking back into use.

After four days, Sylvie allowed herself to believe that she was now dry, clean, fixed. Normal. Alive again to all the possibilities of life. She couldn't believe it, waking in the morning with a dry bed, and none of the old sharp burning pain as the urine raked over her sores. All gone, all healed. She wallowed in the luxurious pleasure of feeling comfortable and normal again.

What now? She let her thoughts drift, let her mind find the path. Life was about to change again, this time for the better. What did she want to do? She knew immediately. The main thing was to sort out her family. Start work again, get them all back into high school. Oh, the joy of that thought, knowing what it would mean, to Gregory in particular, but also the girls. She let the happiness of it spread through her, and let herself feel her body again, welcoming life with it rather than battling it.

So back to the hotel again? Why not – if they would have her. If not, perhaps her old boss, Kaleb, would help her find somewhere else. A hotel or a shop would be best for her with her bookkeeping experience.

And hair! She could regrow her hair, feel the joyous weight of it once again. Maybe even braids again, shorter now that she was older. She broke into a spontaneous smile as she stretched her neck, imagining it.

As for the rest of it all, she needed not to stress about every other aspect of life or try to plan everything. For sure though, Ivan was gone and over. She was moving forward, not going back, and he belonged a long way back. Her friends? Well, maybe she would pick up again with Rita or Justine, but their life experiences had been so different, she didn't know if they could find common ground again. Whereas she was sure she would be seeing a fair bit of her new friend Ruthie from the camp. It turned out that they lived in the neighbouring villages.

She was letting her thoughts ramble on, but she brought herself back. She knew she had to think about Edmond, concentrate for a minute in the midst of the dancing joy in her head. Edmond, Edmond.

What was that all about? Friendship, yes. More? She thought he would like more. Not yet, her inner sensible voice screamed. But never again? That was a big thing to say. Maybe no need to think about joining the nuns yet, maybe there would be a time for her to love again in the future. The voice of reason was still there: for now, just get yourself right first, one thing at a time. Family first, find work and let them be confident you are there for them.

And Edmond will wait, her other inner, not-always-so-sensible voice now said. Surely, he will wait.

But there was a problem there, and one she had to address. Edmond had been avoiding her this week. He would come to say hello, but have to rush off somewhere immediately, have something urgent to get to. What was going on with him? She was going to track him down – she needed to ask him if he would accompany Jonny and herself back home anyway, but she also needed to understand what was wrong and put it right.

She called Jonny and explained they were on the lookout for Edmond.

'Hide and seek?' asked Jonny, excitedly.

'Kind of, but go quietly, because we're not really allowed rowdy games in the hospital, are we, and actually Edmond doesn't know we're playing with him – it's a surprise!'

Within a few minutes Jonny had cornered Edmond in the medical ward office and was tucking into a biscuit as a prize for excellent seeking. Sylvie slipped into the office and stood against the door. No escape. Edmond looked a little anxious and withdrawn but managed a proper smile nonetheless. Something was not right, though. She studied him carefully.

'What can I do for you, Sylvie?' he asked, too polite.

'Oh, Edmond, do you think you could come home with Jonny and me tomorrow? I'm a bit nervous about managing him as well as myself.'

'Sure, yes, no problem. Shall we take the bus in the afternoon?' He started shuffling papers on the desk.

'Thank you, that would be great. Jonny, can you take this note to Sister Irene please, then come straight back here?'

She watched him hurtle off happily. He seemed to have put his accident completely behind him, and turned his attention to thoroughly enjoying everything the hospital had to offer for entertainment. Such capacity for joy, she thought as she shut the door and turned to Edmond. To be encouraged, always.

'Edmond. Please can I ask you something else?'

'Of course.' He smiled a little blandly.

She plunged on, despite the lack of encouragement. 'It's just that, well, I think life is about to change again, in a good way. A very good way! I will need to look for a job.' She paused.

'Yes?' Edmond was watching very attentively.

'So I will probably not be going to the water pump every day at four in the morning.'

'No.' He waited. He could hardly bear the thought, but maybe she was trying to say goodbye? He had been dreading this conversation, expecting to be excluded from her new life, now that she was back to the beautiful unattainable girl he used to admire from afar.

'So what I want to ask you is, when are we going to see each other? Can you find time for me, Edmond?'

She smiled at him. Sunshine. Bells were going off in his head. She was not walking out of his life. He was to go with her into this new phase. He let his eyes meet hers, rich caramel, full of happiness.

'Always, Sylvie. I will always want time with you.'

She fairly beamed now, gave a little happy laugh. 'Good!' She hesitated, then added, 'I have a long way to go to get properly back, you know.'

He shook his head, still smiling. 'Only the external things,

Sylvie. You have done the difficult part in your soul and with your body. The rest will come.'

She nodded, holding his eyes. 'Thank you, Edmond. You were there with me. It means a lot.'

'It meant a lot to me,' he replied, gently taking her hand, letting their fingers slowly entwine.

Just then Jonny banged through the door, his pretend errand complete. Edmond and Sylvie sprang apart. Full of emotion and nowhere to put it, she gathered her little brother up into a big hug, much to his surprise. He hugged her back though, then demanded she accompany him on a dinosaur hunt.

'I know there's one – Doc Jule told me she saw a tail. It must be a din'saur! Come, Sylvie!' He grabbed her hand and fairly dragged her out of the office. She looked back over her shoulder at Edmond and winked.

Chapter 33

Juliet and Jan

JULIET FELL BACK AGAINST the pillow, panting slightly, her face shining with sweat. Jan leaned over her to brush the damp hair off her brow and let a kiss follow his fingers. He was grinning widely.

'Well, I think we finally found your wildness! All okay there, Stardust?'

'Yes, oh, yes . . . that was . . . that was thorough,' pronounced Juliet definitively.

He chuckled. 'Such a romantic, aren't you?'

'Certainly, I am!' she protested.

'And I don't agree with your assessment anyway. There's more, you know . . . more and more.'

She opened her mouth to object further, but he interrupted her with an intense kiss, rolling onto her as she tangled her fingers in his unruly hair.

Two hours and one cold bucket wash later, Juliet was feeling fine, just fine.

There was no room for dinner. The one table was covered

with eviscerated radios, dials and screws and oily bits scattered in no semblance of order. Jeff was presiding over it all, happy as a pig in muck, fiddling about with various metal rods.

Jan tutted at him, and sat on the step of the veranda to eat. Juliet however unceremoniously dumped a handful of metallic detritus on the floor to make room for her plate and sat at the table. She fixed her eye on Jeff, with a pitying look and a melancholic sigh.

'Every night picking on some poor machine, Jeff. Can't be good for them or you. Maybe you should read a book, give them all a rest?'

'Ah well, dyslexic, y'know,' he muttered, concentrating on threading a wire into a coil. 'Just like Einstein.'

'Oh, yeah, just like him,' said Jan, copying Juliet's disregard for the parts and joining them at the table.

'Wait a minute – is that true? Einstein was dyslexic?' Juliet asked sharply.

'Oh, yes, well known.'

'So is $E = mc^2$ a mistake then? Was he trying to write something completely different?' She started to giggle.

Jan burst out laughing. 'Hilarious. He was maybe writing his shopping list, and suddenly Bam! Mysteries of the universe explained! Ha, ha!'

Jeff looked down his nose at the two of them laughing, and did not rise to the bait.

After dinner, they made themselves comfortable in the hammocks on the veranda. There was a brief interlude of after-dinner quiet, then Jeff seemed to get a second wind.

'Have you two remembered the boss is coming for a visit next week?' Jeff still managed to sound bored as he dropped that little bomb.

Jan stopped gazing covertly at Juliet while pretending to read, and looked up. 'The Boss? Brucie baby? Tell me now, baby, is he good to you, does he do to you the things that I do—'

'Not that boss, no, and not the mafia one either,' responded Jeff, still in his monotone.

'Well then, why are we worrying?' Jan stretched into the hammock a little, letting his fingers play softly with Juliet's ankle.

'We're not and it's the MSF Africa boss. We're just telling you so that you maybe avoid overly demonstrative sharing when she comes.'

Juliet stared at him, batting Jan's hand away. 'Whatever do you mean? Explain!'

'You know – sharing: hammocks, beds, bodily fluids—'

'Steady, steady – and how could you possibly think that? We're so discreet!' Juliet claimed defensively, a telltale dimple deepening in her slightly rosy cheek.

'It's your fault! You're so noisy! All those howls of pleasu—' Jan's words were cut off by the cushion accurately flung at his head.

'Naughty man! Jeff, I must apologise for the assault on your senses,' began Juliet, laughing but blushing a little more.

'I for one am amazed that the sound carries across the road and round the corner,' interrupted Jan, blushing not at all.

'What? What are you talking about?' asked Juliet.

'Young Jeff here has been most kind in offering assistance to Serena the foxy French radio operative over at the Red Cross HQ . . . helping her all night long sometimes, I think!'

Juliet looked at Jan, eyes laughing but mouth severe, as she remonstrated, 'Now, you know, Jeff here is an expert twiddler of knobs and flicker of switches. I think it's marvellous that he's willing to share his knob-twiddling skills with a volunteer from another NGO, foxy or not.'

'Ha! Yes. Extremely generous. Heartwarming.'

'My contract definitely states that I'm not to be mocked by filthy minded medics. I shall have to write a stern letter to management,' threatened Jeff, grinning happily.

'Will that be a French letter, Jeff? Who could help with that, I wonder?' mused Juliet, with an exaggerated tilt of her head.

'Right, I have very important work to do in my office. I can't lounge about any more with you work-shy docs any more . . .'

Jeff winked over at them, making no attempt to move from his extremely relaxed position in the hammock, arms behind his head, a beatific smile on his face.

'Aw don't leave, Jeff – let's have a beer and drink to celibacy, may God save it for someone else.' Jan crossed himself as he clambered out of the hammock he was sharing with Juliet and headed for the fridge.

'Is the boss coming to decide about the changes to the mission, Jeff?' asked Juliet while they waited for beer.

'Guess so, although I think a lot of decisions have been taken. The number of landmine and UXO incidents is now low enough that this hospital can stop being a surgical outpost. Edmond and Chinua will stay to run a minor injuries unit, and we will get a second ambulance and driver to assist with transfers to Adigrat. Maternity will stay, run by an Ethiopian and a Cuban: government docs, not MSF. Very junior, but we're lucky to get anyone, they're so short up here.'

'Oh, wow. So there are to be two new VOGs but no new surgeon? I suppose there are hardly any surgeons in the country, presumably none to spare for the refugees away up here.'

'What do you mean *two* VOGs?' Jan sounded shocked as he handed out the beers. 'Impossible! There can be only one. Or at least only one that you would want – a fine manly Viking one—'

'Hmm – can I remind you people that we are supposed to be politically correct, humanitarian, neutral, non-sexist.' Jeff made the sign of the cross, his voice: full-on sanctimonious monk.

Jan was far from sanctimony. 'Is that gender-neutral? No problem for me, we eastern Europeans are well ahead on these awake things.'

'Woke, not awake. Oh, no, does that mean they're going to change the colour of the scrubs?' Juliet joined in.

'Goddamn it! I look good in green!' said Jan in mock fury.

'You do, it beautifully brings out that kind of jaundiced

look you get after a night of it on labour ward.' Juliet wrinkled her nose up.

'Hey, if we're both gender-neutral, is it more okay for us to, y'know, do dah, etc.?'

'Not for the Dutch boss, not here. You can do whatever you like in Holland I think, very liberal, but not here.' Jeff was beginning to sound like a nursery teacher running out of patience. 'I think we need to invite the other NGOs over – your conversation is making my brain hurt.'

'It's probably shrinking. You should do maths and eat fish – I think that protects the brain.' Jan nodded wisely.

'Continuous bullshit, that's what's doing it.'

'Fish? Now that's something I miss.' Juliet was a sentence behind, and off on a ramble. 'Not much good fish here, is there? Lovely big sea bass with langoustines, that's what I'm going to order – first restaurant I go to at home. Or maybe monkfish. Even trout would do, although they're best caught in the rain and fried by the lochside, eaten when you are starving after hours of waiting for a bite.'

'Fish? Pah! Not for me. My brain will have to just manage – what I'm going for is a big burger. Home-made, from a cow that had actual grass to eat, fat chips, ketchup, a few Buds—'

'That's what you yanks have for all three meals, isn't that right – breakfast too?'

'Damn right, that's the secret of our country's success.' Jeff shrugged, somewhat smug.

'Ah, explains a lot. Scotland is always going to struggle to compete with haggis versus burgers.'

'What on earth is haggis?' interposed Jan.

'I think it's all the stuff you get from animals that no one wants to eat, maybe with some of the stuff that's dropped on the floor, then you squish it up into a ball with some oatmeal and spice, and boil it in the stomach lining of a sheep—'

'No! Revolting! Surely illegal?' He looked aghast.

'Nope, quite tasty actually. You eat it on the twenty-fifth of January after saying a long poem to it in the Scots language, then stab it with a big knife.'

'God, you people are weird.' Jeff sounded genuine for once. 'How did television and penicillin and all that other stuff come from you? Penicillin maybe not so surprising, with those eating habits. Anyway, are you looking forward to going home to talk to horrible food?'

'Well, kind of, I guess,' Juliet replied haltingly. 'I mean, it's not in my top ten things that I miss.'

'Which are?' Jan was looking carefully at her, maybe wondering what competition he had for her. She raised her eyebrows a little and smiled at him.

'Oh, the usual, you know: friends, family, plumbing—'

'Plumbing?' interrupted Jan. 'And here I thought you enjoyed the bucket system.' He glinted wickedly at her.

She shot him a look. 'Sometimes I do.'

She wiggled a little in the hammock, very aware of him revelling in the watery wanderings of his thoughts. Jeff rolled his eyes.

Juliet coughed a little to stop the bucket thoughts, then added, 'And bad weather – weirdly enough I miss bad weather. Luckily, I'm going back at the start of winter, so I'll get plenty of that. Probably enough in the first hour to do me for the year.'

There was a bit of weather the next day, as though the heavens had heard Juliet and wanted to demonstrate that it wasn't all relentless sunshine in Ethiopia. Mostly it was, obviously, but not this morning – the wide African sky was grey and motley white, and rain was falling on the dry ground like a blessing. Quite an insistent blessing.

Juliet was on the veranda, thoroughly enjoying the cool and the wayward drops blowing in at her every few seconds. There were so many memories woken up by each splatter of cold and wet. Busy traffic and shoppers battling cheerfully through late afternoon November rains in London streets, all lit up by headlights, traffic lights and shop signs, gleaming reflections in the puddles.

Or wild, windy rain out in the hills back home in Scotland, making every dog walk a Scott-of-the-Antarctic type adventure; coming back to lovely warm soup in the house while it battered on the windows, berating her for having deserted it in favour of the cosy kitchen.

She would be back there very soon now. Making a new path for herself in Scotland, starting again in that place of memories and ancestors. She felt ready for it now, ready to face it all.

And alone? Her mind yelled at her. Without him? Would

they square up to the changes coming soon and talk about it? Big questions, and she had no answers. Somehow though, in her heart she felt secure, despite her mind bemoaning the lack of words exchanged about the future.

Jan emerged blearily from the house and pulled a chair up to her. They sat companionably watching the sheeting rain. He studied her eyes as she drank in the monsoon for a minute. Less stormy? he wondered. She felt his gaze on her and turned to him, a blast of piercing blue waking him up fully.

'Sunday morning,' she said. 'Late ward rounds today. Maybe too early to have left bed, do you think?'

'I almost always think that, *moja laska*.' He laced his fingers through hers and led her back inside. 'Come.'

Chapter 34

Juliet and Sylvie

WHERE WAS SHE? JAN zipped around the female ward, poked his head into minors theatre – no sign. He wanted to discuss a difficult case with her, to get her surgical opinion. He grinned wryly at his hopeless self-deception. He should just admit that there was no urgent thing to discuss (the lady had had multiple symptoms for at least a year) – he just wanted to be around her. Chat, make her laugh a bit, see those eyes sparkle. Breathe the same air for a little while.

He found himself looking for this thoughout the day and night; he had to hold himself back, not drive her mad. He was endlessly drawn to her though, understanding her more and more. He wanted to watch her, listen to her, note the changes.

Because he had seen changes in these past few weeks, oh, yes. She was still sarcastic and teasing to him and Jeff, but at other times she was so open to him, so quietly honest. He felt that she was no longer blocking him from her inner sanctum, not pretending to be the hardnosed professional anymore. Was letting him see the striving and the energy at the heart of her. Energy was the right term, he thought. She was like a volcano bursting with life. And at the moment, with joy and with a seemingly insatiable appetite for him.

He grinned to himself. He was more than happy to meet that need, was entangling himself deeper and deeper with her. It would be a tough few months without her. And did she also feel that they were weaving themselves together, that everything was better when they were side by side? He supposed that he would have to wait for an answer, but not for too long hopefully – he was laying his plans.

And there she was, sitting under the makeshift gazebo with Sylvie and Jonny. It looked as though they were drawing things with him. He leaned against the doorway, enjoying the view. Every so often there were hoots of laughter. After a minute or two, Jonny clearly needed to move, and took off on a hobbling run around the tree. Jan caught the looks exchanged between Sylvie and Juliet as they watched him go – relieved to see him so mobile and happy. All the shadows that used to lurk in both of their eyes seemed chased away now.

He went to join them, throwing himself down on the ground to lounge beside Juliet.

'Hello!' she smiled. 'Shouldn't you be working hard somewhere?'

'No, not at all,' he replied promptly. 'I should be here with you two soul sisters, listening to your scary plans.'

Sylvie laughed. 'They're not so scary! At least, not for you, unless you have a job to give me?'

He sat up. 'I might! Lots of work to be done with all the other ladies and patients – education awareness blah, blah, blah – what do you think?'

She laughed again but shook her head. 'You're kind to offer, but to be very honest, I want to try and get my old job back – I was doing well there. But you know, I'll come and help if you come back for another camp—'

'Thank you, that will be lovely,' Juliet interrupted, squeezing her shoulders.

Sylvie inclined her head affectionately towards her, 'Also, the truth is I don't want my future to be all about what happened to me; I want to have a life away from all of that.'

Juliet nodded. 'Of course you do, and you will have it! We're just selfishly wanting to see you when we come back, isn't that it, Jan?'

'Absolutely.' He nodded.

Sylvie beamed at them both. 'Edmond will keep me informed as to when you're coming back.' She cleared her throat, slightly embarrassed. 'You know, he lives near me.'

'Oh, yes, very handy,' twinkled Juliet, and the two of them burst out laughing again.

'Talk of the devil!' Jan looked up at Edmond approaching. 'Hey, man! Are you taking this special girl away from us now?'

Edmond gave them his slow smile, his arms out to catch Jonny as he hurtled towards him. 'Yes, bus will be coming.'

They all got up, ready to walk down to the gate, Juliet holding Sylvie's hand, Jonny on Edmond's shoulders.

'Sylvie,' began Juliet, then stopped, a lump forming in her throat. She waited a moment then tried again.

'I want to say something to you. You may not realise how much you've helped me. About Drewie. I feel as if he's come back to me in a way, and it's you who made that happen. I want to thank you. I'll always be grateful to you.'

Sylvie halted and turned to her. 'You're thanking me, and I am thanking you, so much.' She smiled, meeting Juliet's teary eyes, her own full of warmth and hope. 'We're both ready for life to be better.' She enveloped her in a big hug.

'Now, no crying, girls, the bus driver won't stop if he sees that,' called Jan, already at the gate with a bag containing Jonny's bucket, cube and drawing things plus clothes which Juliet had given to Sylvie, since she'd arrived with nothing.

They released each other from the hug, and moved slowly to the gate, just as the bus pulled up a little way along. Juliet waited at the gate, watching as Sylvie took Jonny's bag in one hand and Edmond's hand in the other, walking quite naturally beside him away from the hospital, the surgery, and the past. Onto a better life, hopefully, as she had said.

She smiled as a collection of big and little hands shot out of the top windows of the bus and waved madly at her. She waved back, leaning against Jan and watching as the bus lurched off again, until it disappeared down the track in a cloud of dust. So, Sylvie was on her way. Juliet couldn't help a little stomach contraction of worry at the many hurdles still ahead for her. But at least she was through the first big one: the surgery. There were so many other girls still stuck in misery . . . so much work to do. Strangely, she felt a little cheered at bringing it back to work. She liked work, would always work, would make things better through work. Yes.

Chapter 35

Juliet

Last Days

JULIET BOUNCED INTO THE office. 'Jeff! Just the man I need to see!'

'Oh, really?' Jeff automatically tried to get behind the desk, looking for any defence, while recognising with a sigh that she was on a mission, and he was likely done for. 'So, eh, what can I do for you?'

Please God, not much, something close to the rules at least, he was thinking . . .

'The big boss is coming next week for two nights, yes?'

'Yes.' Jeff could feel his heart sinking.

'Well, I was thinking, wouldn't it be nice if she covered labour ward for one night so that I could go up to the other camp to see it when Jan does his round there? Since I'm leaving in two weeks, a little special treat for me? Maybe call at Axum, see if I can find the Ark?'

He blanched at her. 'Ark? What ark? Are you expecting a flood?'

She tried to give him a winning smile but he was under no illusion – this was no off-the-cuff request, and could easily develop into an intense pain-in-the-ass campaign . . . he would have to capitulate early.

'Not that kind of ark: the Ark of the Covenant, you know, Old Testament stuff. It's apparently hidden in a secret underground church in Axum – Solomon brought it there when he was in hot pursuit of the Queen of Sheba. Or maybe she was after him; I'm not sure of the dynamic there. Anyway, it's all very ancient and brilliant. So, is it okay? Will you see if Helen will cover? Top ruins, you know!'

Her enthusiasm was spilling out of her, starting to infect him.

'God's sake, I'll be the ruin by the end of this. Okay, I'll ask her today. Run along and play in the hospital now. I have work to do.'

'Thank you, you're the best!'

'I'm much better than the best, I assure you!'

Jan stepped out of the kitchen into the little yard behind, to better see what on earth was happening out there. Goretti was sitting on her chair at the back door, clapping her hands and laughing at Juliet.

'What the f . . . what are you doing? Are you ill?'

'No! I am practising the chicken dance – ready for our big once-in-a-year night out in Axum!'

Jan frowned. 'What is the chicken thing? Are we bringing chickens?'

'No, no. It's the dance, you know, the Ethiopian funny thing with the jerky neck, chicken style. Goretti has taught me – see?' She strutted around the yard some more.

'I don't think she has quite finished the job yet, have you, Goretti?'

'Okay, Rudolf Nureyev – I'm getting there. Bear in mind, you don't normally do it to "hard rock anthem" before you judge me.'

'And you look a bit swanish I'd say. Stop trying to make your neck longer. Maybe imagine you're trying to swallow injera . . . that's much better! Yes, you look just like a native. I think we're ready to party!'

'Still five days to lift off. I think if I put in a good hour a day of practice, I'll be unrecognisable as a mzungu.'

Goretti smiled at their backs as they disappeared off to the hospital, arguing over who was least mzungu-like.

A week later, Juliet stood on the clifftop by the amazing painted church, catching her breath, taking in the incredible view spread out before her. It was a land like no other: deep rents in the fabric of the earth, the stone whitened by centuries of hard sun, old forest to the south. The cradle of humanity; the beginning of all of it. A place to feel you are at home on the earth, part of the amazing story of life here. She felt a strong arm coming across her shoulders and leaned back against Jan's chest. At home with him, her inner voice added. She let her breathing slow down to match his, looking over to the hospital, the camp, the hill they had run up on so many days.

They were on their way back from Axum. What a wonderful trip, she thought: top ruins right enough, although no Ark in sight. Fabulous dancing at the hotel (so weird to see a whole dancefloor of people who were all moving in time to the music! Very different to the UK or probably anywhere in the western world), the two of them allowed to openly be together. Altogether a night to remember.

Today, they had got Man-U to divert the car just before getting back in order to climb up to the church they saw on their daily runs, and really for Juliet to say goodbye to the mission. *Au revoir*, not goodbye, she thought. I'm coming back. Helen, the boss, had seemed very positive about the idea of fistula camps, especially when Juliet had promised to fund her own travel and expenses. MSF would pay the patients' expenses – brilliant organisation that they were. So, nothing to stop her, apart from life, she thought. Nothing.

'So, that's three hundred and sixty-five days done here. How were they?'

'Ah . . . so rich. Full, so much life. Surgery, Africa, all those patients, my fistula girls, babies coming . . . '

'Yes, so much. Anything else?' he asked.

'Oh, well, let me see, the skies, the birds, the colours, the food: not so much – I still hate injera, but oh, I know—'

'Yes?' Jan interjected hopefully.

'The music, and the Chicken Dance!'

He shifted his weight to be able to look at her, saw the deep dimple and the naughty eyes and laughed. 'You witch! When are you going to say: "And the Visiting Obstetrician and Gynaecologist"?'

'Oh, I forgot!' She laughed back at him, then moved slightly to fully look at him: his dark blue eyes with tiny white tiger stripe lines at the sides – evidence of many days squinting in the sun, his gentle smile, lines deepening between the Viking cheekbones and relaxed jaw.

'You. You and me. Day in, day out. Surgeon and VOG. You and me.'

'Me and you, you and me. Sounds good together! Catchy! And making good days?'

'Mm, yes, definitely . . . thank you, Jan. Good days with you. True.'

'I'm hoping for some more.' His eyes were locked on hers now, his *yes* sure in them. He carefully tucked a lock of blond hair behind her ear, leaving his hand on her neck, his gaze unwavering.

She broke it with a small mock frown. 'I mean, I do pay my debts, and I do owe you one weekend. Although clearly I'm going to be very busy and important and will need to check my diary with my secretary . . . So, when will you come?'

He smiled at the direct demand, met her burning look

placidly. 'March, I think. Have to wait for the new guys to come and help them settle in a bit, I guess.'

'Yes, you will. Okay. March. Good,' she said shortly, and turned her attention from diaries to much more fun things.

Chapter 36

Juliet

Goodbye

IT WAS THE LAST morning. Juliet was leaving at ten o'clock, starting her journey back to Scotland, via Addis, Amsterdam and London. The thought of all those places was so alien to her. She had become accustomed to the wide spaces, single dusty road and sparse buildings of the camp and hospital. Imagining her reimmersion in busy streets, traffic, crowded trains and shiny airports was very odd. She parked the thoughts – plenty of time in the jeep to think of it.

She only had three hours left. She looked down at Jan, fast asleep beside her. They had had rather a busy night – an emergency each at midnight, then a few hours of lovemaking, both unwilling for their time together to stop. And now it would. They would wake up, burst into action; she would rush about saying her goodbyes yet again, tease Jeff for the last time, and then leave. Leave him, leave this odd place, this strange somehow out-of-life existence she'd had for a year. Leave African Juliet here, and go back to UK Juliet. No, that wasn't right. There was only one Juliet, changed from before, and with Africa in her now for good.

She didn't want to set the day off, though. Maybe she could claw back one more half hour. She traced a pattern on Jan's chest with her fingertips, watched him stir and reach for her.

The scramble to get ready and leave began a little later. There had been formal farewells to Juliet from all the staff last night – Chinua, Edmond and Irene being the prime speakers.

Sebastian, the wonder anaesthetist, was there too, but he was not a man to speak publicly. They had had a heartfelt hand grasp though, going on for over a minute. She could only thank him, hope he understood how indebted she was to him. She had been quite overcome at their obvious genuine sorrow that she was leaving. She had to repeatedly promise to keep in touch, and to return.

Edmond, in particular, would correspond with her through email in the office; he would be the one to set up a fistula camp with the new doctors, assuming they agreed. She would let him know about funding and dates, and whether Dr Val would also come.

For now, Man-U was revving the car, not too insistently, but maybe a little. Jeff was standing talking to him, waiting for her to get in. She could not find Jan, and was panicking a little.

'Edmond! Where's Jan?' she called, spying Edmond at the ward door.

'Section!' he called.

Typical. 'I won't be a moment, Man-U,' she yelled, barrelling into theatre.

He looked up as she entered, over the little boy he had just extracted from his mother. He didn't say anything. She stayed at the door, holding his eyes for a long moment, a tight smile containing her emotion.

'March,' she said. He blinked his eyes at her. She smiled more convincingly, nodded and ducked out of the door, feeling every step which took her away from him, having to force her feet to take them.

Stepping away into a different life. She would be walking a new path in a new spot, working out the physical and psychological landmarks there, finding her place. All so different to Ethiopia. And would the thing they had between them translate to that new place? Or was it just a product of here? Of MSF and Africa. She so wanted to believe it could stand on its own whatever the air around it. She couldn't just stay on in Ethiopia, though – she needed to step into the next phase, try the life at home she had trained for. And hope that he would follow her, try something with her. She kept walking.

Chapter 37

Juliet and Jan in Inverness

JULIET WAS WAITING FOR Jan to come out of the airport, leaning on the bonnet of her car, enjoying the breeze. It was an unseasonably warm March Saturday: high clouds making good leeway over the mountains; the land and the air unrecognisable from snowy February.

She had bunkered down somewhat in those cold wintery days, thinking through all that had happened in the past year, and before. A blast of pure joyous sunshine had lightened everything one dark morning, when she had received an email from Edmond with a message from Sylvie:

> *Dear Juliet. I have been back at work for a month and guess what today is? Start of school term — and my sisters and brothers are all there — even Gregory. Thank you, Juliet.*

Inexpressibly precious.

So now the jigsaw pieces were coming together for her, too, a recognisable shape forming. A pattern of life with work, friends, hills and sea. There were big gaps, though, which needed to be filled. Africa-shaped; Jan-shaped.

She didn't quite know how she would manage to complete her jigsaw picture, not yet. Maybe this weekend would provide some clues. Assuming he came, of course. Her heart plummeted suddenly at the thought that he might not. Might decide that she had been tempted into a bourgeois comfortable life, which was certainly not for him.

No. Because it wasn't true. She might be happy, but not in a giving-in and conforming kind of way. She still had the burn to work, to do something. It was all very well for Voltaire's Candide to retire to his garden, but she was braver than that. There was new life bursting through the recently defrosted earth, and new possibilities in her. If he came, he would see that.

But where was he? Butterflies were skittering madly in her stomach.

At last, she saw him, emerging from Arrivals. She felt her heart speed up and that reflex happy warmth spread through her as he walked down the pavement, looking around for her. She waved and he caught it, came straight to her, smiling, holding out his hand for hers, all the while looking at her steadily, carefully; drinking her in, and she him.

'Hello,' he said, crinkling his eyes just a little.

'Hello, too,' she said, meeting his gaze with her own.

'So . . . how are the days?'

She laughed, brushed her blowing hair off her face, not

letting go of his hand. 'Colourful . . . lots of air . . . all full of promise.'

His eyes widened and his dimples deepened. 'Yes, I felt that as we flew in.' He leaned into her. 'And the nights?'

She felt a tremor of anticipation go through her. 'Maybe about to get a whole lot better?' She leaned in, too.

'Why wait for night?' he murmured, pulling her to him and bending to kiss her.

After a few minutes, Juliet pushed him gently back and pursed her lips at him, their apparent severity belied by her sparkling eyes.

'I do applaud your enthusiasm, but we're in a car park in the middle of the day—'

'True.' He looked around appreciatively, taking in the fields around the small airport, the hills behind and the Moray Firth shimmering below. 'Great location for an airport, this.' And dived down for another kiss.

'And,' Juliet went on, after a few minutes, feeling that he hadn't quite got the point yet, 'I thought you wanted to conquer mountains and vanquish midges? There's a lot to do!'

'Also true!' He looked at her lopsidedly for a moment. 'Maybe too much for one weekend? Good to be flexible. Visiting Obstetrician and Gynaecologist is super-flexible. Especially if willing to work for no promotions and minimum pay.' His gaze veered off into the distance and then back to her, his eyes laughing.

'So . . . I'm sorry,' She paused, taking it in. 'Do you mean you're visiting for a while?'

'Same as you, I guess!' He raised his eyebrows at her.

She just looked at him for a long minute, then nodded, a big smile taking over her face.

'Open return tickets to Inverness and to life . . . Okay. Well, then. Let's go and make our visit.'

'Yes, absolutely, and for goodness' sake let's hurry up . . . ' He smoothed her wayward fringe back, caressing her cheek and drawing her close again.

ACKNOWLEDGEMENTS

HUGE THANKS ARE DUE to the following people. Firstly, the fabulous people who made the publication a reality: David Robinson, Sir Alexander McCall Smith, Edward Crossan, Jan Rutherford, Hugh Andrew and everyone at Birlinn publishing. Thanks to Sharon Zink for early editing.

Secondly, my fellow workers against fistula:Brian Hancock and Michael Breen (mentors, tutors, friends), Ishbel Campbell and Christine Wood (instigators of the Nail Bar), Kate Darlow, Ian Asiimwe, Alphons Matovu, Joan Nabaggala, Musubika Joanita, Catherine Reimers, Kristie Greene, Lesley Reid and Sarah Fraser. It's a pleasure and an honour to work with all of you.

Next, my first readers and ace encouragers: Helen Collie, Leonie Chaffey, Julie-Clare Becher, Tamzin Cuming, Liz Lewis, Susie Dinan-Young, Kirsty Stewart, Afra Jiwa, Susan Crow, Wendy Graham, Jessica Ross, Catriona Collie, David Collie, Julia Richardson, Sally Collie, Christine Edwards, Karen Geddes, Di McNab, Kath Campbell, Carol Whyte, Mhairi Pottage, Denby Mantle, Jean Anderson, Katy Homyer, Meg Beddow, Wendy Timmons, Stephanie Taylor and Iliyana Nedkova. Thanks for all the positivity you generated!

Thanks to all my colleagues in Edinburgh who support my trips away.

Lastly, thanks to my wonderful, supportive and understanding family: Mum, Rob, all the Uttleys and cousins, and most especially Bill, Lachlan and Isbeal.

Uganda Childbirth Injury Fund
https://www.ucif.co.uk

WE ARE A SMALL charity dedicated to helping women in Uganda who have suffered permanent injuries during childbirth.

Our volunteer nurses and doctors have been visiting hospitals in Uganda to help provide treatment for obstetric fistula for over 30 years. Many of the patients live in rural areas where there is a shortage of trained surgeons and nurses. We have formed close working relationships with our Ugandan colleagues and continue to share their work to treat these injuries. Together we treat over 200 patients per year.

Fistula Foundation
https://fistulafoundation.org

FISTULA FOUNDATION PROVIDES MORE life-transforming fistula repair surgeries than any other organisation in the world. Its mission is to end the needless suffering of women who experience obstetric fistula and other childbirth injuries. The Foundation raises funds from donors worldwide and directs those funds to local hospitals and surgical teams that provide fistula care in areas of high, unmet need. Since 2009, the Foundation has provided more than 85,000 surgeries to women in 35 countries across sub-Saharan Africa and Asia.

Freedom from Fistula
https://www.freedomfromfistula.org

FREEDOM FROM FISTULA HELPS more than 30,000 women and children every year in Madagascar, Malawi and Sierra Leone. The Scottish-based charity manages hospitals and clinics that provide free surgeries to treat fistula, maternity services to prevent fistula, treatment for child and adolescent victims of sexual and gender-based violence, and primary healthcare for children. One hundred per cent of donations go to the projects in Africa as the UK administration costs are covered by The Gloag Foundation.